ORESTES

AND THE LIFTING OF
THE FAMILY CURSE

ORESTES

AND THE LIFTING OF
THE FAMILY CURSE

Hazel Marshall

ARCHIVE publishing

First published in the United Kingdom by
Archive Publishing
Shaftesbury, Dorset, England

Designed at Archive Publishing by Ian Thorp MA

A CIP catalogue record for this book is available from
The British Library

ISBN 978-1-906289-64-5 (Paperback)
ISBN 978-1-906289-74-4 (Epub)

Front cover: *'Iphigenie'*
from a painting by Anselm Feuerbach (1829-1880)

www.archivepublishing.co.uk

Printed and bound by CMP (UK) Ltd

DEDICATION

Little Owl of Athene, *Athene noctua*

Give me wisdom that sitteth by thy throne,
and reject me not from among thy children

(Wisdom of Solomon 9: 2)

PREFACE

The Myth of Orestes is almost certainly fiction. In the 1980s I came across a set of pictures and never forgot the story woven into them. It was about a young boy born into a troubled family; a powerful story well worth re-telling. Only much later did I find out the origins of the tale, written down about two and a half thousand years ago by several Greek playwrights I'd barely heard of. Those old writers — Euripides, Aeschylus, Sophocles — were finding this story such a good one that each of them added to and recast it, making it right for their own much later time.

I am no academic, no student of the history, philosophy or poetry of Ancient Greece. I would like to let these characters live again in my own era, making this splendid tale more accessible to ordinary English-speaking readers like myself, re-telling it as a myth, a dream of the race, and trusting it will chime with our own times. The story of how Orestes deals with the double bind in which he finds himself marks a vital stage in humanity's progress from barbarism towards wisdom and compassion. How can such an impossible situation ever have a happy ending? — and yet it does.

I invite you, dear Reader, to pause at various points in the story, perhaps closing your eyes, drawing in your awareness and recreating the scene in your imagination. You might ask yourself, 'What on earth would I do in Orestes' shoes? — How can he possibly cope with this? — What does this remind me of?' You will find your own unique response within.

FOREWORD

Ideas can change the world and Hazel Marshall's new book is about just such an idea. Our hero is bound by honour and family tradition to avenge a past wrong, for this is a tale of *vendetta*. Long-lasting family feuds are not rare; in his play *Romeo and Juliet*, Shakespeare wrote of such a case and, as so often, things did not work out well. Vendettas can also sour relations between tribes and between nations; we need only recall the long-standing conflicts all over the world: 'past wrongs *cannot* be forgiven and must *never* be forgotten'.

Vendettas are about revenge and retribution — the situation young Orestes found himself in. Family honour obliged him to avenge his father's death but in doing so, he laid himself open to retribution for his action. He was in a desperate situation, one without any prospect of a happy ending — that is, until the gods themselves stepped in. The goddess Pallas Athene had a brilliant idea.

She solved Orestes' difficulties by finding another way for honour to be satisfied; she set up a Court of Justice. Invoking the sense of justice we all carry deep within our hearts, she chose *twelve good men and true* to hear the evidence presented by both sides, and to weigh that evidence in their hearts. Which case best appealed to their sense of justice?

Revenge arouses our baser passions; but Athene invoked a higher principle, our sense of what is *right*. Trial by jury has formed the basis of our own legal system for many centuries; ordinary, good-hearted people can take the heat out of a situation, their judgement less clouded by their passions. Athene's seminal idea has given us a basic strand of European culture, a way that has found increasing acceptance around the world. Until I read the drafts of Hazel's book, I hadn't realised just how much we owe to those wise, ancient Greeks. You may find similar gems in this fascinating retelling of a little-known Greek Drama.

Frances Aitken

CONTENTS

PART III: ATHENE AND THE FURIES

PART IV: RESTITUTION

DRAMATIS PERSONAE: PEOPLE and PLACES

The House of Atreus at Mycenae in Argos

King Agamemnon	of Argos
Queen Clytaemnestra	his wife
Iphigeneia	their elder daughter
Electra	their younger daughter
Orestes	their son

Their Ancestors (see Family Tree, P.10)

Tantalus
Pelops
Atreus
Thyestes

In Aulis

Calchas	Oracle of Artemis, a Priest
The Old Man	Servant to Agamemnon
Achilles	Greek Warrior-Hero
Odysseus	a Greek Leader
Menelaus	Brother to Agamemnon

In Sparta

King Tyndareus	of the Spartans
Queen Leda	his Wife

At Phocis

King Strophius	of the Phocians
Queen Anaxibia	his Wife, Sister to Agamemnon
Pylades	their Son
Demetrius	a Tutor

On Mount Parnassus

Delphi	Apollo's Temple
The Pythoness,	Delphic Oracle of Apollo

At Mycenae
    Theodore   Head Groom
    Philip   his Assistant
    Zephyra   Orestes' horse
    Helen of Troy   Wife to Menelaus
    Hermione   their Daughter

In Tauris
    King Thoas   of the Taureans
    Larysa   Leader of the Choir

The Gods
    Zeus   God of Thunder, King of Olympus
    Artemis   Goddess of the Hunt
    Apollo   God of the Sun and of Light
    Hermes   Messenger God of Travel
    Athene   Goddess of Wisdom and Justice

INTRODUCTION

The Myth of Orestes is a symbolic story, one of many carrying truth through the ages. It is a fearful, a desperate myth. Attend to it only if you're feeling strong, only if you can cope with the appalling situation our hero found himself in. And it really wasn't his fault. No lame excuse that, but the very fact of it.

If we too have fears, the universe may seem to show its friendliness by echoing our own state of being, rather than trying to persuade us out of it: for a dark mood, a dark story. This is also a heroic story. The hero is the one who learns to disobey, to survive the guilt, to overcome the fear. From this myth, where others go before us and yet live, we who are afraid can take the courage to do what we must and face the shame. It is said that fear arises only when we are ready to deal with it. By developing the courage to share it and challenge it, we meet with our own wisdom and know its befriending.

Orestes' story is a dark and powerful tale of strife and bloodshed, retribution and revenge, in which fate plays a significant part. At its core lies the conflict of two opposing principles, the feminine and the masculine, mother-right and father-right. Their collision has a familiarity; it illustrates the turbulent yet ultimately immensely creative inner struggle in which many of us find ourselves today. Orestes carries the conflict within his own being and at last comes to a resolution.

Bound by the unbreakable gossamer hawser spun from duty, love and guilt, many people live their lives in the shadow of other people, terrified, frustrated and helpless. Orestes' whole family was under a curse; it was his turn to be placed by the gods in a classic, agonising and completely impossible double bind. However, when he turned to face the gods, something different happened … and that's the point of this story.

A PAUSE: *Whether or not you are already familiar with the myth, I invite you, the Reader, to set out in an intuitive, imagining mode, a 'story-time' way of being. Let your awareness hover, attending to what lies just behind reason and judgement. By the end dawn is not far off.*

* * * * *

PART I

THE WINDS OF WAR

CHAPTER 1

EXILE IN PHOCIS

1: Map of Ancient Greece

He'd been a baby ten years ago, bouncing along in the carriage tossed between the arms of his beloved nurse, his elder sister and, occasionally, his mother. His nurse had told him how his mother would seize him, gazing down into his small puckered face, whispering to him words of love and affection. 'My child, my hope, my little one, your name is Orestes. We're so happy because your sister Iphigeneia is to be married when we arrive.'

She'd turned to his sister saying 'Here, take your tiny brother, the son of Agamemnon; hold out your arms for him.' Then, to the nurse, 'Look, he's asleep — the rocking of the carriage has made him nod off. Wake up, little fellow. Wish your sister luck, for your father has arranged a marriage. She's to be wedded to a great hero.'

It was a happy party on that journey to the distant port of Aulis. Once more his mother had taken him on her knee. 'You're too young to remember this day, Orestes but it will be a part of your history: the day your sister made this wonderful match.'

He could picture that rocky journey to Aulis, almost feel the wheels bumping along the highways and tracks between home and the sea. It was true of course that he remembered nothing of it. However, his nurse, Laodameia had known it all. When he was still very young she had told him of the events that followed their arrival, expecting, of course, to be welcomed by King Agamemnon, his father. But it hadn't worked out that way. He'd never seen that sister again, only his other sister Electra. Something terrible had happened next and he didn't know what.

* * * * *

Now, he was bored. That was more than ten years ago. Nothing ever happened here. Education! He ought to be out there, living in the palace at Mycenae where he was born, getting ready to make his way in the world. After all, he was the only son. They said he was a prince. He was nearly twelve — well, just eleven. His father, King Agamemnon, was said to be immensely famous, but he, Orestes, was stuck here, far away in Phocis. Exile, that's what it was.

And now he'd had a message from his sister Electra: that very father, a character as mythical as his lost elder sister, was due home at last. How he wanted to be there to welcome him, the son running through the palace to greet his father, the great leader, returning triumphant and in splendour.

Instead, he was up here in exile, stuck in Phocis. Yes, King Strophius was a pretty decent guardian on the whole, and his Queen was kind. But he ran the palace like a kind of boarding gymnasium, with several other sons of notables captive there too. The sports were all right, in fact Orestes enjoyed them all; but the indoor part, music and poetry and the old myths, though having its moments, could get really heavy. And the crusty, middle-aged, well-respected tutor Demetrius, was hard to get round.

'I should be there. Back home.' He clattered his stylus down on the tablet. 'Father coming back and just Mother and her — boyfriend — to welcome him. Wonder how that'll go. I know she doesn't want my father home, but she'll pretend. Father won't like it either, I should think, with that man hanging around.' Elbow on desk, chin on fist as the tutor droned on, Orestes gazed from the schoolroom over the rocky terrain that bounded the Phocian palace. Electra had been putting into his head her own furious images of their would-be step-father. Those images were imposing themselves on the solid reality of Mount Parnassus hovering in the hot sky beyond. He was helpless, stuck for weeks and weeks until he could get away. *Then* his father would see him, surely? After all, his birthday had passed; surely he was old enough now to decide things for himself.

For the vacations, he didn't go to Mycenae; he'd scarcely been back home there since he was small. He knew his mother and *that man* were best avoided. After all, that's why he'd been sent here to Phocis. His grandparents Leda and Tyndareus, who ruled in Sparta, quietly took him instead. They were good to their daughter's son, making him welcome when at last he was briefly freed from exile. 'Best stay away from your mother, lad. You never know with Clytaemnestra. You're stopping here where you're safer.' Safer from what, they did not say.

He didn't much mind not seeing his mother; but he did miss Electra. He hadn't seen her for many years. She was all right, though he remembered her as a bit bossy and insistent about things. It was great, that one time when his Grandmother had arranged for her to be there in Sparta as well, for his fifth birthday. Sure, his sister was older and a bit embarrassing; but feisty too, a pretty decent friend really. Being a girl, she didn't have to bother with school and he envied her freedom. He sighed, thinking of his grandfather's palace in Sparta overlooking the Eurotas river. Wish we were there now messing around, exploring the town. He thought about the other sister, much older, the one he couldn't remember — Iphigeneia. She was said to be away with the gods, having gone when he was a baby, lost on that fated, bumpy journey to the sea.

He missed going home less because of his family than because there in Argos he'd be able to talk to Laodameia. She'd looked after

2: Orestes in Exile © Tricia Newell

him as a baby and now she sent him messages regularly. She was a kind nurse and a great gossip. She *would* tell him things. 'This Palace,' she'd explained when he was small, 'is the House of Atreus. The town is Mycenae, founded here in Argos by Atreus. This House will be yours when you grow up and you will be a great king after your honoured father Agamemnon.' No one except Laodameia ever mentioned his lost elder sister; she'd told him and Electra some story about a deer being sacrificed at a wedding ceremony, but he'd been too young to make head or tail of it or be much interested.

Despite the nurse's welcome on his visit long-ago, a menace seemed to brood over his mother's palace. He felt uncomfortable in Clytaemnestra's presence — always had. His detested would-be step-father was really Agamemnon's cousin, known to the children as Uncle Aegisthus. When he'd appeared Orestes, at five years old, had been sent away. He remembered how he'd resolutely refused to call him Father; why should he, when he had a perfectly good father of his own, sailing the seas (so it was said), fighting wars and saving Greece. All right, he hadn't seen his real father since that other day when Agamemnon had noticed the tiny baby and claimed him as his son; but then, he too had vanished.

Electra often sent messages, but she didn't tell him much. She'd been a small child at the time of that fateful expedition, left at home, too young to know any more than he did what had happened to their sister. Instead, she recounted her day-to-day quarrels with Clytaemnestra. She detested their mother and her hatred seemed returned. Nothing quelled this impossible girl. The queen would try: 'You wait till your father gets home!' to which Electra would yell, 'He's not my father, he's your wretched boyfriend. Why didn't he join the army too? I hate him, I wish my *proper* father would come, NOW!'

Yes, Orestes reflected, he was probably well out of it. In fact, he was certainly better off in the palace of King Strophius than he would have been in the House of Atreus. Argos was full of upheaval and quarrel, while here in Phocis all you had to do was learn, practise your sports and find out who you could and couldn't trust. His Aunt, Queen Anaxibia, was all right and there were several pretty good people around, he considered; but luckily, no girls in Strophius' establishment, and he had a good friend in Pylades, such as every man needs.

Pylades was King Strophius' own son. At twelve, slightly older than Orestes, he was full of humour and determination. He rejoiced in trying to bait the tutor, Demetrius. It was a fairly even match, because although Demetrius usually won, as of course he should, occasionally he was overcome with chuckles at some master-stroke of rhetoric from Pylades and would turn away to hide a grin. Straight-faced, the boy counted those occasions as victories; 'Did I make you laugh, Sir?'

Demetrius was fond of both boys and concerned for their welfare. Each was the son of a royal house and would one day inherit a throne. Pylades should be all right, thought the tutor; his lineage was sound and his family decent. His father Strophius King of Phocis, who lived here and ran the place, was an excellent employer and a trusted landlord to the local farmers, dispensing justice and sometimes benevolence. He lived in the palace with Queen Anaxibia, who was a sister of Orestes' father Agamemnon, and the king saw his son Pylades every day.

With Orestes, Demetrius had a deeper connection, back to when the boy was only about five. His family was both royal and troubled —

some said, cursed — and the son was not lucky in his parents. It was well-known that after the king had been away for a few years, fighting a war whose outcome was uncertain, Clytaemnestra had taken a lover. Agamemnon's cousin Aegisthus had settled in and, in her husband's

3: Family life: Orestes' concept of himself with
Clytaemnestra and Agamemnon © Tricia Newell

absence, professed to wish to marry her. However, best not. With the children's father probably still alive, though long absent, Aegisthus had simply taken over the throne as substitute King of Argos.

Six or so years earlier, with Agamemnon overseas and that cousin of his newly entrenched in the palace, Laodameia the nurse, sensing danger for the little boy, had made contact with King Strophius. And Strophius had sent Demetrius himself to Mycenae. 'Tell Clytaemnestra that my wife Anaxibia, Queen of Phocis, is longing to see the child. Say the King and Queen beg you to allow him to visit us. That way you'll rescue the boy and bring him to safety here.'

Demetrius, who saw Agamemnon as a hero, had been glad to go. 'Just think,' he'd reflected, 'There he is, that Aegisthus, acting as step-father to the son of the king, living in the palace at Mycenae, enjoying the ruling of a kingdom, with a woman in his bed, money in the coffers, power comfortably in his hands, and all without the trouble of matrimony. This being the case, the boy's life will be worth nothing.'

'Uncle' Aegisthus himself would not have described his rule in Argos as comfortable. The trouble, in the view of the pseudo-King, was her wretched children. They were frightful, though he was careful not to say that to Clytaemnestra. Electra, little madam, was exasperating, knowing everything and liable to round on him at any moment with furious words. He could never refute them effectively. She was an unmitigated nuisance and a threat to his well-being. And she didn't seem to like her mother any more than she liked him.

He'd hardly seen the other child, Orestes, now far away, thank the gods. He'd been sent to Phocis to be fostered by Strophius, who was keen on education and good behaviour. On the one occasion when the child had visited the Mycenae palace Aegisthus had taken good care to be out, leaving Clytaemnestra to cope. At least Electra had seemed to like her young brother well enough and having him around had kept her quiet for a bit. But surely, thought Aegisthus uneasily, the boy will grow up and come home soon. He'll be dangerous.

Clytaemnestra had been only too glad to be rid of one more nuisance. She parted from the five-year-old Orestes with scarcely a murmur. 'Let his nurse go with him. But then she must come back here.' So Laodameia had wrapped him well up in a beautiful robe — she long remembered the wild animals woven into it — and, escorted to Phocis by Demetrius, had accomplished her mission. She'd returned perforce to Mycenae where she was useful as the only person who could manage the other child, Electra. Orestes himself had come back only once, long ago.

Back in Phocis, Orestes' situation troubled the tutor. 'He's eleven now. He ought to know what goes on in his family; it's neither fair nor wise of his mother to keep him in ignorance. He knows nothing about the War, nothing about his ancestors. And what of the elder sister, that awful story?' wondered Demetrius. 'Above all, he's unaware of the threat hanging over his head. He hardly knows he's in line for the throne. It's time he understood what's before him. I'll talk to the King.'

'Ah, Demetrius. Come in my friend.' King Strophius was a kindly man. Six years before, he and his wife had taken Orestes in because it was expected of them and he had since grown fond of the child. 'Yes, you bring to light something I too have been considering recently.

I'm glad we are fostering young Orestes. He is the child of my wife's brother, our brave Agamemnon and it's an uneasy situation at home, to say the least. He's a good friend to my son. But you are right; it's time he knew something of his background. I will have to talk to him.'

Next day after the Rhetoric class Demetrius called Orestes back. 'What have I done this time?' Orestes whispered to Pylades.

'Bungled your astronomy again, I expect.' His friend slapped him on the back. 'Good luck!' and he raced outside to target practice with the others in the afternoon light. Orestes, half-expecting a lecture about his poor performance with the chunk of Homer he'd been trying to learn, or maybe his uncertain grasp of the starry constellations, was startled when his tutor told him, 'Orestes, you're to go and see the King this evening. Don't be late. He has serious matters to discuss with you.'

Serious matters? Heart sinking, Orestes ran off to join Pylades for the archery session; but unease deflected his aim and would spoil his supper.

A PAUSE: *In Ancient Greece, as in many other places, life about four hundred and fifty years before Christ was dangerous. Powerful people often killed those they feared: it was expected of them. Exile saved Orestes as a child. Children sent away from home 'for their own good' may have a particular take on life. Is there any resonance here for you?*

* * * * *

CHAPTER 2

THE HOUSE OF ATREUS

'Now, Orestes.' King Strophius' voice was sombre. 'Sit down. It's time you learnt about your family. If I'm right, neither your mother nor your uncle has told you much. What have you picked up about your relatives, about where you come from?'

'Nothing, Sir, not really.'

'Well, what of your grandparents?'

'I like them, you know, I stay with them quite often, in Sparta. She's Queen Leda and my grandfather's King Tyndareus. She talks to me but they don't really tell me things.'

'Those are your *mother's* mother and father. What about your *father's* parents, your other grandparents?'

'I've no idea, Sir, I didn't think I had any other … I know I had another sister, older than Electra, and she's disappeared, but I don't know where she is. I keep thinking she'll come home … '

Strophius frowned, staring down at his hands. How can I tell him, how impart such terrible knowledge, wipe the innocence from a young boy, all in one short hour? Try as he might, the effect on his protégé of such an appalling story would be appalling too.

Orestes sat before his foster-father in silence. His *father's* father? 'Grandfather' meant kindly Tyndareus. When he was tiny, he knew his mother herself had once taken the family to visit her parents in Sparta; they'd stayed there for some time because of some vaguely-sensed trouble at home in Mycenae. What trouble? Surely it had just been a holiday, a chance for Clytaemnestra to catch up with her own mother, Queen Leda, and for Electra to begin to notice the Spartans and their warrior-skills. He'd been far too young to question any of it.

'You've done nothing wrong, Orestes,' Strophius began, 'and you're very welcome here. But your proper home is the House of Atreus at Mycenae, isn't it, where you should be living with your mother and sister and your Uncle Aegisthus. But I have a story to tell you, and I want you to listen till it's finished. It's about your father Agamemnon and his father, your grandfather Atreus. Your great-uncle Thyestes comes into it too. I wish it were not like this …

'You must be strong, because you are the next in line and in this coming generation it will be you who must act.' The king stopped and eyed Orestes. 'What I am telling you today is that your house is cursed. Cursed by the gods. To be cursed is a terrible thing, Orestes, and I wish I could spare you this, but you need to know.

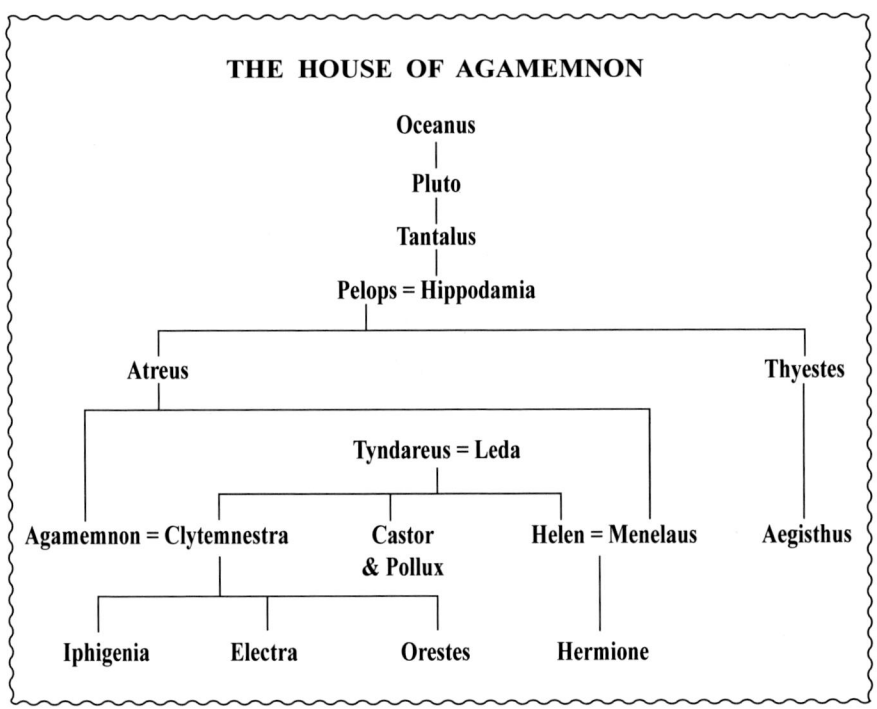

4: The Family Tree

Strophius produced a sheet of papyrus on which had been etched a diagram. 'Here's your family, Orestes. Here are Tyndareus and Leda in the middle, and your mother. The trouble comes with your other grandfather Atreus — see him up there? He came from a line of disasters. His father Pelops had dreadful deeds done to him by his own father, Tantalus. When you're older you will learn what they did and what happened to them. But it's enough now to know that Tantalus mocked the gods, the gods cursed him in return, and that is the curse on the House of Atreus. My story begins with your grandfather.'

A long pause followed, in which Strophius wiped his forehead and heaved a silent sigh. 'Atreus and his brother Thyestes both somehow survived their upbringing, but they went on to quarrel. Do you know the word *retribution*, Orestes? Paying people back; taking revenge; that's what the curse on the House of Atreus is. It's what each generation does, and has to do by command of the gods. They take turns in punishing the latest dreadful deed. You take my stylus, so I smash your slate, so you kick my shins, that sort of thing, on and on: revenge must be sought to find peace. Though your family certainly haven't found much peace yet ... ' The king stared out into the fading evening.

'Where was I? Your great-uncle Thyestes — here,' he poked at the chart — 'seduced the wife of your grandfather Atreus. You know what that means? He ran off with her. And that infuriated Atreus, who quite naturally took revenge. But what he did to Thyestes was so unspeakably terrible that I cannot spell it out to you this evening, Orestes. Suffice it to say, it was unforgiveable. It involved the secret killing of his brother's children — but you'll find it out eventually, I'm afraid. Only one child survived. And your Uncle Aegisthus — well, he's a cousin really — is that surviving son of Thyestes.'

Orestes was horrified. He didn't know what to say or feel. Hearing that his wretched uncle Aegisthus had been the only survivor of a massacre did make him feel more sympathetic towards him. But what was that about going off with other people's wives. Wasn't that what Electra said his 'uncle' was doing with his own mother? He was overcome with confusion? Where did this leave his father? Where did it leave him? Did it mean he in turn would have to do some horrible deed some day?

The king went on. 'There's worse to come. Do you know how your grandfather died? No, of course you don't. Well, a few years ago, in payment for that terrible, unspeakable deed, Aegisthus himself killed Atreus, thus avenging his father. So your uncle who is now your mother's lover is the very man who killed your grandfather. Do you see what all this means?'

Into Orestes' understanding, a chink of sallow light was falling. So that's why my family went to Sparta for that holiday; to keep out of the way of that other grandfather's funeral ...

'You must spend your time here well, Orestes,' Strophius went on. 'Learn all the martial arts. Some day you will need them. Talk to Demetrius, you can trust him; but I'd advise you not to share this with your fellow students. Or only with Pylades, perhaps. Come back to me if you'd like to talk more about this.'

Neither Strophius nor Orestes had much rest that night. Strophius lay awake in the dark in his bed in the palace. What will Agamemnon do when he finds his wife with that man? He'll be home soon, by all accounts. What will follow? How will this boy cope? Will it all be too much for him?

Orestes, mind racing, lay on his couch in the silent dormitory. What about my father, away my whole life? Electra says he's coming home soon. What will he think? That awful man, our false step-father, living with my mother, pretending to be king. 'Uncle' Aegisthus. So, he's a murderer. He killed my grandfather, my father's father. I can believe it … Tossing and turning, he decided to make every effort to get to the palace at Mycenae. Then he'd find things out. Electra would be useless.

5: Orestes in Phocis

And she'd be no fun any more, all sullen face and enraged whispered mutterings about their mother and uncle. What did she know? Clytaemnestra? No, his mother would tell him nothing. He imagined her stiff greeting: 'Oh, you're here, boy, are you. I trust you're working hard with your classes, not letting sport take you away from your lessons? Phocis, isn't it. When do you go back again?' And off she'd go.

No, she'd better not know he was there. He would talk with his old nurse Laodameia. She would understand, she would tell him. In her chamber, warm and quiet, he would be welcomed with hugs and offered drinks and a lovely supper. He could pour his heart out to this childhood ally, a friendly listener who would treat him as an equal, help him understand, never patronise him. Yes, he'd send her a message … tomorrow … he had a plan now … And at last Orestes fell asleep.

A PAUSE: *There was a curse upon the family of the House of Atreus. They believed it had come from a quarrel among the ancestor gods. A thousand years before Orestes, the Old Testament was telling how 'I, the LORD thy God, am a jealous God, visiting the iniquity of the fathers upon the children unto the third and fourth generation … ' (Deuteronomy 5:9, written c. 1,406 BCE.) Some families certainly seem more afflicted by family struggles than others. How do you feel about this?*

* * * * *

CHAPTER 3

LAODAMEIA REMEMBERS

While the eleven-year-old Orestes brooded in Phocis, Laodameia was recovering in the palace in Argos from yet another frantic evening. House of Atreus it may be, but oh the fuss! Alone at last in her chamber, the nurse sank into her chair. At last she could stop for a bit. The excitement of the servants was buzzing in her ears: 'Hurry, hurry, Agamemnon's coming home at last, the war is won, Troy's defeated. A great victory, a great leader!' Silly girls, didn't they realise the trouble there'd be in the palace, one almighty clash the like of which had not been seen here for — well, not for years. *She*, Queen Clytaemnestra, was floating around, entangled in it all, giving orders, inspecting everything, getting in the way. *He*, the king's substitute whose name wouldn't pass the nurse's lips, stayed out of sight, absent without leave, showing up most days this week only in time for the evening meal — and bed.

She sighed. It didn't take an Oracle to see what would happen next. Electra, poor child (well, she was fifteen now) became daily more disagreeable. Her name meant *amber*, full of electricity, but she had few of the further attributes of amber: patience, balance, calmness. And poor little Orestes (not so little these days) was still far away thank the gods, in that Northern academy where as a small boy she'd taken him herself, learning to fight and do his lessons and become a man. He'd need to.

She'd barely put her feet up — 'just five minutes' — when a knock came at the door and before her stood a breathless young man. 'Mistress Laodameia?' Quickly and softly, lest the palace had ears, he closed the door behind him. 'A message. No, it's for you — yes, you — you only. Shh!' Finger to lips. 'It's from Orestes. He's coming to see you from Phocis as soon as he can, in a few days if he can get away. Yes ma'am, I know he's only eleven. He said to give you his greetings. He wants to discuss something with you — yes, only with you,' whispered the lad again. 'It's of great importance, he says. But please not to broadcast his arrival.'

Offering the tired young messenger some sustenance, the nurse's feelings soared, crashed and soared again. That beloved child, coming home. But into what? Suppose his mother, or the usurper Aegisthus, caught him here when he was supposed to be away? She must be careful. There was no love lost between Orestes and his uncle and, heaven knew, a rich history of disappearings in the family. 'Oh, it'll be good to see him again,' she blurted.

The door closed behind the messenger and he slipped away into the night. The nurse settled back and closed her eyes once more. Orestes, her favourite. He'd been a dear little boy and she'd done her best to ensure that neither his father's absence nor his mother's abysmal attitude to the children affected him too badly. He'd played quite happily with Electra when he was old enough, and that hard-hearted girl (a handful all along) seemed surprisingly fond of her small brother.

But what of the older child, the missing one, the girl left behind that terrible day? Until then, they'd all been a family, with her a part of it. That princess never mentioned had been beautiful and happy, devoted to her little sister and her new baby brother, a delightful presence. Laodameia had secretly mourned her ever since. 'I'm the only person left who knows what happened. The queen knows, of course, and him, but they aren't talking.' In her heart, she called, 'Iphigeneia, girl, where are you?'

So what did happen ten years ago? I must get the story straight in my head, ready to tell Orestes. Surely that's what he's coming for. Agamemnon, in charge of the army and the kingdom, had decided to sail away to wage his war, intent on winning back that tart, his brother's wife Helen. A prince called — what was it? — Paris, that's it, Paris, son of Priam of Troy, had stolen Helen away from her husband Menelaus, Agamemnon's brother. The young pair had run away to Troy across the seas, or so it was said. And just look at the trouble that's brought, thought Laodameia. A thousand ships!

She recalled how she had been busy with the new baby when the queen had sent for her. 'Prepare for a journey, nurse.' Agamemnon had sent a message, a wonderful surprise. Iphigeneia was to be sent to Aulis, the sea-port where he, his men and his umpteen ships were stuck. Apparently the wind wouldn't blow and they couldn't sail. The nurse had never seen Clytaemnestra so happy and excited; she'd grabbed her baby and kissed him. 'She's only fourteen, but she's to be wed. To the great hero Achilles! Apparently he caught a glimpse of our lovely daughter when visiting Argos and wishes to marry her. My husband praises Achilles to the skies, says he absolutely refuses to sail with them unless a bride is sent from our family. I'm not *sending* her; I'm taking her myself. Oh, Laodameia, isn't this a happy day for us all? Here, hold the baby. I'm bringing him too, to show him to his father for the first time.' And the queen had hurried away to share with Iphigeneia this amazing piece of news, delighted to be marrying off a daughter to this hero.

6: Iphigeneia's Bridegroom-to-be, Achilles

Now, ten years on, hardly anyone knew what had happened; only she, Laodameia, who had been there herself. She'd made sure both Electra and Orestes were well aware there had once been a third, who was not here now, but Electra remembered Iphigeneia only as the big sister who had gone away, and Orestes not at all. She had told them the story of that exciting day when the messenger from the king arrived in the palace and how Iphigeneia, though still almost a child, had been thrilled to the core: the great hero Achilles had noticed her, wanted to meet her, marry her, love her. Laodameia told the children how excitement had shone in the girl's eyes, how even their mother had been excited. Days had been spent in preparing the wedding finery. 'You, Electra were left with a stand-in nurse. You were only four. But the baby was too young to leave, so I was to bring him too.' They had set out for Aulis in the chariot, to greet Agamemnon, meet Achilles and celebrate the marriage.

Always, then, Laodameia had broken off and changed the subject. 'Come on now, that's enough. Wash your hands for lunch. Electra, you can do your face as well.' Ever since, the children had half-believed that Iphigeneia was safely married, but far away. What had really happened? It had remained a disquieting mystery.

The nurse knew, only too well. Eyes closed, she recalled the bumpy ride, with the queen and the girl and the baby and the maid. Outriders too, of course, for there were brigands on the roads. Arriving at Aulis, they'd seen Agamemnon's splendid ships mustered. She was proud to be carrying Orestes, who was not crying but trying to look around him. Oh, Iphigeneia would be happy. Though so young, she'd be settled, with a glorious bridegroom. The queen too was overjoyed.

As they approached the town a group of soldiers gathered, excited, hoping for a glimpse of the new bride. They ran after the chariot as it rumbled into Agamemnon's compound, shouting 'Princess Iphigeneia, Princess Iphigeneia!' Everyone was thrilled and buzzing with talk. 'Oh, the Queen's come too, Agamemnon's queen, our commander-in-chief's lady. Her father is Tyndareus. He's well-liked, a good king. Come out, Queen Clytaemnestra, climb down from your carriage,' and they chanted her name too.

Clytaemnestra was in her element. She knew how to handle a crowd and when the chariot stopped she made a speech, her voice rising to reach the men, who listened closely. 'Soldiers, your warm greeting and courteous welcome make me feel good luck will be ours; better by far than the usual portents of good fortune. Our expectations are high: I bring this bride, our daughter, to a most suitable and happy marriage.'

Laodameia could remember, as if ten years were nothing, the cheers that resounded as Clytaemnestra's voice rose again. 'I've brought wedding-gifts as a dowry. Please unload them carefully and take them indoors.' This queen was one to be obeyed; the soldiers unloaded the gifts. When the horses began to bucket around she commanded, 'For heaven's sake, somebody, stand by their heads and get their attention; of course they panic in strange places. Talk to them, calm them down.' And the soldiers obeyed, soothing the horses and dealing with the chariot.

A group of women from the neighbouring town of Aulis clustered around offering helping hands. Clytaemnestra confided, 'The princess is like a child still, quite tender and fragile. Take good care of her.' And she turned to her daughter, full of fuss and concern, 'Now my dear girl, be careful, don't trip over your dress. You women, help her safely to the ground and show her where to sit.'

Iphigeneia almost panicked at the cheering of the soldiers and their delighted awe. But the women addressed her directly. 'Come now, you're Agamemnon's famous daughter. You look pale, but don't be shy. There's nothing to fear. We are strangers here too and visitors from Argos are welcome.' She could hear them murmuring to each other, 'Mind the steps. Give her your arm — gently — gently — ' In the warmth of their kindness and her mother's good humour, Iphigeneia climbed down from the chariot and began to enjoy herself.

'And now,' Clytaemnestra was saying, 'would one of you give me a hand, so that I can get to my seat with reasonable grace.' The crowd roared its approval and the queen's commanding presence filled the precinct. 'And, the child. The son of Agamemnon. Put him into my arms for a moment, nurse. His name is Orestes. He's still a tiny baby, you see? There-there, my dear child, you've nodded off, haven't you. The carriage rocked you to sleep. Wake up, little fellow, wish your sister luck, for the son of a fine man, a most desirable ally, is going to marry her.'

The queen gave Orestes back to Laodameia, the soldiers wheeled the chariot away and the women withdrew. 'Now, my child,' said Clytaemnestra, 'sit here, close to me as a daughter should, to show these people what a lucky woman I am in my children. We make rather a good family group all together, do we not?'

That was Laodameia's last happy memory of Agamemnon's family. From then on — doom. Only she could remember what had happened next. Agamemnon, far from happy to see them, had seemed enraged. Only later did the reason become clear: his family would witness the dreadful thing that had been planned. From that day the queen became 'the memory womb of child-avenging fury,' as was written of her.

The curse, whatever it was, fell again and Iphigeneia did not return to Argos.

A PAUSE: *Happiness is under a cloud: something's wrong and you're not sure what. Laodameia picks it up out of the air. It has been said that 'intuition is the imagination, trusted'. On the surface all seems well, but her intuition can tell it is not so. How much do you trust your own intuition, that sixth sense? Where does it come from, and how reliable do you feel it to be?*

* * * * *

CHAPTER 4

AGAMEMNON

So what *had* happened, that fateful day in Aulis?

Agamemnon was not a happy man. He'd bungled things. Bungled them disastrously. Oh these wretched Oracles! But you had to listen to them, hadn't you, especially if you were Commander-in-Chief of an irritable army and saw the navy frustrated by both the weather and the impatient soldiers. He didn't like that priest Calchas: a slimy type, he thought. But he was the local Oracle of the goddess and, like him or not, you couldn't ignore him.

7: The Goddess Artemis

And what a goddess. Artemis the huntress. She certainly liked spilling blood. The priest had hurried along the road from her shrine just round the corner to the seaport where the ships were holed up, impotent, restlessly tossing, waiting for the wind to change. He'd butted into the precinct, gate-crashing the headquarters, telling him, the king, that Artemis had her sanctuary here in Aulis. 'You angered her. You killed a deer on the way here. What arrogance! That's why the winds are in the wrong direction.' Worse, Calchas had told Agamemnon what he had to do about it. 'Artemis herself decrees that you must (oh, indescribable) offer your daughter (my child, Iphigeneia!) as a sacrifice. Only then will the winds change and blow you out to sea. Only then will the navy take over and the army settle down. Only then can you sack Troy.'

Over several sleepless nights Agamemnon had pondered aloud, confiding in his servant from Mycenae, known affectionately as the Old Man. He wasn't in fact very old (he could run for miles) and he had an earthy wisdom the officers lacked. What are we sacking Troy for anyway, wondered Agamemnon; and why *me* in charge? How on earth did I get talked into this? It's all Menelaus' fault.

8: Helen of Troy

His brother Menelaus had married Helen mainly for her looks. She had soon left him and run off to Troy with Paris, the young Trojan prince. Now all this to bring her back and save her husband's pride. Sack the city! It was no more Troy's fault than his own. 'Kill my daughter, indeed. Never! I'll announce the disbanding of the whole army first. I couldn't conceivably ever be so brutal as to kill my own child. Never. How could I, Old Man?'

'Clever, sir, but dangerous,' said the Old Man, 'pretending you're bringing her here to marry the son of an immortal, when really she'll be given to the temple to be butchered … '

'Don't say that!' yelled Agamemnon. 'It drives me mad to hear it, my head's splitting.' But when his brother, who'd talked him into this stupid war in the first place, heard him swithering he had begged and wheedled till the king gave in and agreed to the damnable business. 'If you don't obey Calchas,' said Menelaus, 'then you, dear brother, will certainly be the victim of your own forces. The soldiers will mutiny. It'll be your own blood … ' Nasty thought.

And so he had been persuaded a week or two earlier to write a letter, folding it and folding it again. And he'd sent it to Clytaemnestra, telling her, 'Send our daughter here to be married to the great hero Achilles.' He'd filled the letter with lavish praise of Iphigeneia's supposed suitor (his mother was purported to be a sea-goddess, daughter of an ancient god of the sea), adding, 'Achilles absolutely refuses to sail with us or bring his crack troop of Myrmidons unless my daughter is sent to return with him to his own house.' He was sure this pack of lies about their daughter's marriage would persuade Clytaemnestra to send Iphigeneia to Aulis. Then she would be sacrificed, Artemis would be appeased, the winds would change, the ships would sail and all would be well …

No it wouldn't! It wasn't too late to change his mind. Leaping out of bed, Agamemnon grabbed writing materials once more and began a second letter. No-one knew what he'd been intending. Or did they? Well, just the priest. And Menelaus. Oh, and Odysseus and one or two more of the top brass. And the Old Man, of course. They were in on the plan. Frantically he wrote and re-wrote the new message, lumps of discarded papyrus all over the floor, telling Clytaemnestra that he was changing his orders. He sealed and unsealed letters in his private hut in the dark till finally he had the perfect version:

Further to my last letter, Daughter of Leda, these are my new instructions: do not send, repeat, do not send, your daughter here to this peaceful harbour of Aulis. It seems we must celebrate her marriage at some other time.

The candle guttered. 'Wake up, Old Man! That letter you took to Argos the other day. I was wrong. I'm changing my decision. I'm disbanding the army as I said before. Come here.' His hoarse whisper resounded through the pre-dawn darkness. 'This is life and death. I've changed my mind: she must *not* come. Only this letter will stop them sending her. What an appalling plan it was, to tell my wife I was sending for the girl to marry Achilles, when really I was giving her to

Calchas to be butchered like a deer — a mad-making idea. 'Run, my friend, run like the wind, like a boy, get this second letter to Mycenae in time.'

'As fast as I can, my Lord. What's that? No, of course I won't sit down in the forest by a spring and fall asleep. As if I would sir, really!'

'They'll be on their way already. Don't let them slip past you at some fork in the road. Stop her, don't let her arrive here, don't let them get her. Even if she's only just leaving Mycenae's gates, stop the chariot, grab the reins, drive her straight back inside the city walls.'

'Just a minute though, Sir. Why should your daughter believe me when I tell her all this?'

'The letter's got my seal. Make sure it's unbroken. Get moving. It's up to you to save me.'

And so the Old Man ran off, happy enough to be heading home to Argos. Agamemnon watched him go, his back to the brightening sky; for, as the poet said, *'the four-horsed chariot of the sun was galloping towards the eastern horizon, flooding the sea and sky with light.'*
[Euripides, Iphigeneia at Aulis, tr. Don Taylor, P.12]

Back in his hut his breakfast did nothing for the king's state of mind. He was weighed down by an impossible burden of grief, resentment

9: The Judgement of Paris: Hera, Aphrodite and Athene with Hermes

and bad luck. At Menelaus' wedding the family had promised they'd
help his brother should Helen, being so beautiful, ever be seduced
away. He was only redeeming that promise.

But what had he been thinking? Wage a war, just to drag that harlot
back to his own cuckolded brother? Stories about Helen were legion.
Although she had the looks, she wasn't worth it, for goodness' sake.
Apparently it was the Goddess Aphrodite who'd given her to Paris, the
Trojan prince. He'd been holidaying in Crete with the local shepherds
when he found Helen *'where the sighing reed beds whispered beside
the river'* [Iphigeneia at Aulis, tr. Don Taylor, P.13] — oh those poets.

Evidently Aphrodite, glistening from her bath in a fountain of spray,
had granted Helen to Paris as a prize after that ridiculous beauty-
competition between three goddesses, Hera, Athene and Aphrodite
herself. They'd asked him to judge which was the fairest of them all,
pleading with great bitterness for his vote. And of course he'd chosen
Aphrodite. Well, who else would a gorgeous young man choose but
Love, voluptuous with sex, against the wifely power of Hera or the
spear of the law that went with Athene?

While Agamemnon pondered thus over his breakfast, the Old Man
was not getting very far with his letter. He'd left the precinct of the hut
and reached the road to Argos when he ran into Menelaus, out early,
keeping fit and incidentally keeping an eye on Agamemnon. 'We don't
want any changes of heart, do we?' The upshot was that the second
letter now lay in Menelaus' hand. The Old Man's protests were useless,
though he gave almost as good as he got. Held by the scruff of his neck
and dragged back to the hut, he was yelling for his master at the top
of his lungs. 'My Lord Agamemnon, this is an outrage. Come out Sir!
Your brother has torn your letter from my hand by force, quite without
conscience.'

Horror! Agamemnon emerged and yelled at his brother in turn. But
he knew he'd been worsted, and Menelaus, quick to twist the knife,
threatened to show the letter to the army unless it were scrapped and the
plan to sacrifice the daughter confirmed. The two of them exchanged
practised insults. Menelaus reminded him of his fall from grace in
the eyes of the people and the mutterings of discontent in the army.
'They're calling you an unlucky General,' he told Agamemnon. 'When
Calchas first suggested you should offer your child to Artemis for fair
winds and an easy passage, you jumped at it. You weren't forced. Now,

you think you've changed your mind. But you haven't. You say you'll never be your own child's murderer. But you will, you will!'

Agamemnon rallied and came back reasonably enough. 'Well then, sacrifice your own daughter. Why *my* daughter?'

'It wasn't me who killed that deer, brother, it was you. The goddess wouldn't accept Hermione. It's one of your children she wants,' responded Menelaus.

'All *you* want is to get that lascivious woman back in your arms and into bed, when you've been lucky enough to lose her with no trouble to yourself,' countered Agamemnon. 'All *I've* done is change my mind. The gods know the difference between genuine vows and oaths sworn foolishly or under duress. I will not kill my daughter. You won't get revenge on your worthless wife at the expense of my guilty conscience for an unforgiveable crime committed on a child of my own flesh. So there you are.' He was vaguely aware that these words completely contradicted what he'd said on earlier occasions. But he was not going to kill Iphigeneia. No — that would be wrong.

Menelaus was just returning some self-pitying plea when a messenger appeared in the precinct and Agamemnon's worst fears were realised — no, worse than worst. Clytaemnestra herself was in the chariot outside the gate. She hadn't *sent* their daughter as instructed, but *brought* her to Aulis. His wife was here, now!

The messenger was babbling on. 'They've brought your son with them, the baby Orestes as well as the Princess Iphigeneia. It will be good to see them, Sir, won't it? And your lovely wife. You've been away so long. They're resting just outside the gates by the stream, the horses are happily grazing and here I am, bringing you the good news. The army knows all about your daughter's arrival. There's a big crowd trying to get a look at her, asking who's to be the lucky bridegroom. Some are saying it's a consecration to Artemis, Virgin Queen of Aulis, to prepare her for marriage. So where are the flowers, the floral crowns? Lord Menelaus, you must organise the music and the dancing for your niece. The day should be all happiness for the girl.'

Completely abstracted in his misery, Agamemnon managed, 'Thank you for your news. Go inside and pray the gods are with us.' With which the somewhat crestfallen messenger had to be content. God help me, what do I do now? I'm ashamed to cry, ashamed not to cry. What in heaven's name shall I say to my wife? How can I face her, look her in the eyes, welcome her to Aulis? But — how dare she come here uninvited? What did I expect, though? Of course, that's what she *would* do. Knowing her, she'll find out my unspeakable plan soon enough.

And Orestes will be here, my little son. He can't talk yet, but surely he'll understand why I had to do it? His baby crying will speak for him, straight to my guilty heart. And — oh poor young maiden! I can hear her voice: 'Will you kill me, Daddy — you?' No, it's all Paris' fault, Priam's son. His love for Helen has destroyed me. And under a tide of self-pity Agamemnon sank. Oh Gods, save me! 'You've won. I've lost,' he told his brother.

10: Agamemnon Trapped at Aulis

Menelaus was touched. 'I pity you. In fact, I'm weeping myself. I'm sorry for all the nasty things I said. Putting myself in your shoes I've changed my mind. Don't do it, brother. Don't kill your child for me. I see how wrong that would be, while my own children live and thrive. I can replace Helen any time I choose. I've been thinking stupidly, selfishly, like an adolescent. Anyway, your daughter is my relative too. Kill my own niece so that I can keep Helen? No I don't think so. You're right. Disband the army as you were planning. Send them all home from Aulis.'

'Thank you,' said Agamemnon. 'I'm grateful. I hate these quarrels, it's unworthy of us sons of Atreus. But I must refuse you, brother. I *can't* do anything. It's a desperate situation. I'm boxed in like an animal in a net. The navy is longing to sail; the army is thirsting to fight. There's no alternative. I must murder my child. Why? Because Calchas the Oracle will go public and the troops camped all round will know everything and turn on us.'

Menelaus tried to be helpful. 'Let's kill him then, that priest.'

'That'd be no use. Odysseus knows everything too. He stirs them up. They'll follow him.'

'Well, there's two of us and only one of Odysseus.'

'Yes, but he's clever, ambitious, wily, and very popular with the men. He's highly dangerous. He'll stand up in front of the army and explain every detail of that wretched priest's prophecy, line by line. He'll tell them I, Agamemnon, promised to go along with the goddess and make the sacrifice and then went back on it. He'll stage a coup, take command of the army and you and I will both be killed, as well as my daughter. And if we don't escape, he'll bring the whole army to Argos, kill us all and occupy the country. Oh I'm in an appalling situation. I'm trapped and in despair …

'Perhaps you could you do one thing for me, Menelaus? Make sure that Clytaemnestra doesn't hear a single word about this. Or not before I've taken the child away from her and seen the whole horrid business through — when she's dead, I mean.' And Menelaus, subdued by the thought of Odysseus plus his army coming after them both, meekly agreed and went off to do Agamemnon's bidding.

Clytaemnestra was enjoying herself. Her daughter, happy and composed in the kindness and care of the women, was sitting alongside her on the seat outside her husband's quarters and whispering, 'Mother,

I can't wait to see my Father. Don't be angry with me if I beat you to it and cuddle him tight before you do.'

'Hush! Not yet, child.' Raising her voice for the onlookers, Clytaemnestra spoke as a queen, calling upon Agamemnon to appear. 'Come out, my lord, we're here at your command.' And out he came. Forcing his head up, his shoulders down, swallowing hard, he emerged from the frail hut like a general and stood tall before his wife and daughter. Iphigeneia was unable to contain herself. 'Mother, don't stop me' and she leapt to her feet, ran and flung her arms around him. 'Dear Father, I've missed you so much!' Clytaemnestra hid her embarrassment; this display of affection was not seemly.

For Agamemnon, the conversation that followed was torture. He struggled to wrap himself in deceit. The girl's innocent love evoked his love in return and it mixed most agonisingly with his dread. He tried. Goodness, how he tried. But Iphigeneia, delighted to be there, couldn't think why he was not equally delighted to see his own child.

'I'm so happy to see you. Aren't you glad to see me? You've arranged this wonderful match for me and I'm so pleased. Stop frowning Daddy, fill your eyes with love. Why are you crying? Please don't.'

'I'm crying because we'll be parted so soon, and for such a long time,' blurted Agamemnon. 'Oh child, you speak so honestly I can't help crying.'

'I'll talk nonsense then, if that makes you feel better,' offered Iphigeneia (dear God, how can I avoid telling her?) 'Don't go to war, Father. Stay at home with your children. What's that — you've been stuck too long with these ships here in Aulis. Well, what's prevented you sailing at once? You say you're going on a long journey and leaving me behind? What? Am I going on a long journey too? Well then, can't we travel together? You could arrange it.'

'No, no, your journey is different. You must remember me … ' (He'd almost let the cat out of the bag there; must be careful.) But she went on, 'Will my mother come with me, then? No? So I'll have to travel just with my new husband, but without my father or mother. Well then, where am I going, Father?'

'That's enough!' he said sharply. 'There are some things young girls shouldn't know. But' — he couldn't stop himself — 'I must perform the proper sacred rituals before I go. Yes, that's a fact, I must do the proper rites. And you'll be there too at the altar. Yes, part of the ceremonies with the holy water.'

What could he say? Oh to be as blessedly innocent as she. 'Go inside now, child. Give me a kiss, hold my hand tight. You'll soon be gone from me, a long way away, and for too long a time.' (I must stop talking like this. Even to touch her makes me cry, in spite of myself.) 'Go into my quarters, child.'

And no sooner had she obeyed than he must turn to Clytaemnestra, who hadn't missed a word. He must face his wife.

A PAUSE: *Agamemnon is in a double bind. Driven by fear, will he keep his promise and do something terrible; or change his mind, confess himself wrong and break his word? Have you ever found yourself stuck as Agamemnon is between a rock and a hard place? What happened for you? Could it have been different? And what do you feel about the making and breaking of vows?*

* * * * *

CHAPTER 5

ACHILLES

Agamemnon had to begin this conjugal meeting by accounting for his tears. They were caused, he explained to his wife, by the heart-breaking thought of losing his daughter to Achilles, she so young, after he'd brought her up with much love and care. Clytaemnestra swallowed her irritation (*he'd* brought her up, indeed!) 'I feel the same, dear husband. But what of the bridegroom?' she asked. 'Is he really of good family? Where's he from?' Agamemnon had the hero's antecedents ready: Achilles had excellent parents and he'd been tutored by Chiron the Centaur himself. 'When's the wedding, then? And what about the

11: Clytaemnestra Suspects

sacrifice you'll have to make to Artemis?' went on his wife. Hiding a shudder, he reassured her that the sacred animal was being prepared. 'And where's it all happening? What about the feast, and the party for the women?'

'It will take place here before the Greek army, in the shadow of the Greek ships,' declared Agamemnon. And, deafening himself to her protests, he went on, 'I shall be the one to give away my daughter and I will light the torches for the marriage. You won't be needed here. You will go straight back to Mycenae and look after Electra and the baby. Take it or leave it.'

For the first time since arriving in Aulis Clytaemnestra knew there was something wrong. Forcefully her words stung him. 'No! That's unheard of, an outrage to all decency. It's a *mother's* duty to see her children married.'

'It's an outrage to see women like you in an army encampment!' Agamemnon's flash back at his uninvited guest won him a temporary victory. 'It's a wife's duty to be at home looking after the children. Go into my quarters now.' She objected yet more loudly; but here in Aulis he held sway and for the moment she gave in, sweeping angrily away.

Self-disgust consumed Agamemnon. If he couldn't even manage to get rid of his wife, how on earth was he to escape this appalling double bind, avoiding both his own personal danger and the nation's shame at the landlocked ships. If only I'd married someone else. A sensible man keeps a quiet, reliable, domestic wife who stays at home — or no wife at all. He went straight across the precinct to his hut and banged the door.

As he disappeared there strode into the courtyard an extraordinarily good-looking young man, shouting for the Supreme Commander. 'Is this Agamemnon's headquarters?' he demanded of the staff officer. 'Tell him Achilles is here and must see him immediately. I'm sick of lying around sunbathing, stuck in this wretched port for the mere lack of a breeze. My Myrmidons are sitting on their hands grumbling, demanding to sail or go home, while Agamemnon and his brother squabble uselessly over what to do next.'

However, it was the queen, not the king, who came to meet him. 'I heard you say your name. Achilles, isn't it? I came out at once. I'm so glad to meet you.' Achilles couldn't think why, but he replied with practised flattery, and thus began a most embarrassing conversation, he having no idea who she was or why she was here in the camp.

12: Clytaemnestra meets Achilles

'Clytaemnestra is my name. The King Agamemnon is my husband. Let's shake hands and pray for happiness, since you're marrying my daughter.'

'What, Madam? I'm not marrying anybody! I've never even met your daughter. The Atreus brothers have said nothing to me.'

Clytaemnestra staggered under this blow, but rallied. She and Achilles put their heads together and worked out that each had been deceived and insulted; they'd both been made to look like fools. Clytaemnestra was scarlet-faced, Achilles furious. 'I'm going to find your husband,' he declared. He swung round, almost crashing into the not-so-old Old Man who'd crept up unobserved.

'Shh! I'm a slave,' the Old Man whispered to Achilles. 'I'm with the Queen. With good luck and good thinking I shall save a life.' Obviously this man knew something. 'My loyalty's yours, ma'am, more than your husband's,' the servant assured her, bowing. 'Your daughter — ' he glanced behind him — 'he's planning to kill her! Yes, her own father — shh! — is going to murder her. That priest, that Oracle, has told him Artemis demands this sacrifice before the ships can sail.' And the Old Man divulged the whole plot, reminding her and Achilles of the elopement of her sister Helen with Paris, of Menelaus the cuckolded husband, and of Agamemnon's need to make war on Troy, capture his brother's wife and drag her home.

'You're saying my Iphigeneia must *die*. To ransom *Helen?*' gasped Clytaemnestra.

'Yes. Her father's sacrificing your child to the goddess. He tricked you, thinking you'd be happy to send her to marry Achilles.' He told them in uneasy whispers of the change of plan; how Agamemnon, in a fit of relative sanity, had sent him with a second letter cancelling the order to bring her to her death and how Menelaus had intercepted, stolen the letter and caused this disaster.

Sinking on to the bench where she had been sitting so happily with Iphigeneia not half an hour before, Clytaemnestra appealed to Achilles. 'He's used the promise of marriage — to you — to lure my daughter to her death.'

'Yes.' The hero flexed his muscles a little. 'Your husband has angered me and that has consequences.'

Clytaemnestra flung herself on her knees before him, declaring she would do anything to save her daughter. 'Stand up for me, I beg you. Defend me from this unmerited calamity. And stand up for her too, though she's not yet your wife. My lovely daughter whom I've brought here with flowers in her hair to be married to you. I've led her like a sacrificial victim to the slaughter. And make no mistake,' she went on, the more anguished as the truth sank in, '*You'll* be blamed too unless you save her. Your honour will be impugned. I have no friends here among all these soldiers and sailors where casual violence is taken for granted. But you can persuade them. Defend us! They will follow you.'

Achilles had had a moment to reflect. 'Much as I would like to help you, Lady, we must follow a middle path here between the anguish of grief and the exhilaration of triumph,' he pronounced. 'Excellent as my instincts usually are, in this case sensible thought should win out over intuition. I'm a generous spirit. I'll do all I can to protect you. No, your daughter will certainly *not* be killed by her father, not now she is engaged to me. He's tried to use me as an instrument for his conspiracies. I can't let him murder your daughter in my name. But it's his fault, not mine.' And, uttering threats of increasing pomposity, Achilles swore by his ancestors ('some of whom are immortals,' he added for good measure) that her father would not lay a finger upon Iphigeneia to harm her. 'I know I must seem like a god, but in fact, I'm just a mortal. So far — '

Clytaemnestra detested her own helplessness. Even as queen, she must trust this man, so like Narcissus, so absorbed in his own reflection. She must thank him, with flattery. 'I was tricked into thinking you were to be my son-in-law. It's my heart that's breaking, not yours. How admirable, that still you should promise to help someone less fortunate than yourself.' Begging for pity, she reminded him how, if Iphigeneia were sacrificed, he would never forget how he had failed her. 'Think how you'll feel on your wedding day to someone else. Only you can save her now. Why, if you wish I'll call her out to meet you herself — ' But even as she spoke, she knew he wouldn't save Iphigeneia.

Achilles said, 'No, don't bring her out just for me to get a look at her. People would laugh, would gossip. Never mind, I'll find a way. I never lie. If my promises prove worthless, let me die on the spot. You have my word that I shall save your child.' He then talked Clytaemnestra round, putting the onus back on her. First, she must try to persuade her husband to reconsider.

'But that's hopeless,' she protested. 'He's a coward. He's scared of the army.'

'Beg him, then,' said Achilles. 'Go down on your knees. If he agrees, I'm out of it and still his friend. If he doesn't, come straight back to me.'

'But supposing he won't agree, how can I find you? My situation will be desperate. You're the only one who can possibly help me. Where in all this camp will you be?'

'If you need me,' declared Achilles airily, 'I shall be there, never fear. To stir up a commotion by asking around for me would not work; anyway, it would be a disgrace to your father, King Tyndareus. Make no fuss and you'll find me.'

'Of course you're right.' And, clutching at this frail straw, Clytaemnestra went on applying balm to his self-regard. He soon left for the army camp and she, in near-despair, for her husband's quarters. She could see it all. These men. Her husband. His brother. The priest. This Achilles. They would garland Iphigeneia like a heifer, put a crown of flowers on her golden hair, lead her to the altar and cut her throat. 'You, my child whom I nurtured to be bride and mother of kings, you will be lost, trampled, stifled by their self-interest. Brotherhood has gone rotten. And they've forgotten all about the vengeance that will be exacted by the gods.'

A PAUSE: *Trickery and a crashing disappointment — not only no Achilles, but death for Iphigeneia, helpless bereavement for the mother and horror for the nurse and the queen's maid. The women have a poor deal in this story. What do you think really needed to happen? Does this have any resonance in your own life?*

* * * * *

CHAPTER 6

CLYTAEMNESTRA

The queen went straight in and told Iphigeneia what was about to happen to her. She stayed a little while, but couldn't long bear her daughter's moans and screams of anguish as she absorbed the truth: 'My father plans to kill me!' The queen left her in tears with Laodameia and went to seek Agamemnon. 'Talk of the devil,' she muttered. 'Here he comes, the father planning the most unnatural crime of all, the murder of his own child. He doesn't guess that I now know it all.'

13: Clytaemnestra and her Daughter

'Ah, my dear wife,' he began. 'I have things to tell you while Iphigeneia is inside, things not suitable for a young girl to hear before her wedding. There are rituals to be observed, altar fires lit, the victim prepared. There are chalices to be made ready for the red blood from the hind's pure white throat, cut in honour of Artemis to celebrate the marriage.'

'Your words sound fine, husband, admirable. Will your actions be admirable too? Come out here, Iphigeneia,' she called. 'You know it all now, every one of your father's plans. Bring the baby.' And her daughter obeyed, weeping over tiny Orestes wrapped snugly in her dress, his face pink and puckered, portending tears.

Maintaining the charade, Agamemnon cried, 'My child, why are you crying, wiping your eyes on your gown? No more smiles for me now? What's going on? Have you two been rehearsing this tearful performance together?'

Dear gods, how shall I begin? muttered Clytaemnestra through her teeth. Aloud she said, 'Answer me one question. Your daughter. My daughter. Are you going to kill her?'

'Am I *what*? What an appalling question. How foul of you to suspect ....'

'Have you any brains left, or are you quite stupid? I know it all, your whole filthy plot. You listen to me, it's my turn now.' And she hurled at him not only her fury at what he was planning but a married life-time of resentments and hurts. All Agamemnon's wrongs were thrown back at him, everything she had suffered, the whole business of the curse on the House of Atreus into which she had been forced to marry. 'You grovelled before my old father Tyndareus till he gave me to you — against my will. And I accepted it and have been a model wife ever since. It's a lucky man that has such a wife. I've kept house for you, given you two girls and a son.

'And now you're taking my daughter from me? Why? So that Menelaus can have Helen back. Why not Menelaus' own daughter? Why mine? What a glorious action, to ransom a whore with a child's life, to buy back the cheapest thing in the world with what is most precious. So you'll do that, will you, and go off to war, for years perhaps, leaving me alone at home with her empty bedroom in the children's wing, singing the same sad song: "Your father killed you, little girl. He gave you your life and then he took it."

'Don't do it!' she spat at him, 'Don't imagine the gods reward murderers just for the asking. When eventually you return to Argos, you'll get the welcome you deserve.' Clytaemnestra was threatening as well as reproaching him. 'What sort of homecoming will you expect? Will you open your arms for your children to hug you? How could they trust you, knowing you killed their sister? Have you thought this through at all, husband, or merely considered your position as general of the army? A real general would have stood up and spoken with wisdom and justice, like a leader. *Soldiers of Greece*, he'd have said, *if you really want to fight this war, then draw lots to see whose daughter must die.* Let Menelaus kill his own daughter Hermione in front of *her* mother. Instead, my daughter must die, while Helen, whose behaviour has caused this disaster, can bring her own girl back home. For the gods' sakes, husband, I beg you, don't kill our daughter. Listen to me if you've any brains left. Change your mind.'

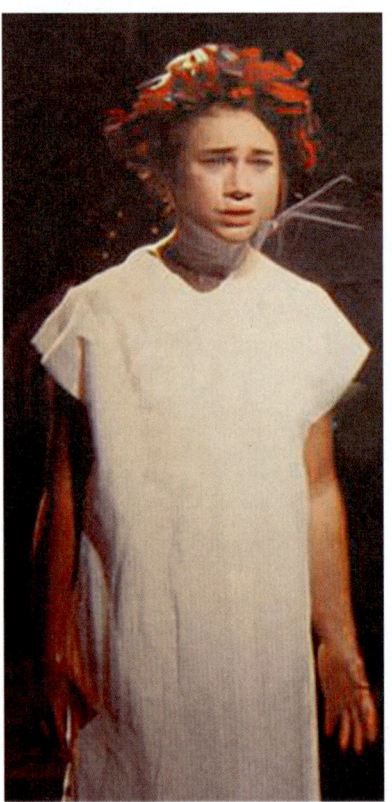

14: Iphigeneia at Aulis

While he was reeling from this, Iphigeneia handed the baby to Laodameia and came weeping to stand before him. 'Father, don't end my life before I've lived. I'm far too young to die. Life is precious. Even the plain daylight is completely beautiful. You can't drive me down into the darkness of the grave. Not yet. I am the first of your children to call you Father, the first you called your child, the first to clamber up on to your knees, to smother you with kisses and be kissed in return.'

She moved close and laid her hand upon his cheek. 'Remember what you said when I was small: "Well my little girl, shall I live to see you happily married, living in some other man's house in a manner worthy of Agamemnon's daughter?" And then, remember what I said, pulling at your beard just as I'm stroking it now. "When you're an old man I'll look after you, because you looked after me and brought me up and that makes it fair." You must have forgotten that, if you're prepared to kill me now. Menelaus and my Aunt Helen, what are they to do with me? I beg you, why should their marriage cause my death?'

To her father's increasing agony she went on, her voice drowning the baby's howls. 'Little brother, you're old enough to cry, as I'm crying, to implore your father not to kill your sister. Pity me Father. I'm young. Spare my life. Far better live in misery than to die even the most glorious death.'

'It's Helen's fault,' said Agamemnon. 'I love my children. Only a madman doesn't. Wife, listen! I'm pushed to these desperate extremes. It's terrifying to do it, but it's equally terrifying to refuse. I've got to do it. Look around you: this massive army, these stationary ships.' He took Iphigeneia by the shoulders. 'They won't get to Troy unless I sacrifice you, daughter. The Oracle says so — tells us the goddess requires it.' Pushing her away, he turned to the queen. 'The men's energy is terrifying, and their lust for retribution. Don't you realise, they'll come after us. They'll kill both our girls in Mycenae and you and me as well, and my son, if I refuse to obey the Oracle. Don't you understand: this isn't about Menelaus. It's for the country that she must be sacrificed.' He raised his voice. 'We must not allow the wives of Greece to be ravished from their beds by barbarians such as Paris.'

And Agamemnon turned and marched grimly off into the camp.

A PAUSE: *In that era the perceived demands of the gods had to be honoured. Clytaemnestra's suggestion does tend towards justice: 'Draw lots to see whose daughter must die.' She would be willing to have some other girl sacrificed for victory, thus betraying the feminine principle without a backward glance. Which gods do we honour and obey now? The gods of money, power, fame? — of beauty, nature, truth? Or ... ? For what would you make a sacrifice?*

* * * * *

CHAPTER 7

IPHIGENEIA

Clytaemnestra sank down, supported by the local women who had greeted them so recently. 'Oh my child, your father sells you as a bride for death, and then he runs away.'

But Iphigeneia was rallying. She could see the hopelessness of her cause and her father's last words had stirred her. 'If I'm not killed we'll *all* die, Mother. You and Father and baby Orestes, and Electra my little sister back home, all will be wiped out.' There was something to be done. 'My father commands me to obey, then betrays me, then — yes — runs away. No one will defend me. So come on, Mother,' she said. 'I am going to die. We'll sing a last threnody together, you and I, a song of death. My way leads to darkness and cold eternity but, far from resisting it, I must embrace it. It's my life that will be the sacrifice, not a deer's or a heifer's. My blood must launch the ships for Troy.'

What was that uproar? Men were shouting, someone was bursting into the precinct from the army camp. Clytaemnestra started to her feet crying, 'It's him; it's Achilles.' At once Iphigeneia, ashamed to be seen by her supposed bridegroom, jumped up to run and hide indoors. 'Not now!' snapped Clytaemnestra, grabbing her arm. 'You're in no position to be fastidious. Swallow your pride, girl, it's your last chance.'

'I tried to do as I promised,' gasped Achilles. 'I got into a fight myself. They stoned me, the whole bloody army.' And the men had indeed been throwing stones at the hero; some had found their mark and he was certainly the worse for wear. 'There's a riot. It's your daughter. They're saying she must be killed.'

'Well, speak for her then,' Clytaemnestra shot back. 'Defend her! Where are your crack troops now?'

'My Myrmidons? They threw the first stones. They said I'd been bought off by marriage. I said, "Don't you lay a finger on my wife," but they shouted me down. However,' and he stood taller, 'I'll still fight them for you.'

'One man against an army?' Clytaemnestra couldn't see that

working. 'Well, God bless you for your courage.'

'They won't dare sacrifice her, not while I live.' Achilles was gathering himself together, though more men were forcing their way in. 'There are thousands of them. Odysseus is in command. Don't worry, I'll stop him. If not, they'll drag her away by her golden hair. You'll have to hang on to her tight with your bare arms.'

15: The Anger of Achilles

Iphigeneia faced Clytaemnestra. 'Listen to me, Mother. Don't be angry. Not with my Father, nor with Achilles. That's pointless now. No one can easily bear what's unbearable. Sir, you deserve our thanks. You've tried to help us; but you mustn't lose your job — maybe your life — for our sakes. It won't work. No.' She turned to face the menacing soldiers. 'I must die. So let me do it decently, with dignity and courage. No, Mother, you know I'm right.'

The men in the courtyard were quiet now, no longer throwing stones, listening, hearing Iphigeneia's clear voice. 'If I die, no Greek woman will ever again be dragged from her home by force. Troy will be sacked and the whole world will see what happens to Paris for stealing

Helen. I shall win that by giving my life. I shall become famous as the woman who set Greece free.

'These sailors, these soldiers,' and her words rang out, 'are ready to defend their beloved fatherland because it has been wronged and insulted. They will risk their lives, Mother. They'll die if need be. How can my single life stand against that? Why should Achilles take on the whole Greek army single handed, and probably be killed, for the sake of one girl? What use are women in war? One brave man is worth ten thousand of us. And if the great Goddess Artemis demands my body, who am I, a mere mortal, to oppose her wishes?'

16: Achilles does his Best

Swinging round, she stood, fourteen years old and beautiful, and addressed the men. 'I dedicate my body as a gift for Greece. Take me! Sacrifice me. Go to Troy, plunder the city, leave it a ruin. That will be my memorial. Your Greek victory will be the marriage I never celebrated, the children I never had. My name will be remembered through the generations. Greeks must rule barbarians, barbarians must never rule Greeks; for freedom is our birth-right.'

And the soldiers burst into huge cheers. At that moment, Achilles, standing by Clytaemnestra and nursing his black eye, fell in love with Iphigeneia. 'Oh, if only I'd been allowed to win you for my wife. You're a blessing, a model of nobility. How can the goddess demand such a sacrifice? I envy both you and Greece. Your words are worthy of your fatherland. The gods are too powerful for you and so you've wisely faced the inevitable. Such strength of character only increases my passionate desire to have married you. I'm angry and disappointed not to be able to save you, even if that had meant fighting the whole Greek army.'

Iphigeneia cut in. 'Listen to me. I have no hope now, and no fear either. You mustn't die, my friend, nor kill anyone on my account. So leave me, let me save Greece if I can.'

Achilles did his best. He promised her that he would be present at the sacrifice and if she changed her mind he would fight for her, force her killers to stop. 'Even you, when the knife is at your throat, may see things differently. If you regret this momentary impulse, remember my promise. No harm will come to you, not in my presence. I shall stand right by the altar and wait there till you come.' And off he went with his weapons to the sanctuary of Artemis.

As soon as he had gone, the black-robed priestesses of the goddess appeared, sent by the Oracle, ready to prepare Iphigeneia and take her away. Clytaemnestra sobbed as if her heart would break. 'Mother, why are you crying? I'll be frightened if you cry. And please promise you won't wear black for me, or cut off your hair because you've lost your daughter. I won't be lost, but remembered for ever. There won't be any grave to grieve over because the altar of Artemis will be my tomb.'

'Oh my darling, it's not the grave but the death I'll grieve for. But I know you're right … '

'Tell Electra that I'm the lucky one, dying for Greece. Tell her never to wear black for me either. Just say goodbye to her. And when Orestes is bigger' — she took the baby and cuddled him close — 'tell him to be a man for me. I'll never see you again, my little darling. You did your best, didn't you. Oh Mother, don't hate my Father. He's your husband. He'll be terrified now. He doesn't want to kill me; he's doing it for Greece.'

17: Iphigeneia goes to Artemis

'It's a disgusting sham!' Clytaemnestra burst out. 'His ancestors would disown him.'

'Who will escort me … ?' She stopped for a moment. 'Oh no! Will they hold my head back by the hair? No, you mustn't come with me, Mother, that wouldn't be right. And don't hang on to my clothes. Stay here. That'll be better for both of us. Now,' she raised her voice, handing the baby back to Laodameia who was standing by in misery. 'Don't cry, Nurse. There, I love you. Please could one of my father's guards escort me to the garden of Artemis where I'm to be sacrificed. Not one tear Mother, not one!'

Silently the temple priestesses came forward to prepare her for the sacrifice, dressing her hair with flowers, garlanding her body, washing her hands with holy water. The music began. 'Chant a hymn for me, women of Aulis. Sing of my fate in honour of Artemis, daughter of Zeus. Let all the sons of Greece throughout the camps be silent, for this moment is holy. Let the priests prepare the instruments of sacrifice. Let my father circle the altar according to the ritual. My sacrifice will bring salvation to the Greeks. And victory!'

And at Aulis the crowded harbour rang with the shouts, blown on the contrary wind, of soldiers fired for war and waving a forest of weapons. 'Glory to the fatherland!' cried the princess. 'I shall never see my home in Argos again. Goodbye, for ever, sun, great torch of the world, goodbye. I go to another life now, another time, unknown and strange, my eternal home. Goodbye daylight, for ever and ever. Goodbye.'

And so the procession led Iphigeneia away to the sanctuary for the ritual to be enacted. Clytaemnestra, unable to bear any more, withdrew into her husband's quarters. But the doors could not shut out the prayers of those around her: '*May Agamemnon, the greatest soldier of the Greek nation, end this tale crowned with immortal glory.*' And at the moment of the sacrifice, the army and the navy fell silent and the wind changed.

A PAUSE: *Iphigeneia recognises the limits of her situation: If the Goddess demands my body, who am I, a mere mortal, to oppose her wishes? Useless to resist. So, before Achilles' intervention, she does something extraordinary. She turns a dire situation into an opportunity, bringing glory to her father and her country with a heroism that in fact brings her name into our own time. What instances of courage and self-sacrifice have you come across in your own life, or in story?*

* * * * *

CHAPTER 8

ARTEMIS EXACTS HER DUE

For Clytaemnestra, nothing could be worse than this — except what happened next. A young captain of Agamemnon's personal guard came rushing in from the sacrifice, shouting as he came, 'Daughter of Tyndareus, come out! I've something extraordinary to tell you.'

A note in his voice made her get up, distraught and close to collapse as she was. 'What now? I can't cope with anything more.'

'It's your daughter!' What else? A few of the local women stood with the queen as, breathlessly, the captain saluted. 'Something amazing has occurred. The Greek army was on parade in the sanctuary garden. Your daughter was made ready for the ritual. Agamemnon was weeping like a child, I tell you, face hidden in his cloak. She came close enough to touch him and, near as I can remember, this is what she said. "I am a willing sacrifice. I won't make a sound. I'll stretch my neck out without any fear. May you win victory!" Everyone was immensely impressed at this young girl's extraordinary courage and sense of what was right.'

'Well? Go on.' And Clytaemnestra heard of the call for silence, how her daughter was crowned with flowers, the whetted knife drawn and displayed, the holy water, the solemn circling of the altar. Agamemnon and Menelaus were there, but it was Achilles who prayed, dedicating on Agamemnon's behalf the sacrifice of an innocent virgin. *Grant us in return, Artemis, a fair wind, good passage for our ships and victory in Troy.* 'The girl's father and uncle and most of the soldiers stared at the ground as the priest prepared to perform the deed,' the captain told her. 'I did too. I felt terrible.'

At his next words Clytaemnestra's grief was turned into incandescent rage. Her husband had sent this captain to tell her yet another tall story, still deceiving her, still treating her as a fool. The young man's voice was rising in excitement. 'Something wonderful happened, my Lady, a miracle! There's no doubt a throat was cut, but — no girl lay stretched on the ground. The gods had substituted a deer for your daughter. We saw it, a hind bred to run like the wind on the mountains.

Calchas the priest spoke up, all joy, telling us that this sacrifice was acceptable to Artemis — that she might even prefer a deer to a girl whose nobility could stain her altar. She would now grant us all we asked for.

'Your husband himself has sent me to tell you the news, particularly about the glory it confers on him, our Commander. And your daughter's been transported to the heavens, to live among the gods,' finished the captain. 'No longer grieve for her, Ma'am. And don't be angry with your husband. Death is turned to rebirth, darkness transformed into light.'

The queen looked around at the precinct, empty but for a few women. 'Then where are you now, Iphigeneia my child?' Her words were deadly quiet. 'And you, Captain? You bring me plasters for a broken heart. Do you expect me to believe this story? It's a lie, concocted for my benefit, to soothe me and keep me quiet.'

At that moment, Agamemnon himself came in through the gate, stiff and tall, his face breaking into a ghastly smile while hers was a mask of stone. His words could not have been better calculated to inflame her fury. 'Our daughter is among the gods. Your duty now, wife, is to take good care of Orestes, that little soldier of mine. Go back home. I'll be busy and won't get to Argos for some time. I hope things go well with you.'

Though she was not born into the House of Atreus, simply married into it, the curse now well and truly descended upon the queen. Rage turned to ice. She looked at her husband with arctic coldness, turned and left without a word. Their marriage was over. Agamemnon turned his corpse-like smile towards the women standing around, and they slowly began to leave. Nothing was ended. Much was just beginning.

* * * * *

Ten years and more passed. Laodameia, in her room in the palace at Mycenae, was deciding what to tell Orestes when he made his clandestine visit. No one in Argos knew how Agamemnon had traded his daughter's life for a breeze, how the queen had been deceived, made ridiculous, shamed, deprived of her child then left to cope alone. The secret had been well kept and this knowledge seemed set to die with her.

Laodameia never forgot the journey back from Aulis to Mycenae. Stunned with sorrow, she'd concentrated on Orestes, deftly handling the baby, fearing for her mistress' sanity. The queen was alternately huddled in misery in her corner of the chariot, or staring desperately out. And as the wheels bumped over the stones she was muttering, 'I'll get him! He'll be punished. Oh, how to avenge this crime?' She seemed driven less by grief for her daughter than by the insult to her own person. Back in Mycenae she was never heard to speak Iphigeneia's name again. She ignored her younger daughter also, as far as she could, and the nurse feared for Electra. And for the baby too.

Life in the palace had rumbled on for those ten years. The king was absent, fighting a war in Troy that all hoped would yield a tremendous victory. The palace servants remained in ignorance of the disaster at Aulis, believing the elder princess safely married and gone; for, like Laodameia, the queen's maid who had accompanied them in the chariot kept the secret of Iphigeneia's fate. It was too horrible to be divulged.

As soon as he was old enough Orestes was sent away to Phocis to be fostered by King Strophius and put out of Clytaemnestra's mind. Deprived of her father, Electra certainly missed her brother, though she found other children to play with, including her cousin Hermione, older and less obstreperous, who was living with them since her mother's abduction. But taking the little boy to Phocis and leaving him there had broken the nurse's heart. Though wary on his behalf, Laodameia had longed for that one brief return he was allowed, a visit to her warm room never to be repeated.

Electra grew taller, feistier and more full of words. She was a sharp child, dark-haired, thin and clever. Before he was sent away, she taught her little brother to disobey. She wheedled the attendants into doing her bidding. She defied her mother at every opportunity, infuriating Clytaemnestra by demanding, 'Why's Orestes been sent away? I want him here? *When's* my father coming home? Why isn't he coming? I want my Daddy?'

When she was still only eight or nine the children's 'Uncle' Aegisthus appeared in the palace to pay a visit to his cousin's family. Not that there was any love lost between the visitor and the absent Agamemnon. The curse on the House of Atreus had passed through both their fathers, who were brothers and had hated each other. Things had happened that were far too horrible for the children to hear about.

However, Aegisthus was no blood-relation of Clytaemnestra's and the fact that he detested her husband warmed her to him. It took no time

18: Aegisthus

at all for his visit to be extended; they ended by cuckolding Agamemnon and comforting one another. He moved into the palace at Mycenae. Each had been disastrously wronged and there was a kind of glee in stoking their rage and planning revenge. They did not marry, since there was evidence that Agamemnon would probably return; but in his absence Aegisthus assumed the kingship, lived like a lord and took over the ruling of Argos 'together with my consort Clytaemnestra', as he put it.

The servants mostly accepted the situation. They assumed the queen was missing her husband and her now-married elder daughter and they didn't begrudge her a lover. They found Aegisthus useful. He filled a gap, saw to the palace affairs with some degree of efficiency and kept their mistress relatively quiet. He soon found a governess for Electra who could keep her mostly out of the way, and he packed the boy off to the relatives in Phocis as soon as he decently could. Out of sight, out of mind. 'You'll need protection, little fellow, both now and in the future,' Laodameia had whispered to Orestes.

For over all their heads hung the threat that weighed upon them like a shroud of darkness: the doom of the curse on the House of Atreus.

A PAUSE: *It is said that any buried rage or fear or hurt which the parents fail to deal with in their own lives is picked up and carried by the children. In this story, Orestes is such a victim. Family secrets kept and stored can act corrosively as time passes. If you know of any such secrets, how might it be if their contents were wisely dealt with?*

* * * * *

CHAPTER 9

THE RETURN OF THE KING

In the tenth and final autumn of that war so catastrophic for Troy, the storm had broken in Mycenae. The watchman, who'd spent the whole year filled with gloomy forebodings, was crouched on the palace wall on his elbows, gazing towards the mountains. He had been given fresh orders by the queen: 'My husband is returning to Argos *tonight*. It's not just rumour this time. Shout from the roof-tops the moment you see the signal-fire. Cry victory or it will be the worse for you. Let the city know that Troy is taken. Greece has triumphed. Agamemnon has won the war!' The watchman, struggling to keep awake, came to with a jerk

19: Queen Clytaemnestra

and stared out from the tower, terrified of missing the vital sign. Look! There it was, a tiny flame flickering from the hilltop.

'Wake up! We've won,' he shouted through the darkness. Beacons would soon be lit all over Argos, and in the towns and villages there would be dancing in the streets. 'The King is coming home this very night.' His voice was echoed by that of the town-crier and by Clytaemnestra herself as she emerged from the palace with her entourage, lit the altar-fires and raised her own cry: 'Victory — joy — Agamemnon comes home tonight in triumph!'

Clytaemnestra did not feel afraid of her husband's imminent return, though she would have preferred the war to go on for ever. With the two remaining children out of the way, the guards suitably armed and rewarded and Aegisthus out of sight but close by, she was mistress of the situation. She had grown familiar with the fury within her consort's heart and her own, their loathing stoked by their nightly conversations. They had their plan. The adoration of the people for the warrior-hero Agamemnon, nourished by his absence, did not dismay her. Her lover was powerful, a more than adequate pseudo-king. But the gods' love for Argos was a violent love.

Waiting, she knew that even now Agamemnon would hear no word against the Oracle in Aulis. He would never blame Artemis for all those lives laid down in the attrition of a useless ten-year war, let alone for the life of Iphigeneia. She remembered how her husband had dreaded the doom that would crush him if he didn't obey Calchas, yet also feared the doom that would crush him if he did. Which was worse? Desert the fleet and fail the Greeks, or change the winds with his daughter's blood and feed the war-lust of the soldiers? Agamemnon, under the curse on the House of Atreus, had been damned if he did and damned if he didn't.

Well, her husband had chosen. 'The law's the law. Let's hope for the best,' he'd said as he obeyed the goddess and sacrificed the loving daughter who had once sung her joyous songs for palace guests. A woman's death for war, grief, pain and misery. Where would the curse go next, the ancestral trap his father, his uncle and his grandfather had also fallen into? Clytaemnestra did not sleep well these days; for, as the poet put it, 'drop by drop at her heart, the pain of pain remembered came again' (Aeschylus, 'Agamemnon' P.109). She tossed and turned the hours away, haunted by images of her husband ordering the acolytes to gag the girl, since any cries would curse the house, choking her so that she could not call him Father.

But this night Mycenae was buzzing. Citizens were rushing to the palace waving torches. 'Is it true? He's coming home? Victory at last?' And the queen stood tall before them and proclaimed, 'Yes! The gods have rushed the fire from Mount Ida, beacon to beacon, a chain of fires to relay my husband's signal to me by way of capes and mountains. The Greeks have taken Troy, won Priam's citadel. Now, let no new disaster strike. Let the best win out, clear to see. That's all I want.'

'See, my Lady too is full of joy and longing for the return of her husband. Spoken like a man,' shouted someone. 'Praise the gods!' And now, the courier of the king himself came running, bearing fresh news. 'He comes, Ma'am! The son of Atreus, lord of men, is just outside. Give him the royal welcome he deserves.'

'Open wide the gates,' ordered Clytaemnestra. 'Tell him to hurry. The people's darling. How they long for him! And his wife? He will find me true to him, faithful to the last. I have not changed. He and I are bound for ever.' They believe me, she thought. In ten years, how well I've learned my part. She turned sharply and went into the palace.

A PAUSE: *Clytaemnestra is full of the zest for revenge, the glee that comes with the idea of punishing the hated person. Vengeance is built deeply into the fabric of humanity, the longing to hurt the offender. In this story such longing is played out. How do you feel about the modern punishment of offenders? What of the call for the death penalty, muted but still alive in our societies?*

* * * * *

CHAPTER 10

CASSANDRA

The watchman on the wall saw Agamemnon's chariot rumbling into the palace courtyard, his plunder borne with him. He watched the horses below him coming to a standstill and the citizens of Mycenae pressing forward, calling 'Well fought, Sire, well won! How can we praise you enough, son of Atreus, we who have been faithful to you all along?'

Agamemnon stood up in the chariot, 'We must thank the gods by performing a sacrifice,' he said. 'We have raped and defeated Troy because their son Paris stole Helen away. And by the gods, we've taken her back. We were right to do it.' And although Clytaemnestra came out at that moment with her women, who were carrying a dark red carpet, Agamemnon did not interrupt his speech but went on telling the crowd stories about the conflict, about the loyalty of Odysseus, about the need now for a national tribunal. 'The gods who sent me to war have brought me home,' he finished. Only then did he step down from the chariot and look at his wife.

Clytaemnestra was staring at him. She turned to the citizens. 'I'm ten years older now and my loneliness has been terrible. I am not ashamed to tell you how I love this man. The rumours alone have almost killed me.' Which man? Which rumours? She was facing him again. 'And so our child is gone, not standing by our side.' What did she mean? Her words could be taken several ways. 'By rights our child should be here.' The king grew pale beneath his helmet. Who? Which … ?

'I'm talking of Orestes,' she went on. 'You seem startled, husband. You needn't be. Strophius the Phocian is taking good care of him. He warned me how we were doubly threatened, should you lose your life in the war and anarchy rise up here at home. So our child is gone for his own safety. I have cried and cried, watching late at night till I have no tears left. For you alone I've endured it all. But now we can bring the boy home — your son. We have suffered long enough.'

She reached towards Agamemnon. 'Climb down from the car of war, my Lord. Now for the red carpet.' She turned and called, 'Women, spread it before him, let it lead him to the palace doors. Come to me now, my dearest. Here's a red stream for you to walk on. May it flow and bring you home. Leave all the rest to me. We will set things right, with the gods' help, and do whatever Fate requires.'

Agamemnon's feet ached as he descended from the chariot. He was hungry, he was weary, he was longing to be bathed, fed and comforted in his own home. Quickly he got over the shock of what he had feared his wife was saying. She's all right, he thought; she's the keeper of my House, my home. But I'm not keen on this blood-red carpet. In fact it scares me stiff.

'You're treating me like a woman,' he told her. 'You needn't fawn over me. I'm no god, just a human being. I don't want some gorgeous carpet. The plain earth will do me fine.' But Clytaemnestra insisted and, too tired to argue, he surrendered. 'All right, I'll walk on it if you're so determined. Just this once I'll enter my father's house trampling royal crimson as I go. Help me off with these boots, someone. They've served me well.'

Who's that? wondered the queen … there, half-glimpsed among his entourage? Surely he hadn't dared bring some girl here? Booty from Troy — unbelievable! But yes, Agamemnon was giving his hand to a young woman stepping from the chariot. She was dressed in Apollo's sacred regalia and carrying his sceptre. Her hair flamed red. The child of a god? The king was commanding the servants to treat her with gentleness, telling how she had followed him from Troy; though everyone knew she would not have had much option.

Agamemnon walked the red carpet uneasily — such luxury! He hoped the gods were not watching, ready to strike him down with envy from on high. 'This thing must have cost a kingdom's worth of silver to weave,' he said. 'I'm ashamed.'

'Be proud of it,' returned Clytaemnestra. 'We can afford it, we're wealthy; we don't do poverty. At last you're back to your father's hearth, the master come among the shadows of your house. Like the sun in winter, you bring us warmth. You're fulfilled now.'

And so Agamemnon came home. His bodyguards were taken to the kitchens to be fed, while the king and the queen entered the palace together, the doors closed behind them and uneasiness was left murmuring outside. Sensing danger, the more far-seeing of the citizens were praying their fears would prove false: they could almost hear the chanting of the dirge of the Furies.

The captive young woman, meanwhile, had been brought into the servants' hall by the women. They obeyed the king, treating her kindly though they found her difficult. She would neither eat nor talk, though they believed she understood what was said to her, and her hair was strangely wild and unruly. While Agamemnon was preparing for his first supper at home, Clytaemnestra herself slipped downstairs and found the girl. The chief maid was coaxing her, without success, to eat and speak and be normal.

20: Cassandra is mute

'Won't you come up and be with us?' The queen smiled at her husband's mistress. 'I know your name. You are Cassandra, a princess, King Priam's daughter. Come and celebrate with us, Cassandra. Your city was burnt behind you, but don't be proud; lots of people get sold into bondage and endure the bitter bread of slaves, but you've landed on your feet here. We are rich, we'll see you're all right. Come now … '

Cassandra remained silent, her face impossible to read. The maid who had taken charge of this enslaved princess whispered to her, 'You better obey, you really had. Else you're in trouble.'

'Can she understand you?' Clytaemnestra wondered aloud. 'She may speak her own barbaric talk. Perhaps she uses sign language? But' — sharply —'she must do as I say. And do it *now*! I have no time to waste down here.'

'She's a stranger, a wild creature,' ventured the maid. 'She needs an interpreter. Don't you dear?' No response.

After a fruitless pause Clytaemnestra, declaring 'She's mad', turned on her heel and marched up the stairs. The staff tried everything they could think of, but Cassandra remained transfixed. They were all staring at her when she startled them with a great shriek. Everyone jumped. 'Apollo, my destroyer!' she screamed. 'Let me die … '

'So she *can* speak our language,' murmured someone, recovering.

'Where am I?' cried the young woman, staring wildly round.

'You're in Agamemnon's palace. The House of Atreus. Did you really not know?'

They tried to reason with her, questioning her gently, hoping to understand this strange person. But gradually their awe was overtaken by fear. Surely there was a god living within Cassandra, for words began to stream from her in an increasing torrent of passion and foreboding. Their dread deepened as the frightful events in Agamemnon's family (too horrible for Strophius or Laodameia to recount) were detailed in jerky, detached, rambling words and sentences. Soon the servants' hall was filled with fear. And now she was presaging murder in the house. 'She's raving. The queen's right. She's crazy, out of touch,' murmured the women.

'Come, dear,' said the maid. 'You say you see the future, but we in Argos, we don't go in for that kind of thing.'

'Oh no, what horror,' cried Cassandra, oblivious, 'what new agony is here, growing deep in this house? A plot, a monstrous, crushing thing. And rescue's far away.' She raved on, something about beds and baths and nets and a lunge of death.

'It's no use, she's lost, talking in riddles.' The kindly maid, groping

21: Cassandra Foretells the Return of Orestes

and helpless, had done her best.

'Avenge the victim. Stone them dead!' shouted Cassandra. 'Look out! She'll trap him! Oh why am I brought here, tormented? Why, unless to die with him? Poison waits for me. Then off with the veils that hid the fresh young bride. We will see the truth, though you won't believe me. The Furies cling to this house for dear life.'

All below stairs tried gamely to understand their visitor as she poured forth her obscure prophecies. 'Our language is strange, yet still you sense truth?' said someone else. 'Which god has taught you these skills?'

'The raging Mother of Death is here and seems to be rejoicing. He is safe home from war, saved for her. But soon you'll see her face to face. Yes, you'll admit I told the truth. Agamemnon, you will see him dead.'

'Hush, poor girl!' cried the maid. 'Don't say such things! Put those words to sleep. What man would do such a thing?'

'*Man*? You haven't heard a word I said,' Cassandra cried. 'She will kill me too. At this very moment she is gloating, as she whets the sword'

22: The Slaying of Agamemnon © Tricia Newell

for him and mixes her drugs for me. He brought me home and we will pay in carnage.

More quietly, Cassandra foretold what would follow. 'We will die, but not without some honour from the gods. He will come home, the son. Born to kill his mother, born his father's champion, a wanderer, a fugitive driven off his native land. As his father lies upon the ground, the God Apollo will draw him home, with power like a prayer.' Incredulous shock stirred amongst the kitchen staff.

'No one believes me,' she went on. 'They never do. Yet now I must be brave. It is my turn to die. I pray that when the avengers come and cut the assassins down, they will avenge me too, a slave who died, an easy conquest.' And Cassandra, princess of Troy, Agamemnon's slave and concubine, went out through the doors of the servants' hall and up into the palace.

Within the halls above, horror struck. As her husband came out of the bath Clytaemnestra came forward to wrap a towel about him, but instead threw over his head a tent of net she had woven herself. Entangled like a fish, Agamemnon perished. Cries broke out: he had been found stabbed in his bath. Aegisthus had emerged from hiding and held him till Clytaemnestra could gore her husband through. Cassandra lay nearby, poisoned to death as she had foretold.

A PAUSE: *In that era, people often dealt with their enemies by extorting 'an eye for an eye.' (Leviticus too had enjoined it a good hundred years before the Greek playwrights wrote our story.) As Strophius tells Orestes, it is by command of the gods that revenge must be taken. Nowadays we rarely slay each other in practice, but we have other ways of getting even. By what means do individuals pay each other back today? How do you react if someone wrongs you?*

* * * * *

PART TWO

RETRIBUTION

CHAPTER 11

DEMETRIUS

Orestes' plan to visit Laodameia in Argos was going well. His messenger, an older friend, had ridden there from the academy and warned the nurse that her favourite, Orestes, was coming secretly to visit. He had come back to Phocis undetected. 'I told her you can't wait to get there. Now it's your turn, kid,' he said. 'Pylades will go too, there'll be horses ready for you day after tomorrow and may the gods be with you.'

Too late.

Rumour, followed by definite news, had reached Phocis from Mycenae. What horror, and so soon. 'The Queen of Argos has killed the King with her own hand.' Again, the curse had fallen in the House of Atreus. Strophius realised the boy must be told. Couldn't Demetrius do it? No. A troubled conversation with the tutor showed him that he must break this appalling news himself. After all, he was Orestes' guardian. Agamemnon was — had been — his brother-in-law. 'I can't put this on to someone else. Thank the gods I've already told the lad something about his family.'

With huge foreboding the king sent for his ward again. 'Orestes, we have further matters to discuss.' And, stumblingly, hesitantly, as best he could, he broke the news of Agamemnon's death. He spared the worst of the details. The boy would learn all too soon just how his mother had done the deed, how his father had met his end.

'So you see, it all rests on you. You are the rightful heir to the Kingdom of Argos. You're nearly grown up now, Orestes. Eleven, isn't it? Not quite yet, but very soon, you will have to take action yourself. Meanwhile, you are safe here. You must keep out of sight. Don't be tempted to go to Mycenae. I know you have a sister there and are fond of the nurse who first brought you here. But do not leave this place. Do you understand?'

Of the students, only Pylades knew what had happened. Strophius had told him all. 'A terrible thing, son. I have to tell you that Orestes' own mother was the murderer. Keep an eye on your friend. Don't let him stray out of the grounds. Watch out for strangers. You must understand, his life's in danger. I wouldn't trust that pair not to come looking for him themselves. They'll be scared stiff of him. Don't frighten him, but since you now know what his mother's really done, you'll know how to manage. I'm trusting you, my son.'

23: Pylades and Orestes in Phocis

'What an impossible task,' thought Pylades. He shrugged his young shoulders and undertook to obey his father. Strophius had given Orestes only the end result. 'Your father is dead at Clytaemnestra's hand, murdered at Mycenae. You are a fatherless prince'. It was Pylades, young, jumpy and always disconcertingly at his elbow nowadays, who let him pour out his grief and rage. In a daze of bewilderment and disbelief Orestes realised he'd always somehow known that this would happen.

Demetrius the tutor, witnessing the young prince's shock, did his best to handle it. It was left to him to make clear the implications, which he did with understanding, pity and huge foreboding. 'Your mother apparently almost threw his body out of the house, and he was buried hugger-mugger, with no libations. It's said the people of Mycenae were forbidden to attend the funeral. When a father is killed he must of course be avenged. You are too young now, but in a very few years you will have to find out how the gods want you to deal with this, Orestes.'

These boys hear only childish stories about the gods, he thought. They don't *know* the gods. I brought Orestes to Phocis as a little lad and here he is, living at the foot of Mount Parnassus; but what does he know of our mountain, let alone of Delphi, just along the road. He doesn't know of Olympus, nor of Zeus who dwells there. He doesn't know Demeter, who I'm named after, or Athene, or Apollo — their power. And what of their Oracles? He mustn't stay ignorant any longer. 'You must visit Delphi,' he told the boy. 'It's not far away. Look at the mountain, lad,' and he pointed away across the green-gold farmland of Phocis to where the snowy summit of Parnassus floated against the blue, the lovely landscape of Greece spread at its feet. 'Delphi lies between two of its peaks. We'll go there and find the temple of Apollo. It's looked after by a famous priestess, the Pythoness. She is the Delphic Oracle. She's very wise and later you can consult her and find out what Apollo requires of you.

'Meantime, spend less time on your indoor studies, Orestes, and learn the martial arts. Practise hunting and horsemanship, archery and swordsmanship for all you're worth. Imagine you're a Spartan. Toughen up, lad.'

24: The Temple at Delphi on Mount Parnassus

Not wanting to bring trouble to Strophius' kingdom, Orestes obeyed, his planned visit to Laodameia put on hold. Reeling with shock, he kept out of sight as far as he could. Good as his word, Demetrius took him and Pylades on a covert expedition to nearby Delphi. 'Here, prophecies are channelled by the mysterious Oracle. With her divine wisdom she speaks the very words of the God Apollo.' Orestes was beginning to understand his own precarious position. So my mother and her lover killed my father in cold blood, he thought. Oh, poor Father! Though Electra won't have been surprised.

But what he did not know was why. Why had Clytaemnestra killed Agamemnon? What possible reason could she have had? Surely his parents had loved each other, at least when he was born? He thought of Laodameia's tale; but she had told him very little of what had happened to his mother on that mysterious expedition at the start of the Trojan War when he was a baby. What of that older sister? Surely, if Iphigeneia had really been married, she would have sent some message home by now. Laodameia had always stopped her story mid-way, never recounting Clytaemnestra's point of view either to him or, as far as he knew, to Electra. Obviously a secret had been kept from them. It seemed no one knew why his sister had vanished.

* * * * *

Years passed. At last the boys' education at the academy at Phocis was complete. The world beckoned. 'Now, both of you,' said King Strophius, 'be on your way. You have my blessing, my sons, and that of Queen Anaxibia. Go abroad, explore, and remember, keep out of the way of anyone from Argos.' Agreeing that they would meet in Phocis in one year's time, Orestes and Pylades vanished from Greece. They went travelling, sometimes together, sometimes separately and had many adventures.

When the year was up, both reappeared in King Strophius' palace as planned and were warmly greeted. The tutor Demetrius was still there, older now but fit and enthusiastic as ever. After consulting Strophius, he found the friends and drew them aside. 'It's time,' he said. 'You, Orestes, must visit your kingdom of Argos. You are ready now.'

'Sir, you are my wise friend, my mentor. You've always stuck up for me. When you took me and Pylades to the Oracle at Delphi, I knelt at

25: Orestes makes up his mind © Tricia Newell

the Navel Stone at the core of the world and asked Apollo how best to avenge my father. I didn't tell you then, but what the Pythoness replied was, "Kill his killers. You must do it with no troops, no armour, by stealth. Slaughter them with your own hand." That is what the god told me. That is what I must do.'

'I guessed that, Orestes,' said Demetrius. 'And I'm coming with you. What about you, Pylades? Will you come too?'

'Wild horses wouldn't stop me,' declared the King's son. 'I'm in on this.'

'I've already arranged travel,' said the tutor, unsurprised. 'We'll need to disguise ourselves. I wish things were different, but this is dangerous work. No one must recognise you, Orestes.'

And so they rode from Phocis to Argos in the South. And now all three stood there on a hillside, stars glittering over their heads and a great township spread darkly across from them. 'Mycenae in Argos is a city of gold,' said Demetrius. 'Look at your parents' palace, where you were born, Orestes, your rightful home as the son of Agamemnon who commanded our armies at Troy.'

And there it was, lying across the valley in all its night-time splendour. Gazing towards the battlements Orestes realised that, despite his mother and her lover, he had been longing for his old home, dreaming of it, listening to tales about it. Surely Electra, his childhood playmate, would still be here? He'd last seen his sister when she was about ten and he not yet six. They would hardly recognise each other now, both grown up. And beloved Laodameia, so close. He thought too of his other sister, the one who was lost …

No one was about. By starlight they stashed their supplies in the bushes, then seated themselves in the dark beneath a rocky outcrop. Demetrius told more stories about the curse on the House of Atreus; how the family was bloodied by death and mayhem going back generations. He did not once mention the lost elder sister. Orestes wondered if he even knew about Iphigeneia. And he had nothing to say of Clytaemnestra except, 'And now most recently, Agamemnon is cruelly slain.' Was there no one to speak for his mother, put her side of things? Evidently not.

'When you were a little boy,' Demetrius went on, 'under orders from Strophius and our queen, I carried you away from Argos. Later, when your father was murdered, being in Phocis saved your life. But you were raised to take revenge, Orestes. It's your duty to give back his honour to your dead father.'

The tale of revenge upon revenge lasted until the stars faded and birds sang loud and clear in the dawn. Demetrius finished by describing

26: Apollo gives Orestes his charge © Tricia Newell

the appalling things done to Aegisthus' father by Orestes' grandfather and, unlike Strophius, he didn't spare the details. That final story of the terrible dinner served by grandfather Atreus was the last straw. In that moment Orestes grew up. For years, the shock of his mother's crime and his father's death, his rage at Aegisthus, the loss of Laodameia, of Electra, of his rightful home, the horror of it all, had left him reeling like a ship in a storm. But this disgusting story finally ended his adolescence. He was a man now and knew what he must do.

Out there in the dawn Orestes took charge. 'Listen, Demetrius — you too, Pylades, my most excellent friend — the moment has arrived. Before this house wakes up we must act. Our plan of attack must be worked out quickly. No time to dither. Let's do it.' Their plan was to speak Parnassian with a Delphic accent. Demetrius was to infiltrate the palace disguised as an elderly messenger sent by an ally in Phocis with a sad story. Good news, though, for the queen: *Orestes has been killed in a chariot race — a horrible accident.*

'Pylades and I shall honour Father as the god told us,' Orestes went on. 'We'll go to his tomb and perform the rites. I'll cut off my hair and you can leave the flowers you've brought. Though they're pretty faded by now.' Orestes grinned briefly. 'It will cheer up the royal rulers no end to hear of my sad demise.' But then he paused. 'It makes me uneasy though, pretending to be dead. What ominous fate might that portend?'

'Come on, Orestes,' said Demetrius. 'Lots of people have faked their own deaths, and when they come home alive, the awe they inspire lasts a lifetime.'

'You're right. It's what Apollo commands. It'll pave the way for my new life, avenged and clear.' He stood up. 'I too will rise from death flush with life and flame like a starburst over my enemies.' His enemies: who? His mother? Her lover?

As the sun rose over Mycenae the three of them, disguised as travellers, crept towards the palace, its walls lit golden in the dawn. Inside the huge gates stood a new statue. 'Look! It's Apollo. The god of my own people is welcoming me to the land of my fathers,' whispered Orestes. 'He wants me to succeed, to clean up this House and make it mine. Demetrius, my friend, best of luck to you in there.' The tomb of Agamemnon was on a low rise in the palace grounds. 'Pylades and I will do our bit too, never fear. May Apollo be with you.'

A PAUSE: *Orestes feels better now. He has a plan. When his pent up rage and horror are transformed into a determined intent, he grows up and takes charge with calm clarity. It is said that some people feel better before a decision is made, others afterwards. Which, dear Reader, are you? Has there been a time when suffering or stress or anger could find vent only in action?*

* * * * *

CHAPTER 12

ELECTRA

The two young men watched Demetrius walk away round the corner of the palace, then turned to the tomb and its altar. While Pylades kept watch for the curious, or the suspicious, or the soldiers, Orestes knelt to pray. He called not only on Apollo but on Hermes, lord of the dead, and on Agamemnon himself. 'Here at your grave I call, Father. I am crying out to you. I am your son, but when you died I was not here to mourn you. I was a mere boy, away in the North. I'm an exile, home at last. I haven't brought libations to be poured at your tomb but, as is proper, I'll leave some of my hair before we go.'

Time passed as he knelt, praying for strength and for the gods' blessing upon the retribution he would shortly take. A sharp 'Psst!' from Pylades made him jump. 'Look there! What's that? Hide.' Quickly they ducked round behind the altar. A bunch of women was approaching from the palace, clear in the early light, dressed in black, each carrying a long, slender jar of flowers. 'A procession,' whispered Pylades, peering out through the bushes that had grown up around the tomb. 'Who are they?'

Orestes, finding a good vantage point himself, said, 'If they're coming to honour my father years after his death, why now? Why today, just when I too have arrived? Yes, who are they?'

'Could that be your sister leading them?' Pylades whispered back.

Orestes gazed, remembering the sharp-faced little girl who had teased and provoked and entertained him so many years ago. Electra? Yes, that could easily be her. 'My own sister. Worn out now, grief-stricken. Yet she should look radiant — so young, so lovely. Pylades, I must talk to them.' In his heart he was saying, 'Apollo, dear god, fight beside me now with all your might. Let me avenge my father's murder.'

Pylades laid a restraining hand on his arm. 'Wait. Don't blow your chances now.'

Electra, for of course it was she, was singing as she came. Peering through the leaves, he could hear snatches of the words. '*Out of that palace of pain — lovely the sun, the air — I mourn for my father — great leader — won the war — slaughtered by trickery — no justly-deserved hero's grave for him — betrayed and slain.'* She broke off and called aloud to the women and to anyone else who might be listening, 'As long as I see the stars shining I shall mourn for him and curse his killers. *O you Furies who strike when you see an innocent life taken, or a cunning wife leading a lover to her bed, help me avenge my father's death!'* The next stanza pierced Orestes through. *'And, Furies,'* she sang, *'give me back my brother! My grief is dragging me under. I need help.'*

As the procession came closer to the tomb Electra finished her song and the women clustered around her. He could see them plainly through the leaves, an older woman, attempting to put her arm around his sister, who was brushing it off and turning away. Oh gods how wonderful! Yes, it's Laodameia. He longed to burst from his hiding place and embrace her, his beloved old nurse, the person who from his babyhood had most shown him kindness.

Together they listened as the women talked. 'How long are you going to go on like this, Electra?' Laodameia was demanding. 'All this mourning and bewailing your father; it isn't good for you. I know your mother's terrible; none of us have any time for her, conniving with that evil man Aegisthus to cut him down. But all this grief won't bring your father back from the swamp of Hades.' She added silently to herself, Oh, may his killer be killed, if I'm allowed such a prayer?

'Dear nurse, I know you're concerned and trying to coax me out of my misery. But I can't stop. Let me be. Let me rage.' Orestes heard the mixture of affection and irritation in Electra's voice.

'Well, don't go and die of it then. All this shrill grief will kill you. Why do you love misery so much? Think of your brother. *He* goes on living.' Laodameia paused. She remembered the young messenger whispering to her just before the night his father was murdered that the young Orestes was about to come and see her. That had *not* been good timing. 'Orestes is there somewhere,' she went on; 'but he's restless, in hiding, waiting for the day when Mycenae can welcome him home.'

'I'm waiting too,' cried Electra. 'I've never stopped wishing he'd come. I've carried on despite my sense of doom. No, he's son of Agamemnon but he doesn't care. He writes that he's aching to join me, but for all his aching, he never acts. Has he sent me one message that's proved valid?'

'Courage, dear child. Zeus will handle your quarrel with your

27: Electra at her Father's Tomb

mother. Don't waste your hate on your brother. Time eases us through the rough patches and, believe me,' went on Laodameia, 'Orestes does care. Yes, your father was killed by those who rule in the palace … '

'And I'll never forgive them. Ever!' shouted Electra.

'Calm down, stop stirring up trouble for yourself, provoking fights you'll never win. I care, like a mother you can trust, and I'm telling you: stop re-living old grievances. Orestes cares too, I know he does.' Only Pylades' firm grip on his arm stopped Orestes rushing out to them then and there.

'What you called my *shrill grief* is my way of maintaining respect for people and the law.' Electra always made her beliefs clear. 'We can't abandon the dead. They must be avenged, not dishonoured.'

'I'm here for your sake, daughter, 'said the older woman, 'but also for my own. I too have grievances. If what I'm saying doesn't help, go your own way; but I'm with you always.'

'Forgive me, dear friend, 'said Electra, softening a little. 'But my father's House is still suffering disaster. It began with my wretched mother, who hates me. Aegisthus sits propped on my father's throne in the great hall, wearing his clothes, pouring libations on his very hearth stone. And he sleeps in my father's bed with my mother, if that's the right word for her. Slut! She's not intimidated by the Furies. She revels in her own depravity. Father's murderers control me now. Oh, I'm waiting an eternity for Orestes to come and end this. Inside me I'm dying. He sends messages. He's always going to do it but he never does. It's taken all the hope out of me. How can I possibly be calm or rational or god-fearing?'

Laodameia was running out of arguments. Any understanding she had had for Clytaemnestra, any sympathy over what had happened at Aulis, had been tested to destruction during the years of Aegisthus. 'What about the so-called king? Suppose he heard you talking like this?'

'Don't worry, he won't, they've both gone out for the morning. As you well know, that's the only time I can escape at all. I'm allowed no suitor. In fact, the uncle would kill me today to stop me having an affair and bearing a bastard. He knows any son of mine would avenge my father. As for my brother,' Electra repeated, 'he keeps saying he'll come and not coming.'

'Give him time.' She thought of the little boy she had raised with such love. 'When a man's about to take on something overwhelming, he'll sometimes hold off a bit. Your brother's a good man. He won't let his own people down.'

'I do trust him,' Electra agreed.' If I didn't, I'd have given up. I'd be dead already.'

All the women had come before the altar now, each carrying her vase, and from among the others stepped Queen Clytaemnestra's own maid. 'As we have been instructed by *her* and *him*, our royal mistress and master,' she declared, 'we shall pour out wine and honeyed oil upon the tomb. We have to; we are slaves. But she thinks these libations of hers will appease her husband's ghost and ward off retribution. I tell you, they're both scared stiff. We shall do this, my friends, to honour King Agamemnon. We remember the young Princess Cassandra who died with him. These aren't empty gifts. Soon, the gods will turn the tables.'

'Stop! Don't do it, my dear friend,' cried Electra. 'Don't let any of their offerings touch his tomb. They're from a wife he hates. Take them away, let the wind blow those flowers out of sight. Or bury them deep and far off. Let *her* dig them up. How could she think they'd absolve her of his murder? Give him some of your own hair instead. I'll give some of mine.'

Crouching uncomfortably among the tomb's bushes, Orestes and Pylades watched as the women did as she asked, turning away, pouring the libations into the sand, throwing the flowers upon the wind. Each severed a lock of her own hair for Agamemnon and, renewing their mutual friendship, knelt in turn before the altar. Laodameia's prayer was, 'Remember Orestes, even though he's gone abroad,' and Orestes heard his sister murmur, 'Well said. Amen.'

Electra in her turn blessed her friends. 'I'm as much a slave as all of you. We nurse a common hatred in the house.' He heard her voice soar through the morning as she called to one she believed far away, '*Orestes, pity me! Rekindle the light that saves our House. O my Father, raise up your avenger, bring my brother home. Kill the killers!*' Seizing her knife, she cut a thick lock of her own hair and placed it on the tomb. Slowly the women turned and left.

Silence. No one about. Orestes and Pylades stood up, brushed leaves and prickles from their clothes and stepped out of hiding. 'Now for our own offerings, such as they are. You know, you are the best friend anyone could have, Pylades.' Briefly they hugged each other. Pylades flopped his rather tired bunch of lilies down on one side of the altar, speaking the traditional words, and Orestes took out his knife. 'I have neither wine nor flowers for you, Father. Instead I lay two hanks of my hair. One is for Laodameia who nursed me as a child. I've just seen her, alive and well, thanks be. The other is for Death. I'll place both beside my sister's offering.'

The friends stood at the grave for a moment, then looked towards the palace. 'We'll go there to wait as soon as Demetrius comes back,' said Orestes. 'Then, I pray, our destiny will be fulfilled.' They ducked back behind the tomb to find more comfortable resting places.

A PAUSE: *Orestes has to wait for the right moment. If he leaps in too soon, he blows his plan, makes himself known to all the women and risks betraying his allies. Pylades is a particularly good friend at this point, urging restraint. What would you have done had you been there? What would your own prayers be, dear Reader? For what would you pour your libations?*

* * * * *

CHAPTER 13

DECEPTION

Demetrius, in his guise as an elderly Traveller, had presented himself round the back of the palace with a message for the queen. 'She's out: you'll have to wait.' Later that morning a slightly less grumpy guard admitted him to the lower echelons. 'Here's an old chap, says he's got a message for *her*. Looks harmless enough.'

'Sit him over there.' Just as Demetrius, feeling very much like a weary messenger, was accepting some refreshment, the queen herself, fresh from her morning excursion, came down to the kitchen to see to the arrangements for the evening. Her daughter was coming after her, snarling at her mother — as usual the two were quarrelling.

'I'll pretend I didn't hear that, my child. But you always loved your father better than me.' It was Clytaemnestra's habitual lament. 'You should pity me, Electra. I am not happy with what I did. I am sorry for it. I lost my temper. I went too far.'

'Too late,' snapped Electra. 'He's dead. You did it. Why don't you call Orestes home from exile?'

'I'm afraid,' her mother admitted. 'I know he's angry at his father's death. I must look after myself.'

'Well, what about your "husband"? Why do you keep Aegisthus so bitterly opposed to the two of us? He's proud and stuck up, and he treats me disgustingly.'

'You see? You stir up fresh quarrels all the time.' Clytaemnestra grew annoyed and flushed, Electra pale with fury. 'Enough of this, we're here to discuss tonight's dinner.'

'Madam,' said a quiet voice at her elbow, 'you look like a queen. Might you be the wife of Aegisthus the king?'

'You've guessed right, stranger,' said Clytaemnestra, startled at being addressed so directly but glad to turn away from Electra.

'Greetings, my lady.' Demetrius spoke in a confidential whisper. 'I have some welcome news for you and King Aegisthus. It's from a friend of yours.' And he named the official who ran the Phocian Games up north.

28: Clytaemnestra

'Oh yes, I know that man,' said Clytaemnestra. 'Go on, what's this news?'

He edged a little closer. 'Orestes is dead. That's my news.'

Overhearing him, Electra cut in with a piercing scream. 'Oh no! that's terrible! If my brother's dead, then so am I. I cease to exist. Today I am dead too.'

Clytaemnestra swung round on her. 'Then go bury yourself! Don't listen to her, stranger, she's crazy. Now what was that you said?'

'Your son is dead, 'Demetrius repeated softly.

The queen, hiding her delight, attempted to look devastated in her turn. 'How did he die, messenger? Tell me.'

'It was at the athletic games at Delphi.' Demetrius had his story at his fingertips. 'He was doing really well, the son of Agamemnon. He'd won gold in several events. But then' — his look was tragic — 'then, the chariot race …

'Well, go on, what happened?'

'It was held at dawn. He was in the lead, lap after lap, cutting corners, getting away with it, till his wheel caught the post. It broke the axle-box and he was thrown out. He got tangled up in the reins as he smashed into the ground, and his mares spooked and bolted across the race-track. It was truly terrible,' said Demetrius, wiping an eye. 'Everyone was gasping. They set up a pyre and burned his body then and there, weeping for this brave young man so suddenly and hideously doomed.' He stopped, choked with woe at the terrible news he was imparting. 'I've come on ahead, but messengers are on their way with the urn of his ashes for you, so that Argos, his home country, can give him a fitting burial.'

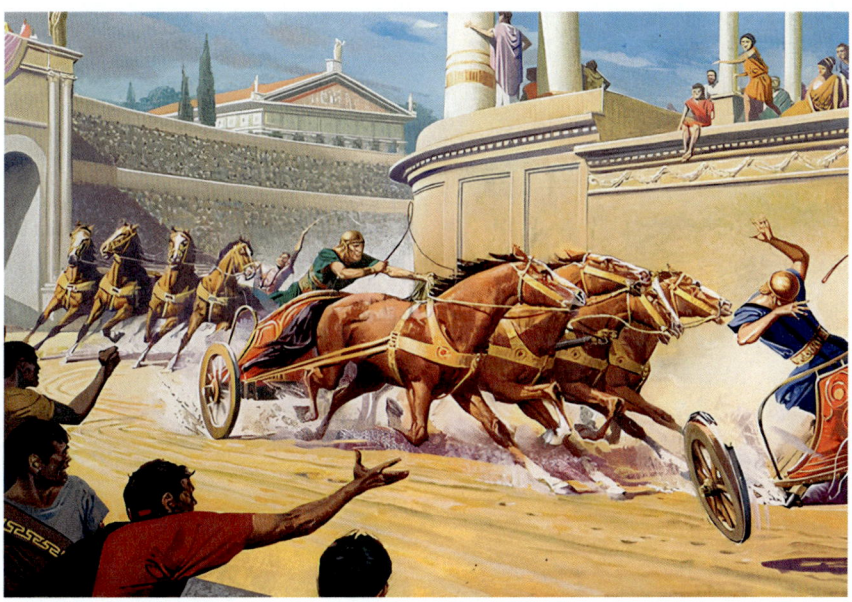

29: The Chariot Race

Oh horror! The kitchen staff listened, huddled, murmuring amongst themselves, 'All the family wiped out — and the son. Our ancient rulers.' It had long been whispered that Aegisthus had offered a handsome reward in gold for Orestes's assassination.

Clytaemnestra did her best. 'O Zeus, what dreadful news! Good, that he was doing so well, yet horrible, that he died so.' She turned to the messenger. 'Although he betrayed me, I don't hold it against him. Even though he deserted me, went into exile, became a stranger. I've been so worried about him, it's been keeping me awake at night.' Silently she thought, of course he'd have hated me for killing his father, He'd have sworn to do something terrible. This blessed calamity makes me safe; as long as Orestes lived, I could die at any moment. Now I needn't be afraid of him. Nor of this girl here. She's been worse, living inside my house, leeching my lifeblood. She can't threaten me now. He's dead. I'm at peace.

While relief arose in Clytaemnestra, her daughter was in despair. 'I grieve your death, brother,' she cried to the empty air, 'but in her heart your mother condemns you. Look! She's rejoicing at your loss.' The queen turned on her again and the quarrel raged on. Demetrius, who needed to get away to meet Orestes and Pylades by the tomb as arranged, tried to seize the moment. 'Then may I leave, my lady, since all is well?'

'No, no, we must offer you hospitality, to repay you for bringing us these tidings. I insist. We'll leave the girl out here, crying for herself and her dear departed. Come.' And the queen led him from the servants' hall.

Electra turned to the women. 'Well, what a display of maternal feeling for a son's ghastly death. What a mother. Heartbroken? Grief-stricken? She makes me sick! As for me, I have nobody. I'm bereft, enslaved by people I despise, Father's murderers. I'm not ever going back up those stairs. I'll live as a dropout. I'll camp in the grounds. I won't have friends. I'll never marry, I'll be a dried up old spinster. Let them kill me, I don't care, I don't want to live.'

The girl was inconsolable, but Laodameia, though not quite certain about this stranger or his message (wasn't there something faintly familiar about him?) hid her own tragic loss by turning, as she had turned for years, in a useless attempt to comfort Electra. Her own life seemed nothing but grief for these children and their impossible family. Zeus, Apollo, where are you? 'Take heart, girl, ' she said. 'There is life after death.'

'Oh shut up!' yelled Electra through her sobs. 'Don't keep on at me. The dead in Hades can't help. I'm heartbroken. Who will avenge me now? There's no-one, if he's dead and lost to me.'

'Yes, child,' Laodameia said, empathy replacing sympathy, 'you certainly are defenceless. And it does seem he will never come home.'

'I'm going to my father's tomb. It's the only place for me now.' And Electra ran out into the courtyard and away.

'I'd best try and keep an eye on my poor girl, though all I want to do is lie down and cry,' and Laodameia plodded out after her. Electra ran past Apollo's statue and returned to the ancient grave-site. When the old nurse joined her, puffing hard, she found the girl gazing in bewilderment at Agamemnon's altar. There were flowers lying there, admittedly rather few and droopy.

'Look! What's this? We didn't put any flowers here this morning, did we, nurse ? Ours weren't lilies anyway.'

'That's right, we threw them out. You left your hair, that's all, you and the rest of us. Look, here's our offerings. Haven't we all got such straight hair. Only yours is wavy.'

'But I only left one ringlet. Look, there's three here now, all the same. Thick hanks, all wavy, just like mine. Someone's been here — just now — bringing gifts for my father. It can't possibly be my mother; she was out all morning. And who else would come? There isn't anyone.'

Even as she spoke, a momentary hope stirred in Electra. That messenger in the kitchen — was he all he seemed? These hanks of hair: could they be a signal from — *could* it be? No, he's dead — but who else? 'If someone's still remembering Father, maybe there's life for me after all,' she said aloud. 'Maybe I'm not so alone, so powerless?' As long as someone kills Aegisthus, she thought to herself, her mind a chaos of events and possibilities. Because if Orestes is dead, the king will certainly put me to death too. Any sons of mine would finish him off. I'll have to kill the man myself. No, I'm going crazy. How could a woman do that on her own?

'For the gods' sakes, Electra,' said Laodameia, reading her mind: 'think sensibly, think ahead. Don't go and do something stupid.'

'No-one else has hair like mine,' said Electra. 'No-one could have cut these two locks except me, and … Look at the texture. It's identical, can't you see?'

'Well, it's certainly not the hair of our royal rulers,' said Laodameia.

'They're far too callous to bother. You're not imagining that *Orestes* sent a gift in secret?'

'It must be his,' said Electra. 'Remember as children, we both had the same curly hair? I think he's come here and cut some of his own to honour our father. He's taken a huge risk. They'll kill him, I know. But no-one else would have hair like this. Look! Oh he'd be the dearest man I know.'

'Now you'll be imagining these footmarks are his too,' said Laodameia wearily. 'Come on girl, you've hardly seen him since he was six and soon your feet'll be matching, as well as your hair.' That was a mistake, for Electra immediately swung round.

'Footmarks? Where? Yes, see here. Boot-prints in the sand.' Her excitement mounted. 'Since we left this morning, two sets of fresh tracks, him and a fellow traveller.' She put her foot into one. 'See, it fits!' and she began following the footmarks. Yet even as she spoke her shoulders slumped and she stopped. 'You're right, nurse, it's idiotic to think my feet would fit anyway. It can't be him. He's dead. I'm powerless. I'm alone and there's nothing left. Life without hope of my brother.' With her feet in Orestes' very tracks she stood by her father's tomb and cried inconsolably.

Behind the grave, Pylades relinquished his hold on Orestes' arm and nudged him forward. 'Go on, now's your moment.' And so her brother, travel-worn, bearded, his tell-tale hair well hidden, emerged from the hiding place among the bushes and came at last towards Electra, carrying the urn of his own supposed ashes. His disguise must hold; if he were recognised by the sister who'd last seen him when they were children, she would be complicit in what he was planning to do. Pylades followed.

'Ladies, I'm looking for Aegisthus.' Orestes spoke smartly in the Parnassian dialect, honing his Phocian accent.

'Well, that's his house down there,' Laodameia answered, pointing. She wasn't fooled. This fellow had been a child when she'd last seen him, but she knew him.

'They've been expecting us for some time. Could someone let them know we've arrived?'

'Why don't *you* hurry down and tell them,' said the nurse to Electra.

'Yes, girl, run.' Orestes looked anywhere but at Electra. 'Tell them that men from Phocis are looking for Aegisthus.' But Electra was staring

30: Pylades, Orestes, Electra and the Ashes

at the urn he held. Surely this was confirmation: yes, her brother was dead. The man holding it was saying how King Strophius had sent them with news of the chariot-race disaster, bringing Orestes' ashes for proper burial.

'Please sir,' she cried, 'let me hold it in my hands a moment.' She reached towards him, took the urn and cuddled it. 'Oh Orestes, you were such a great little boy; how I loved our games. You were sent away for your own safety. But how I missed you. All we did together, all the care I took of you, wasted now. And what a grim death you've died. Better you'd been murdered then after all, if now they're bringing you home in an urn. You were my child, not your mother's. Now, you're dead, Father's gone, our enemies gloat, and our mother is mad with joy. Orestes,' she said to the urn she cradled, 'you promised you'd come home and punish her. And look at you!' She lifted the lid and sifted the ash through her fingers. 'Let's die together now. Don't leave me behind. The dead feel no pain.'

A PAUSE: *Orestes and Pylades are play-acting; and with Demetrius bearing false news and Clytaemnestra disguising her exultation at her son's supposed death, only Electra and Laodameia are straight in their loves and hates. All the deceptions hold — for a while. Have you ever had to maintain a deceptive role? How did it feel? How was, or how might such pretence be resolved?*

* * * * *

CHAPTER 14

REVENGE

I don't know what to say, thought Orestes. He made an effort. 'Can you be *the* Electra? The famous Electra?' She raised her eyes and looked back at him; and then and there to this stranger she poured out her grievances, her misery. How her mother beat and demeaned her, how she lived enslaved by 'that murderous pair', how her life was pointless now that her one remaining relative was dead. And Orestes found himself ever more in sympathy with this girl, his own sister who could not let herself recognise him.

'I do feel for you. Have you no-one to help you? Or stop your mother treating you that way? You've been atrociously abused. And why on earth are you not married?'

31: Electra Holds the Ashes

'The only person to help me is this one. And you've brought him to me in an urn.' They both stared at it. 'Anyway, why do you care, stranger? Or might you be some distant relative?'

No one but Pylades and Laodameia could hear. 'I'll tell you everything,' said Orestes. 'Give me the ashes.'

'No! For the gods' sakes don't take them from me!' She swung away clutching the urn. 'Don't steal him I love!'

'You can't keep this. You have no reason to grieve, or to mourn him. This isn't yours. They're not his ashes, that's just a story.' Gently he took the urn from her and handed it to Pylades. 'He isn't buried anywhere. The living don't inhabit tombs.'

'He's alive, then?'

'Yes, if *I'm* alive.'

'Are you saying — he — is you?'

'Here's my signet ring,' said Orestes, dropping the Phocian accent. 'It's our father's, isn't it? Do you believe me now?'

'Your voice. It's you. You're here!'

'I'll never be anywhere else,' said Orestes, and at last they threw their arms around each other. 'This is my friend Pylades, who has come with me from Phocis to help us.'

'Dearest nurse, look. It is Orestes! He's tricked us into thinking him dead, yet the very trick has brought him back to life.'

Laodameia, who already knew who he was, was herself crying with joy at seeing them together. 'Son of Agamemnon, darling child, at last! Don't worry, I won't tell anyone you're here. We nursed you with tears, and now you've come back to us two who love you still.' And she embraced him in her turn. 'Trust to your power, win your father's House once more.'

'Yes. Don't tell anyone I'm here, not yet; it's not the right time,' said Orestes, with Pylades nodding approval.

'I'm so excited; how can I keep quiet?' Electra was almost dancing. 'I can't hide how glad I am you're back. I never believed I'd see your face again. But there's huge bitterness in the palace. I can't forget the appalling thing that happened.'

'Neither can I; I feel it as you do,' said her brother. 'We both remember what they did. O Father, if only you'd been cut down in Troy, then your name would have been left at home to inspire awe. The idea of your tomb on some far headland would now buoy up the House.

32: Electra recognises Orestes

You'd still be loved by the men you loved. You'd be known to have died in glory.'

'No,' cried Electra, 'don't wish him dead by some foreign river. We would never know how he died. Now we can at least grieve over what did happen.' Fiercely she added, 'I'd sooner the killers die as they killed you, Father, at the hands of friends,' and she was about to renew her diatribe against her own fate; but gently Orestes took her by the shoulders.

'It's the gods who have inspired me to come', he said. 'So don't get too excited, Electra. Don't be so intense. Let go of it. No use going on about how evil our mother is, or how Aegisthus siphons off Father's wealth on his ridiculous opulence; you won't know when to stop. Dear sister, just tell me what I need to know: when will the coast be clear? Where can we ambush our enemies? Don't let anyone guess. Don't look too happy. Stick to your grief, pretend my faked death really did happen. When we've done it, then we can laugh and celebrate and breathe again.' Electra took a deep breath.' I'll do as you say. Come on, dear Laodameia, we'll go and see the coast is clear. Aegisthus is out somewhere, but Mother's at home, and her henchmen too, so danger will be near.'

Before they could move there came a rustling in the bushes and there stood a breathless Demetrius. His voice was a hurried whisper. 'You're not just *near* danger, you're in it up to the ears. They're looking for you. Why on earth are you standing here talking? I tried to put them off the scent. I had to stay for a bowl of wine, but as I left she was shouting "Where's that girl got to, and the nurse?" So stop hanging around; it'll mean disaster. Come on Orestes, get on with it.'

'But who are you?' This old messenger — could this be the tutor who came to Mycenae to fetch her little brother away to his Northern academy years ago? 'I was so young then. But don't I know you? Are you not one of those few we could trust, long before Father was murdered? Yes you are. You're Demetrius. How could I not recognise you? You saved our House by taking Orestes away. Oh blessings upon you! In you I see my father. Know that in one day I've hated and loved you more than any man in the world.'

'Come on now, that's enough.' Demetrius spoke abruptly yet kindly. 'I know you, Electra, and our friend here,' and he grinned at Laodameia. 'We'll have time to discuss things later.'

'What are they saying down there, Demetrius?' Doubt and dread fought in Orestes' mind. 'Do they believe I'm dead? Are they glad of it? What are our chances?'

'Save that for later, when we're done. As things stand, everything's fine. Come *on*,' and Demetrius turned away. But Electra had thought of something.

'Monstrous woman! Only today does she come to his tomb to mourn for him. She stripped him of everything; of his guard of honour, of his life. Yet she hasn't sung a hymn or shed a tear. Why libations now? What on earth possessed her, Demetrius, to send those flowers today? Do you know?'

'Yes, I know. I was there in the kitchen. She'd had a nightmare. She was terrified, so she sent those flowers, unholy woman. She dreamed she bore a snake, swaddled it like a baby, gave it her breast to suck. She woke with a scream, appalled, and sent the libations.'

'Well, it's going to come true.' Orestes' voice became dark. 'Degrading my father so. I will turn into that serpent and kill her.' He was hissing. 'She'll pay, by the gods and my bare hands. Just let me take her life. Let them both die!'

'So be it,' Demetrius replied. 'It's Apollo's will.' He turned to Pylades. 'Come on, both of you, hurry. Right now, Clytaemnestra's alone. Don't give her time to get reinforcements. First we'll do the invocation, here at your father's grave, then go.' The five of them gathered and Demetrius, who'd collected a few sticks and bits of dry grass, lit a small, symbolic fire on the altar. Sparks rose in the evening sky.

'*O Zeus, look down on us,*' prayed Orestes. '*We're in ruins now, children robbed of our father, exiled from our home. Bring our house back to greatness.*' He turned towards the great statue near the palace gates. '*Apollo, I know you will never fail me. Your oracle has told me what I must do. The Furies threaten me with winters of disaster unless I hunt my father's murderers and cut them down. I'll go mad with nightmares, terror will drive me out of the city, if I do not avenge my father. I'll be reviled till at long last I wither and die. I know that the one who acts must suffer, but my heart is strong and warm. Let force clash with force, father-right with mother-right. Apollo, I'm ready to do as you command!*'

Laodameia prayed silently, torn between joy at having her flock together (except for that poor lovely girl of long ago, of course) and utter dread at what was pending, no more to be stopped than a tidal wave. *Oh dear gods, may it all turn out for the best!*

'It's my turn now.' Electra was calling to her father, '*Here at your grave are a girl in prayer and a man in flight and we are one. Your slayers are doomed. We remember the net, the chains of hate they trapped you in. Now, the children take the day. Dear gods, be just. Win back our rights. May this yet be turned to a song of joy.*' As the flame died and the evening faded, they all hurried down from the tomb past Apollo's statue and entered the palace by different doors.

33: With Stealth, Orestes enters the Palace © Tricia Newell

Orestes and Pylades were taken by Electra into the servants' hall, where the women preparing supper were talking sombrely of the purported death of the young heir. 'These trusted bearers of sad news are from a friendly kingdom. My mother has told me to guide them to her chamber with the urn. She is preparing for the burial. I'm going to watch for Aegisthus, who'll join her when he comes home. Come now, you messengers.'

On the way to the queen's chamber Electra left them and the two friends paused in the passageway. For a moment Orestes panicked. 'How can I do this, Pylades? I can't kill my own mother.'

'Remember Apollo,' Pylades shot back. 'What of the Delphic oracle, those oaths you swore? What of the future? What of your sister? Take on people, my friend, rather than making an enemy of the gods.'

'Good advice. Right, you win.' Orestes's hand went to his sword's hilt and they entered the chamber. Clytaemnestra, unprotected, already half-sensing her fate, had some things to say before she succumbed. 'I know who you are. No innocent messenger from Strophius. You are Orestes, here by that girl's trickery, and I'm your mother.' Despite his determination, her words went right through him. 'Let me grow old with you, my son. If you kill me, you will live under a mother's curse.

It was destiny that killed your father. Believe me, he too had failings. Don't you know the appalling thing he did? Tell me!'

'Never judge my father!' cried Orestes. 'He suffered while you sat here at home. Men slave to keep women safe. And you sold me. You exiled me, disgraced me, a free-born father's son, so that you could love this dreadful man here and hate the one you should have loved.'

'I did you no harm by sending you safely to your aunt's house,' responded Clytaemnestra. 'Hear my case, although no one else will. No one else listens, no one else knows what happened. Did you know what that father of yours did? He plotted to kill your sister? Yes, your other sister? He sacrificed her like a heifer. I've kept it all from you. He sent for her, for my daughter, to Aulis where the fleet was at anchor, winning her over with the promise of marriage to Achilles. And there he sacrificed her. He stretched her over the altar, he slashed my Iphigeneia's white throat. Not to save lives — then I could have forgiven him — but to punish his brother's wife, that loose sister of mine, Helen. Then, when he came home ten years later, he had a crazy woman in tow, a visionary. He would have installed her here as his concubine and tried to keep the two of us together under the same roof.

'And as to Menelaus,' she went on, impassioned, 'I ask you, my son, suppose it had been the other way round? Had your uncle been snatched away in secret from his home, would I have been obliged to kill *you*, Orestes, to save my sister's husband and bring him to her side? How would your father have reacted to that, I wonder? Was it right that Agamemnon, the murderer of my child, should escape death, when I had suffered such treatment at his hands? Yes, I killed him. I appealed to his enemy Aegisthus, who gladly shared with me in the killing of your father. Was it not justice, that your father died?'

She paused. Her words had gone nowhere and she understood her fate. 'Mother-murderer!' she shrieked. 'It's in your eyes. You, my child, are the snake I bore. You are that terror in my dreams. I gave you life. Watch out, the Furies will take you. If you dare to kill me, the hounds of a mother's curse will hunt you down.'

With a huge effort Orestes rallied. 'But how to escape a *father's* curse if I fail? You killed him. What you did was outrage. Suffer outrage yourself now. Your death is decreed.' With Pylades at his side, her son drew her over the threshold into the bathroom, the very place where Agamemnon had been netted and dispatched. The doors closed behind them. Clytaemnestra gave a bloodcurdling shriek. 'Assassins in the house! Where are the guards?'

34: Orestes Kills his Mother

Deep in the kitchens the women huddled, shaking. 'Listen! Someone's screaming.'

They could hear the words quite plainly, the queen's voice: 'Aegisthus, where are you? My child, my own son, don't stab me. Pity your mother!'

They heard Electra rushing from the hall and bounding up the stairway, shouting back, 'You, Mother, had no pity for him. Or his father. Go on, stab her! I wish you could stab Aegisthus too.'

And so they could. Aegisthus, coming cheerfully home from the country that very moment, walked straight into the trap Electra had set for him. The friends made short work of him.

And so the curse on the House of Atreus was carried on. Would it never end?

A PAUSE: *The deed is done. Orestes has obeyed Apollo and fulfilled the expectations of Strophius, Demetrius and Pylades — of Laodameia and Electra — even of Zeus himself. So young, how could he have stood against them all, refused to take vengeance and so invoked his father's curse? But he is now the target of his mother's curse. The scourge on his ancestors has now fallen upon him. Have you ever been in a double bind, a cleft stick of this sort? How did it feel?*

* * * * *

CHAPTER 15

CELEBRATION

As the royal couple's henchmen melted from the palace into the night, the triumphant friends, having arranged a temporary burial of the bodies, met together and arranged to celebrate tomorrow. Most of the guards and retainers declared undivided loyalty to Orestes the rightful heir; and the women were rejoicing in a new freedom. Electra and Laodameia invited them all to the feast, together with Pylades and Demetrius. All were glad of what had happened.

All except Orestes. Now that he had done the deed and fulfilled Apollo's command, what next? Standing there in his mother's chamber, sword still in hand, Orestes had seen no end in sight. The concocted image of him as charioteer, out of control, charging towards his own death, plunging off the track, reins flying, haunted him till his heart bolted like the horses and beat him down, horror banging the drum.

I must keep my head, he thought. I must say to my friends in public, Yes, I killed my mother. It was justified. She was stained with Father's murder, cursed by the gods. And I was ordered to do it by Apollo's oracle, the Pythoness of Delphi. I was told, 'Go and pour libations beside Agamemnon's tomb. Lay locks of your hair upon it. Then, alone and crafty, you must exact due punishment from the murderers. Go through with this and you go free of guilt. But fail, and … '

In fact, the Oracle had terrified him. He daren't repeat the punishment for failure, even to himself: to be outcast from society, debarred from holy places, and afflicted with a leprosy that turned his flesh white. 'What bow could hit the crest of so much pain?' as the poet would later put it (Aeschylus, *The Libation Bearers*, line 1031). Too awful to contemplate.

Now, he said, 'Oh Pylades, however can I survive a party? I can't go.'

'Come on, old fellow.' Pylades handed him a branch he'd gathered from an olive tree. 'Hold this. Put on the robes of Apollo. Here you are. Wear this wreath; it shows you've been to the Oracle and heeded the Delphic command.'

With his friend's firm support Orestes managed it. He held up his head and faced the delighted company. 'Look at me. I am Apollo's man,' he managed to declare. 'These are the wreath and branch of a suppliant. Remember, everyone of Argos. Remember how these brutal things were done. When he comes, tell Menelaus how I acted on Apollo's command.'

Yes, Uncle Menelaus to face next. Where would it end, this murderous hate, this Fury? Where could he sink to sleep and rest, now that the curse on the House of Atreus had continued into his generation? Electra's generation. He understood now: Thyestes had stolen Atreus' wife; Atreus had unspeakably slaughtered Thyestes' children; the one surviving son, Aegisthus, had slain Atreus in revenge. Then his mother had teamed up with Aegisthus and slain Agamemnon in his bath.

But Orestes hadn't understood her dying words. 'Your other sister.' What had she meant? Unbelievable, that his father had *killed* his lost sister? Could the gods really have made Atreus' son sacrifice his own daughter? And why? To win back Helen for his brother? Never. She was lying, surely, in the moment of her death? If not, his mother had had a cause after all. If he'd killed their daughter Iphigeneia, Agamemnon had dragged Clytaemnestra right into the curse. And now Orestes, commanded by the gods, had with the encouragement of Electra and the help of his friends, slain both Clytaemnestra and Aegisthus. Payment upon payment, retribution upon retribution. Only remorse awaited him now.

The party went on late. At last Laodameia had had enough and, bidding them all the blessings of the gods, she retired to her chamber. Now she sat alone in the night, remembering. They all had their story, even the queen, so hard to love. Only the old nurse knew for sure what Clytaemnestra had suffered. Only she remembered Iphigeneia. Only she understood that mothers and daughters and sisters also had rights. How could the Goddess Artemis have so betrayed her fellows, her own femininity? But then, it had been a man, the priest Calchas, who had spoken for that immortal huntress. What chance does the goddess have when a man is her mouthpiece? Would there never be an end to this chain of retribution?

Laodameia had kept her place at the palace because Electra had grown up insisting on it. She had become indispensable, the undisputed leader in the servants' hall, dealing with Clytaemnestra's maid when she got above herself, looking after the pseudo-ruler when needed, keeping everyone as contented as possible in this blighted house. And Aegisthus hadn't been so bad, had he? Yes he had: bombastic, ruthless and power-seeking. Yet, as far as she knew, since he arrived he'd been faithful to the queen; and at least he hadn't had Electra done away with. Self-appointed consort, he'd come from a desperately dysfunctional family himself. Again, only Laodameia knew about that; she had sometimes been ordered to wait upon him and he'd told her details of things no-one should know or have to hear about.

Oh great Zeus, life is hard, thought Laodameia. Old griefs, old memories all mixed up, so much pain in the halls of the house of Atreus. And that terrible morning before, worst of all, when she'd believed her darling Orestes was dead, the sweetest, dearest plague of all their lives. She'd burst into tears in the kitchen when Demetrius had told them the news, her heart breaking. She remembered the day the baby was born, the endless nights his wailing had kept her up, how she had paced the halls rocking him in her arms, the care she had given him. A baby can't think for itself, poor creature. You have to nurse it, don't you, read its mind. It can't talk, it's helpless. Does it want feeding, changing? A baby's soft insides have a will of their own. I had to be a prophet, she thought. I tried so hard. I scrubbed his pretty things until they sparkled. A jack of two trades, that was me, washerwoman and wet-nurse. And I nursed Orestes. Oh, and I remember that day by the ships, when I took him from his father's arms. And this morning they told me — the shock of it – the boy was dead. I wouldn't have minded fetching that ruination of the house, the lover, to his death then and there.

But next I learnt something wonderful: the truth. The message was false. Orestes wasn't dead, he was here. Out with Electra by the tomb. I met him myself, saw him, recognised him. It took time to sink in. I held my tongue.

That's why, when that one who calls himself 'king' arrived back at the palace, it was I who gave him the news. 'Orestes is tragically killed. This is what happened.' He relished every word. Later, quick as I could, I told him to leave his cut-throat body-guards behind and go quickly and alone to join the queen, rejoicing all the way. 'Sir,' I said, 'your mistress is calling. Hurry and meet your guests, the ones who brought the news.' And he'd trusted me as ever and gone straight to his doom. I could have warned him, but I didn't. High time too!'

She had knowingly, willingly sent Aegisthus to his death. Her loyalty

35 Laodameia remembers

lay with the children, especially Orestes, not with their mother's lover. Orestes and his friends from Phocis had done the rest, adding his body to Clytaemnestra's with Electra cheering them on. A satisfactory outcome.

Now the bright eye of the halls of Atreus would never fade. *Stealth will master stealth*, as the gods commanded. Success! Apollo's justice had been done, Orestes was home and Agamemnon avenged. Laodameia lay down and slept a peaceful, dreamless sleep.

A PAUSE: *The nurse Laodameia is a vital link in this story, understanding all that has happened, knowing everyone, loving the children and the other women, keeping order, quiet and stable. A warm-hearted, simple person of her time, she believes in the gods as she has been taught and accepts their rule. Has there been such a person in your own life, providing that solid, warm stability? More than one? If not, how would it be if there had been?*

* * * * *

CHAPTER 16

CASTOR AND POLLUX

What of Orestes? Numbly he had bidden his beloved nurse good night. As the evening wore on, his spirits had sunk. Enough of play-acting; he could keep up this 'party' charade no longer. What was looming next? 'Listen, friends!' His face was pale, his tone had changed. 'I must get away. I must get rid of this sword and escape the blood of my mother. I'm being driven from the land. In life or in death I'm an outcast, leaving behind nothing but a name for you all.'

'Orestes,' cried Demetrius, 'What's the matter? Stop it! You're not going anywhere. Cheer up, this is your kingdom now. You've done well; there's nothing to be ashamed of. You've set free the city, the whole land of Argos; you've freed your sister; you've lopped the heads off those two serpents once for all. Don't for the gods' sakes go and burden yourself with guilt.' Electra echoed him, crying her love and praise for her brother. But Orestes wasn't listening.

Demetrius had done enough. He'd played his part, risking his life to guide Orestes through the deed. Clytaemnestra was slain. Now that his protégé was falling apart, there was nothing more he could do and he was getting ready to vanish. Fond as he was of his charges, and thoroughly though he'd done his duty by Orestes, he would rather ride through the night than spend any longer in this accursed house. 'Farewell then, my friends,' he said to the remains of the feast in the emptying room. 'May Apollo look down on you with kindness, guard you and grant you fortune. I'm off, back to Phocis.' And he went to find his horse.

But Orestes took no notice. Beside himself with misery he was thinking, I must escape these people. They'll be too merry to notice my absence. What's that in the corner, in the dark, lurking beyond them all? He heard his own voice screaming in terror. 'No, no! It's women, shrouded. Look! They're like — they're Gorgons, cruel, their heads swarming with snakes, the hounds of my mother's hate. I'm going. Now!'

'Haunted by women?' wondered those who were clearing up after the celebration, much startled. 'Not by us, anyway. Certainly we from the servants' hall don't see anything to blame in what the son of the House has done.'

'Calm down, Orestes.' Pylades stood at his elbow. 'Your mother's hate? — what are you dreaming about, with all you've won? You have your father's love. Steady on, there's nothing to fear.'

36: The Remorse of Orestes

'You can't see them, I can. They're driving me, I must go — ' and Orestes, followed by his sister and his friend, rushed from the hall and out into the night-filled palace grounds. They soon caught up and Electra guided them to a far summer-house where, persuaded to stop, he sat huddled on the stone bench in the darkness, only half aware of his companions. 'Why did I do it? How could I do it? Such a foul and bloody deed! Two bodies. I keep seeing them stretched out on the ground. All for what? To make me feel better.'

'Dear Orestes, it's not your fault,' said Electra. 'I'm weeping too.

What did I do? I vented my fury on our mother. No one will want to marry me now. Who would ever invite me to his home or his bed? I was wrong and I'm responsible. I put you up to it, Orestes. You didn't really want to do it.' She paused. 'Even so, it was proper payment for our father's life.'

Orestes was not listening. Hadn't he done all this to appease and please Apollo? 'You, the God,' he shouted at the night sky, 'you put me up to it. Your Oracle cheated me with her songs. Your justice wasn't just, it was evil. You've brought anguish on me. You've made me a murderer. Where can I go now? I'm exiled. Not just from Argos but right out of Greece. No decent, god-fearing person will tolerate the sight of me. "That's the mother-killer!" they'll whisper.

'Oh Electra, you didn't see how she showed me her breast as I was about to sacrifice her, how she sank to the ground, our mother, such agony in my heart. She put her hand on my cheek and oh, the cry of mourning she gave: "My child, I beg you!" She told me something. She told me a terrible wrong that she had suffered: how our father had killed our sister. But I pulled the hood over my eyes and I stabbed her. I was in a trance. I nearly dropped the sword as she breathed her last.'

'He did no such thing! My father could never do such a deed. Yes, I urged you on; I encouraged you.' She hesitated. 'Perhaps we have committed a terrible act ourselves. Perhaps we did feel hatred for our mother as well as love.' Her voice rose again. 'But at least we've put an end to the curse on this House.'

Unheeding, borne under by a great tide of guilt, her brother floundered into despair. 'What did I do? What have I done? Struck down by my hand. No, not yours, Electra. Oh Mother, the children you bore are your murderers.' He fell to banging his head with his fists. Pylades and his sister got him to his feet and pulled him out of the summer-house into the dewy night. They stood with him as he struggled to breathe, staring down at the diamond-scattered grass. Heavenly starlight roofed the sky but Orestes had no eyes for the constellations. To make things worse, a Little Owl was screeching in the nearby copse.

'Look up, Orestes.' Pylades was holding his arm and pointing. 'Look at the stars. They'll put heart into you. There, see, above the palace roof, up to the left of the Pleiades and the Bull and Orion. That huge pair? They're the Heavenly Twins, Castor and Pollux. They seem to be getting brighter every moment.'

'Remember,' said Electra, gazing skywards, her own brief shame forgotten, 'how those stars are named after Uncle Castor and Uncle Pollux. They'd be glad of what we've done. They'd say, "Why, you've brought an end to the curse at last, Orestes, so pull yourself together. Once you've paid the expected price for the murder you'll be rid of all your troubles and find happiness." No, your friends won't be polluted by this slaughter; of course they'll still speak to you, brother.'

Pylades echoed this, but Orestes would have none of it. 'Those useless uncles!' he cried. 'Gods, are they? My mother's brothers? Died and gone to the stars. Then why didn't they stop all this and save her? Why didn't they prevent me killing her?'

Electra was going on. 'Brother, those uncles would say you're the son of Agamemnon. You have avenged your father. You have done well.' But Orestes could not — would not — hear any more. In horror at the triumphant expressions on the others' faces, he broke away and fled from the summer-house through the starlight, bolting uncertainly beneath the screeching of the Little Owl in the direction of the stables.

37: Little Owl of Athene, *Athene noctua*

A PAUSE: *Electra is confident in herself and in what she has done, ready to take the consequences but free of lasting self-reproach. She will not change her mind (her father simply cannot have killed her sister). Orestes is very different. He sees beyond the immediate situation and blames and hates himself, driven into remorse and self-reproach by the Furies, who represent their mother. With which of them are you most in sympathy? Why?*

* * * * *

CHAPTER 17

IN THE STABLES

Earlier Philip, under-groom at the Palace of Mycenae, had been hard at work in the stalls making ready Demetrius' steed, a tough little bay stallion from Skyros, for his master's long ride Northwards to his home. The horse's sturdy feet had no need for shoes but Philip groomed him till his dark brown coat and black mane were gleaming and his tail contentedly swishing at a stray evening fly. His water bucket was full, his hay-net well stuffed. 'Make sure he gets a handful or two of wheat as well, he'll need it,' his boss Theodore had told him before going off, all dressed up to join the jamboree. Rather him than me, thought the young man, giving the horse's coat a final polish. True to his name Philip was a great lover of horses, but he didn't care much for parties.

One of those loyal to Agamemnon, Theodore the head groom had put in a brief appearance at the celebration, happy to welcome home the rightful heir. Though reserving judgement on what had been done, he knew that the awful pair in power had had what was coming to them. Seeing that Phocian messenger Demetrius slipping away before the speeches and the toasts, the head groom also made his exit, leaving Electra in full cry before her guests. Now he could get back to the stable and make doubly sure the visitor's horse was ready for him. Not that Philip needs checking on, he thought; he's a good lad. Good horse too. But it's a long ride to Phocis.

He and Philip saw Demetrius and his steed quietly away into the night, the stallion's unshod hooves going softly over the city cobbles. Job done. The head groom turned to his helper. 'We'll get off too in a bit, lad,' he said. 'It's late and you've done well. But before we go there's more.' Before morning they must see to the pair of shining golden horses that would draw the chariot for Electra and the other young man. She didn't know it yet, but he sensed that sharp young lady would also be leaving soon.

Theodore was said to have second sight. He knew everyone in the palace and was held in respect and affection. When Laodameia needed

38: A Good Horse for Demetrius

an understanding ear it was to Theodore she turned, plodding round to the stables and the warmth of the horses, chunks of carrot or apple from the kitchen at the ready. He always surprised her with his welcome and his immediate grasp of what was needed, sitting her in the harness-room with one of his wooden cups full of something warming, listening quietly without trying to fix things. 'Born wise, that one,' was her contribution to the kitchen gossip and the others were of the same opinion. Theodore was a wise friend to horses, to people and to her.

She knew that Theodore guessed her feelings for Orestes. Today he would somehow be aware that the baby she had raised and loved had been, all in a few short hours, lost to her in Phocis, killed in an accident, resurrected, recognised, hugged at the tomb, welcomed by Electra as the brother-prince, and become a matricide.

39: The Best Horse in the Stable for Orestes

'Prince Orestes must have Zephyra,' Theodore told his assistant. 'She'll carry him well on his way.' After what he'd done, the newly-arrived son would have to make himself scarce for a bit. Enemies abounded. Though reluctant to see the young hero depart after such a short space at home and despite the lateness of the hour, he added, 'Make sure the mare's ready for the young prince. I know she's your favourite, Philip lad, but she hasn't really got wings. Still, we're giving him the best horse in the stable.'

Orestes, however, was going nowhere. Gasping under the stars, gabbling something about being hunted, he made it from the summer-house to the stables, with Electra and Pylades pounding after him over the dew-laden grass and the Little Owl filling the night with her haunting screeches. But, trying to help Philip with the mare, Orestes crumpled, fell in the straw among her hooves and lay motionless, unconscious at last while she stepped delicately around him to reach her hay. Electra and Pylades arrived almost at once and he was carried into the harness room and laid on a bed of clean straw.

'Philip, go and fetch Laodameia,' said Theodore. Though she had long left the party and was already sound asleep, the nurse woke up at once. She found Theodore in firm charge in the stable and Electra unusually biddable. Orestes looked terrible, thrashing about on the floor and gabbling incomprehensibly. Telling the nurse to join Electra and Pylades and sit quietly by, the groom had seated himself alongside the stricken prince. 'Orestes, listen to me.' Philip, standing behind them, thought his master spoke in just the voice he would use with a terrified horse. After a while Orestes became calmer and lay still.

'You mentioned the stars just now, the Heavenly Twins Castor and Pollux. You, Electra and Orestes, listen: I knew both your Uncle Castor and your Uncle Pollux. So did you, Nurse, didn't you? They died long before you were born, but they were Queen Clytaemnestra's brothers, her and her sister Helen. Well, two of the stars are named after them. When I was a lad like Philip here and working in the stables, those two young princes would come down to see the horses. Loved horses, both of them, didn't they, especially Castor. What a rider, that one. Pollux was different, the quiet one; he *knew* the horses, what they felt like. And, as I think you know, Princess Electra, those two uncles — they would be here for you now. They'd stand up for both of you.'

In the lamp's guttering glow, everyone was listening to Theodore. Orestes had opened his eyes. 'I think they'd tell you that, yes, trouble's going to follow.' He paused. What now? — the gentle champing of oats, the rustle of hay, a skittering mouse, only the owl breaking the midnight silence outside. 'Pylades: I believe Pollux, and Castor too, would acknowledge you for your friendship for Orestes. You have been willing to lay down your life for him. In fact you are still in grave danger on his account. This is what you must do now: you must leave Argos and journey home to Phocis, taking Orestes' sister here with you as your bride. The chariot will be ready at daybreak.' Pylades listened intently and nodded.

'You, Electra, are to be given by your brother to Pylades, to have as his wedded wife. You are to go with him and be faithful to him. We're harnessing for you that chestnut pair you love, and you will take the good chariot.' There was no arguing with the authority in Theodore's voice and Electra remained quiet, barely taking this in. But Orestes was beginning to sit up and take notice.

'Attend, Prince. Your Uncles Castor and Pollux would tell you to take heart. They'd say they had seen you kill their sister, your mother, and Castor would say she has got her just deserts. Good, you're listening,' for, on hearing this, Orestes looked up, briefly hopeful.

'However, *you* have not acted justly,' Theodore went on. 'I think Pollux would add that what you did was wrong. Yes, you obeyed Apollo; but didn't it occur to you that *Apollo* might be wrong? As a god he's assumed to be wise; but the command he laid on you was not wise. What to do if the gods themselves are wrong? Must we not learn to disobey them without guilt?

'You and your sister must now do the bidding of Zeus, who is above Apollo, and follow your fate,' he went on. 'Since you're the son of Agamemnon, this is what the god says must happen.' Theodore spoke with solemn portent. 'You, Orestes, must leave Argos. Now that you have killed your mother you may not set foot in this city for a long time. The terrible spirits of destruction, the Furies who must chase matricides, will drive you hither and yon, a wanderer reduced to madness. You must make your way to Athens and reverently honour the Goddess Athene, whose Owl has been calling to you tonight.'

'But he can't possibly do any of that, poor lamb,' cried Laodameia. 'Look at him, the mite. He's exhausted, he's sick.'

Theodore's voice took on an oracular quality; he was speaking as if for Zeus himself. 'Pallas Athene will keep those Gorgons away from you, Orestes, terrifying them with her own fearful serpents so that they do you no lasting harm. They will hound you, but she will stop them from turning you to stone by holding above your head her shield with its Gorgon-face. Outside Athens,' he went on, 'is the Hill of Ares, where the gods first sat to give their vote on the shedding of blood. From that time on, a seat of judgement has existed there, a tribunal that is most holy and secure. On that hill you will have to stand trial for murder.'

In that moment Orestes, beginning to come to himself, realised that Theodore spoke for the gods. Oracles were not always right. Despite their claims and the fearful power they wielded, the wisdom of Theodore the head groom left those priests and priestesses standing. Aware that there was more to say, Orestes listened.

'We shall not send you from Mycenae alone, Orestes. You will have a companion. The mare Zephyra will go with you. She is not only the best horse in our stable: she is sent by the God Hermes himself to help and protect you. You will take good care of her, and she of you.

'As to this kingdom of Argos, the corpse of Aegisthus must be buried right here; he will have his own tomb in the palace grounds. You can leave it to Menelaus (who is back safely from the war in Troy) to bury your mother properly. Menelaus will be in charge for as long as it takes, ruling for a while in Argos, together with Helen his wife who will be his queen.'

A day ago, Electra would have been furious at this, yelling and rebelling and appalled. Now, frightened by her brother's incomprehensible state of mind and grateful for the help and good sense of Theodore on this extraordinary night, she was beginning to change. She too was haunted by a measure of horror at what they had done. Could some of her earlier certainties be questionable? Almost humbly, she asked, 'May I join in this conversation? You have ascribed our bloody deed to Apollo. What Oracle ordained that I should become my mother's murderer?'

'It was the curse on the House of Atreus,' replied Theodore at once. 'You inherited it from your ancestors and it has destroyed you both. Yes, you put your brother up to it, and that means that you and he must now part.'

'No, that's impossible,' cried Electra, her old feisty self leaping up. 'We've only just met. He needs me. Look at him!'

But Orestes, beginning to be restored to his right mind, was agreeing with Theodore. 'Dear Electra, I know it'll be dreadful to say goodbye, when it's years and years since I last set eyes on you. I love you so much. Yet he is right. We must do as he says. I must go. I'm to be parted from you already.' And he sank down again on the straw.

'Electra, understand that you will have to leave Mycenae, leave the whole land of Argos. Your sister will be safe, Orestes.' Theodore indicated Pylades. 'You needn't worry about her fate, for the great God Zeus enjoys mischief.' Briefly his eye twinkled. 'She has a husband and a home now.'

This was too much. Electra snapped right out of her newly humble state. She had no idea what she thought about Pylades. She'd first seen him that morning and hardly given him a thought. Now, realising a husband had been prescribed for her by the head groom, she swung round on her brother. 'What's worse than being an exile?' she flashed, claiming, as ever, the high ground in suffering. 'So, I'm to leave my home and country and marry someone I've barely met? I don't think so!' Orestes rallied enough to see that Pylades was going to have his hands full.

'Well, dear sister,' he managed, 'I've been in exile myself since I was small. And now I have to turn my back altogether on the House of my father. I must travel, face trial for my mother's murder and submit to the judgement of some strange far-away court. And no, I don't believe anyone will shelter me.'

'Don't be afraid,' said Theodore. 'You have a good horse. You and Zephyra will come eventually to Athens, the holy city of Pallas Athene. Hold your head high.'

Electra and Orestes each felt as if they were dying. So recently reunited, now they held each other close in farewell, hearing how their mother's deathly curse would sever them from each other and from their ancestral home. Electra saw she must make the best of it. 'Goodbye, then, my beloved brother. These are our last words together.'

'Oh my dear, dear sister, must you go already? How can we part after all this? We've only just met, yet I won't see you any more.' He made a huge effort and stood on his feet. 'Pylades, yes of course she must go with you. It's right. Take Electra as your wife, get married, be happy.'

Weeping, Electra broke from her brother's embrace to take her first good look at her prospective bridegroom, while Orestes turned to his nurse for comfort. 'Farewell, dear Laodameia, my beloved friend in Argos. Goodbye, I'm going now.'

But he wasn't. Again, too late. Releasing the nurse from a long hug, weakness overcame Orestes and, lost to them all, he sank yet again to the ground among the straw. Now Laodameia came into her own. 'We must get him into the palace, Princess, and find him a bed. You can see he's ill, he needs caring for.' Everyone rallied to help and Orestes was half supported, half carried from the stable.

A PAUSE: *Theodore speaks for the gods. Occasionally, if you are fortunate, you may come across a person who has wisdom. Under their influence for a while, your life may be changed for the better, perhaps for ever. Has there been such a person in your life? How would it be if you met one today? Are you such a person yourself, perhaps?*

* * * * *

CHAPTER 18

IN THE PALACE

Dangers abounded in Mycenae. Rumours went flying through the night. Not all the citizens welcomed the fate of Aegisthus and Clytaemnestra. Even as Orestes was giving his sister's hand into that of Pylades, plots were being hatched.

40: Orestes is Ill

Beside her brother through the rest of that night and over the days to come, Electra had time for reflection. Apollo put him up to it. And I helped. Was the god really wrong? He certainly did us a favour. But not everyone thinks it's a good thing to kill your own mother. And now my brother's dreadfully ill, full of fever, growing thinner and thinner, driven mad by these awful Gorgon-things he thinks are chasing him. When he comes to himself, he won't wash, won't eat, just lies huddled under his cloak and weeps. Then suddenly he'll leap from bed and rage around like an escaped colt. Laodameia's a godsend, but he takes no notice even of her.

The fact was, they were in grave peril. Theodore had prepared their escape, but it was too late now. Today, a week after the murders, the palace was stiff with guards and the citizens were voting on whether or not to stone them both to death. As a matricide, Orestes was already an outcast; by law, no one might speak to him or give him shelter, warmth or food. Their only hope was Menelaus who, after years of storm-tossed wandering, had reached the nearby harbour at last. Helen had come on ahead of him. She too was highly unpopular in Argos, all those men having been lost at Troy for her sake. Arriving at the palace late the previous evening, she had slipped in under cover of darkness to escape being lynched.

Despite all, Laodameia was glad to be Orestes' nurse once more. 'Thank goodness Hermione's here,' she said to Electra. 'With Helen endlessly weeping for Clytaemnestra and all the misery of the house, being with her daughter again after all these years is a comfort. I know Helen always regretted leaving her, a small child, when she sailed to Troy. Yes,' she added, bathing Orestes' forehead with tender firmness and watching for signs of life, 'a good thing her father brought her here from Sparta and entrusted her to your mother to bring up.'

'I agree.' Electra considered Helen's daughter a pain in the neck, but just now she was glad of her older cousin. 'Hermione's good for Helen; helps her forget her troubles and keeps her out of our hair. But now we need Uncle Menelaus or we're dead.' She gazed out and down the road. 'He should be here by now. This house is so unlucky. Unless he finds some way to save our lives, our hopes are built on shifting sand. We're in desperate straits, Laodameia.'

At that moment her Aunt Helen walked into Orestes' room without knocking. She'd been too tired the previous night, but now in a spate of words she attacked Electra. 'What have you done — you and your wretched brother, how could you, I wept all night for my sister, well it wasn't really Orestes' fault, it was Apollo, you couldn't help it I know,

41: Helen of Troy

but I hadn't seen him since I went to Troy, I was in a god-sent ecstasy
— yes I was, don't contradict — now I'm all lonely and lost. Oh what's
happened to us?'

Despite her new calmness Electra was more practised at fighting
than making peace. 'Orestes lies crushed, Helen. I sit here sleepless by
his pitiable corpse. Yes, he's a corpse, apart from an occasional gasp
for breath. Why blame him for what he suffers? You and your husband,
crowned with happiness and success, come home to find the palace
yours, while we are overwhelmed with misery. The agonies he suffers
have exhausted him.'

'Electra, would you do something for me?' said Helen, paying no
attention. 'Look, I have cut off whole *locks* of my hair. Would you
go and lay them where Clytaemnestra's grave will be and pour the
libations? And could you put these flowers there? I can't go, I daren't be
seen in Argos.'

'Good,' Electra came back. 'It's time you felt some shame for
leaving home the way you did.'

'That was just, Electra, but not kind,' reproved her aunt. 'You know
I'd be in danger from the crowd if I went.'

'Then what do you think *I* would be? Anyway, I must stay with my brother. Why don't you send your daughter? She's family, it would be all right.'

'A young woman shouldn't walk out alone,' said Helen. However, she saw the sense of it. 'Hermione, come here, my dear.' Her daughter, delighted to have her mother back after all these years, appeared and listened carefully to detailed instructions. She knew the right place, but not how to pour the libations and place Helen's locks. 'Put the flowers carefully. And finish up by saying, *O Gods, have kindly thoughts for her two unhappy children, whom Apollo has destroyed.* There now, go quickly and, remember, come straight home again.' She hustled her daughter out as if she were a child, and Electra, thoroughly irritated, was glad to see the back of them both.

'Did you see that, Laodameia? How she had cut her hair off near the ends so as not to spoil her beauty? She's the same woman she always was. O Helen, the gods will hate you for the ruin you've brought on me and Orestes and on all of Greece.' Just then a bunch of the women servants came clattering in to see Orestes, joining her and the nurse. 'Shh! Don't make a noise. Come in, my friends, but tread softly. It's kind of you to come, but if you wake him it won't do him any good. Whisper, be like muted flutes, quieter still, this way, tiptoe.'

42: Laodameia remembers Orestes as a baby

'Don't bump his bed,' cautioned Laodameia as they leant over, peering at him.

'Poor boy,' they whispered. 'How is he really? Tell us about him, dear Electra.' They could see Orestes was deadly sick, scarcely breathing, sometimes crying out in pain. 'How terrible! See, he stirred a bit under his cloak. Is he waking up? No, it's all right, he's still fast asleep.'

When they'd gone Electra turned with a sigh to Laodameia, wiping her damp forehead with the back of her hand. 'O Nurse, it's Apollo who's sacrificed our lives, laying upon us this unnatural, heart-rending deed: to kill our mother, who killed our father,' (… who killed Iphigeneia, Laodameia added, but silently; no point in stirring things.) 'Yes, it was just. However, it was not right. Mother, we're sharing the death we dealt you.'

But Laodameia had stopped listening. 'Come here, Electra. Come close. Look at him. Has he died and we not notice it? He hasn't moved a muscle.' They stood together, watching uneasily. Both jumped as Orestes began to speak, this time muttering in dramatic prose, all without stirring.

'*O magic charm of sleep, with what comfort you came to help me in my sickness. How I needed you O sovereign Lethe, river of forgetfulness, death of sorrow. With what skill you tend the sufferer who invokes your heavenly help.*' His eyes opened and he looked straight at Laodameia. 'Dear Nurse, what was I saying? All that stuff. Where am I? How did I get here? When? I can't remember anything. The past is blank.'

Together they helped him back towards life. 'Your poor head, your soft wavy hair all dirty and uncombed, like a wild man. It's so long since you saw good warm water,' said Laodameia. 'Come on now.' And for the first time Orestes turned over, sat up, put a foot out of bed and with their help eventually stood on his feet.

'To stand up feels like being well. It's good to feel well, even when the feeling's far from true. 'After a few steps, he sat down again and Electra told him all he needed to know about Menelaus being due at any moment, with Helen and Hermione already in the palace. Orestes had recovered enough to add, 'If he's found Helen here, he's found a load of trouble. He'd be happier alone.' They agreed about the viciousness of their mother and her sister. 'You can be different from that wicked pair, Electra,' said Orestes gently. Then suddenly, as if possessed, he shouted at her, 'Well! Don't just say you will be. Let your heart be good!'

Electra jumped again. 'Oh brother, your eyes are so wild. How rapidly you change; one moment health, the next raving lunacy.' Not the right thing to say; once more Orestes was raving as he had for days already, while she and Laodameia wrestled with what they saw as his craziness.

'It's you, *you* that's after me. Who *are* you? *Mother*! No, no, don't let them get me I implore you. Female fiends, bloody faces wreathed in snakes. They're here, coming closer, glaring at me. Gorgons' eyes! They'll kill me, priestesses of hell, dread goddesses.'

'Brother, you're breaking my heart,' Electra wept. 'Stay quietly on your bed. These things aren't real, just your imagination. Oh, who can I call upon for help, now that we have made the gods our enemies?' Theodore had already been in several times; his calm always quietened Orestes for a while. But he wasn't here now and, unnerved, Electra sank to the floor, wrapping her head in her gown.

'Where am I? Why am I in bed?' A lucid moment; the storm had blown over again and there was calm. 'Come now, dear sister,' Orestes was saying. 'Stop crying, unwrap your head. You support and comfort me when I get lost in these insane horrors; and, see, when you weep I encourage you with love. Go and rest now, Electra. Have some supper and a bath, lie down, give your weary eyes the sleep they need. My dear nurse is here and if either of you collapse exhausted, I am lost. All my friends and helpers have gone, except you and she.'

Electra promised she wouldn't collapse or fail him. After all, *she* couldn't survive without *him*. Pylades had vanished, presumably, like Demetrius, on a horse from the stables. 'Lie down. Ignore these terrors. Keep quite still. Laodameia is here. Your sickness is far more imaginary than real, though it doesn't feel like it.' And she went to rest as he suggested. He fell again into an uneasy sleep and Laodameia sat beside his bed. How I do love this child, this boy, this son of Agamemnon, she thought. The House of Atreus may be under an appalling curse, but that was born from the marriages of gods: Hades, Tantalus. Cursed or not, it's the house I've loved more than any. *O Zeus, I pray you, release him, let him forget these mad frenzies. Through no fault of his own he was put in an impossible cleft stick, condemned by the Furies if he obeyed Apollo, condemned by Apollo if he didn't. What else could he have done?*

And, so praying, Laodameia sat rocking herself at Orestes' side.

And over the days as he began to recover she told him the story
Clytaemnestra had begun: how his father had indeed slain his sister
Iphigeneia at Aulis, and pretended she'd been rescued by Artemis at the
last moment. Too shocked already to be shocked again, now he knew
it all.

A PAUSE: *What of convalescence? Orestes is psychotic, driven into illness*
by his conscience in the form of the Furies, who speak for his mother.
Though in mortal danger from the citizens, he is granted time, care
and rest and so begins to recover. What is your own experience of
illness, perhaps burnout, your own or that of others? Have you ever
had a period to recover? If you'd had more time, care, rest, how might
that have been?

43: Map of The Aegean Sea

* * * * *

CHAPTER 19

THE FAMILY

Hermione would have hurried dutifully off as soon as she could to fulfil her mother's behest at the graveside; but Electra gave Helen the slip and told her cousin to defer the visit till tomorrow, as her father was coming. What a relief, thought Electra. Here he is at last, Helen's husband Menelaus, riding in from the harbour, all dressed up in his magnificent fancy robes. Well, he too is of the House of Tantalus, and we need him. 'Hallo,' she shouted, hurrying to greet him. 'Welcome to you who commanded the thousand ships that sailed against Troy. Welcome home, Menelaus.'

He was less bitter than Helen, more gently reproachful. 'Wonderful to be back at my father's house and I'm glad to see you, Electra. But I'm more than sad, too, that you're so miserably enmeshed in crime and anguish. When I was overseas I heard what had happened to my brother; how he died in his bath, slaughtered by his wife. So we were already grief-stricken. Then I was told about this atrocious murder of my sister-in-law. Now, where is Orestes? I believe he perpetrated this act. When I last saw him he was a baby in Clytaemnestra's arms. I wouldn't recognise him now, even face to face.' Menelaus had altogether forgotten how, at Aulis, he had stolen the letter intended to save Iphigeneia's life.

'You'll have to wait a bit, Uncle,' said Electra. 'He is not well and it'll take him a little time to be ready to greet you. But he will be glad of your coming.' With Laodameia's help, Orestes was stirred from his bed and into action. By the evening he was more lucid than he had been since the feast and ready to meet his father's brother. Entering the dining hall, he knelt and clasped Menelaus' knees.

'Yes, I'm Orestes, and I'm appealing to you. Save me, Uncle. You are my last hope.'

'You look awful,' said Menelaus. 'Like a ghost from hell.'

'I know. And I feel as terrible as I look. I murdered my mother.'

'I heard. Don't say such things! Don't harp on horror.' Menelaus was shocked. 'What on earth's the matter with you?'

'Conscience.' Orestes was clear about this. 'I recognise the horror of what I did. My disease is grief. Madness came over me when we took her away, Pylades and I, and buried her. I saw these terrible women, dark as night, powers I will not name, driving me, lashing me into agony. Oh that I could get rid of them!'

'Serves you right! Such deeds must earn such suffering, you know.' Menelaus softened. 'I hope you're not thinking of doing something stupid? To take your own life would be a fool's way out.'

'No, not suicide,' said Orestes. 'I'd rather unload my guilt and misery on to Apollo. He commanded me to avenge my father. The gods can be ignorant, and they can be wrong.' Theodore's words had stayed with him. 'What are the gods anyway? We are their slaves. I obeyed him but he doesn't help me. That's what gods are like. And I did it out of loyalty to my father. Though that's brought no advantage either. In fact, the citizens of Argos hate me now. They won't speak to me; they'd lock their doors on me. They want me banished. I can't ever be king in my father's house. They're demanding my life. They're voting on it tomorrow.'

'Will it be banishment, or death?' Menelaus wanted facts. 'Or something else?'

'They're going to decide. They'll stone us to death, both Electra and me.'

'Escape, then!' cried Menelaus.

'We're trapped. Armed men have taken charge and are on guard all round. We're in a desperate predicament. My hope rests on you alone, Uncle. You've been successful: don't hoard your happiness. You've won; give me a share of your well-being. I am your brother's son. Don't you owe my father a huge debt? Pay where it is due and take your share of grief. Those who abandon friends in times of trouble are not true friends.'

That night Orestes slept uneasily, uncertain of Menelaus, afraid of the citizens and terrified that the Furies would go on pursuing him. Pylades was still absent — maybe he wouldn't return? Electra was strong. She had retained the loyalty of the palace staff, mostly women; they hadn't liked the queen. But there were disaffected retainers, men still loyal to Aegisthus, who had joined the illicit guard now keeping him and Electra prisoner and protecting them for the mob tomorrow. Though the most acute madness had left him, Orestes remained profoundly depressed and his conscience tormented him. Laodameia was his greatest comfort. He could still confide in her as he had as a child, trust her still. She was there for him. Fitfully, he slept.

Early next day came word of another royal visitor. 'Our Grandfather Tyndareus is coming from Sparta,' said Electra as they gathered for breakfast. 'He'll be here soon. He's pretty old now and in mourning for his daughter's death. It'll be tricky.' Around the table, waited upon by her faithful women, were Menelaus with Helen and Hermione, and Orestes. Her brother was dressed and seeming sane; but she didn't like the colour of his face and his clothes hung limply on his frame. Occupying their minds was the citizens' promise that, today, life or death for the mother-murderer would be decided.

Hermione wasn't eating. She was glad her father was there and excited at the idea of seeing her grandfather, but she was scared by her deferred mission: she still had to run the gauntlet of the grounds carrying her mother's libations. Helen, despite herself, was glad of Menelaus' comforting presence. Toying with a few grapes, she was vaguely hoping Hermione would be all right and wondering about seeing her father soon. Menelaus, spreading honey on his third pancake, was trying not to imagine himself and Helen taking over the palace and ruling Argos, should Electra and Orestes be conveniently done away with. After all, he was quite fond of them, wasn't he? Orestes, nibbling the edge of his own pancake, was wishing himself safely back in his room with no one about but Laodameia. Electra was wondering how best, under the circumstances, to deal with Tyndareus when he arrived.

Helen left the hall to see if her father was in sight. Orestes broke the silence. 'My fate is sealed, Menelaus. My grandfather's coming now from Sparta and, after what I did, I have to meet him face to face. He brought me up as a small child. He was kind; he'd carry me about on his shoulder and call me Agamemnon's boy. He and Grandmother Leda always made much of me when I went there from Phocis. They'd tell me stories about our other uncles Castor and Pollux. And now, what a return I have made them, a wretched, reckless wickedness. What dark hole can I hide in from Tyndareus?'

Before Menelaus could reply, Helen reappeared in the hall with Tyndareus himself. He was trying to keep his back to her, but his shorn head and black robes signified his grief for his other daughter Clytaemnestra. 'Tell me, where can I find Menelaus my son-in-law?'

The old king was staring around him, but it was many years since he'd met Helen's husband. 'I was up at the place where my daughter's been buried and they told me he's come safe home to harbour. Take me to him. I want to see my old friend, welcome him, clasp him by the hand.' Menelaus got to his feet and made himself known and they greeted each other warmly.

'Sit down now, dear Grandfather. You've come a long way. Have some bread and wine,' invited Electra, seating herself beside him and Helen.

But Tyndareus had spotted Orestes across the fruit dishes. He immediately attacked him with excoriating words. 'Abominable mother-murderer,' he shouted, 'you snake, adder's eye, you are poisoned lightning. You must be devoid of all sense, conscience, decency. Menelaus, surely you don't speak to this polluted wretch?'

'Why not?' asked Menelaus mildly. 'I loved my brother and this is his son. I'm sticking up for Orestes. He's family.'

'What? This unnatural monster, Agamemnon's son?' Could it be his own beloved grandfather saying these things? Helen hustled Hermione out before the argument between the two men properly took fire. Should

44: Tyndareus at Home with his Wife Leda

people's actions be dictated by the family, or by the law? Menelaus favoured kinship, while Tyndareus, steaming with kingly annoyance, honoured the legal path. The fight that followed between bereaved father and more placid son-in-law was with words not swords; it seemed to favour the king, who grew ever more irascible.

'Let's agree to differ,' said Menelaus at last. He added, irritatingly, 'Anger combined with old age is unwise.'

Tyndareus, despite his years, was far from yielding. 'Why didn't Orestes use the *law* to punish my daughter? Yes, she committed an indefensible crime. But her son should have prosecuted her for murder and expelled her from the palace. That would have been much better than stabbing her to death; and it would have been seen as wise.

'But now you,' and he swung round on his grandson, 'you've done what she did and your life bears the same curse. All right, she's a criminal; but by killing her you've made yourself a worse criminal. You can't go on requiting murder with murder, or where will misery stop? Our ancestors said this crime must be atoned by exile, not by blood for blood. They forbade a man guilty of murder to come near the citizens again. Otherwise it goes on for ever.'

His next words embarrassed everyone. 'I've had a happy marriage, but I have not been fortunate in my daughters. One of them is dead. I grieve for her, but I also reject her. She was a wicked woman. As for her sister, sitting beside me here, I will not even speak to her. You went to Troy, Menelaus, to fetch home a bad wife, more fool you. But with all my power I'll back the law to check this bestial, bloodthirsty rage for vengeance which has destroyed the house of Atreus, and brings Greece near to death.

'As for you, Orestes, you pitiful wretch, clearly the gods hate you. They're punishing you for your mother's death with these raving lunacies and terrors, which show how wicked you are. Menelaus, don't let your wish to help this man lead you to side against the gods, who always punish matricides. The death my daughter suffered was her just desert; but it was not for him to execute the sentence.'

Orestes did not crumble under this sustained attack. Rather, he began to gather strength within, though he could not tell where it was coming from. 'Tyndareus,' he said, 'You're old and I don't wish to offend you. I know I'm a polluted man: I killed my mother. But that is not the sole truth. Ordered by Apollo *I avenged my father*, and for that act I am pure.

Where did my duty lie? As a man, I must support the right of the father against the right of the mother.' Warming to his theme, he reminded Tyndareus how Clytaemnestra had lived in adultery with Aegisthus. 'I killed my mother and, to complete the sacrifice, I killed him too. Yes, it was a crime — but I avenged my father.

'And now, Grandfather, you would have me stoned to death? Think; I have benefitted all Greek men. Otherwise, wives could kill their husbands at a whim and get away with it. If I had approved my mother's act by silence, what signal would that have given? And what would my dead father have done to me? Would he not have loathed me, haunted my life himself with raging Furies?

'It was you, Tyndareus,' Orestes went on, growing stronger and less logical by the moment, 'who ruined my life when you begot my mother. Women spoil the happiness of men. Her shameless action made me fatherless, and so made me a matricide.' After all he had nothing to lose. 'Blame Apollo. He dispenses words of pure truth from his shrine. What he commands, we obey, don't we? My action was a right action, though it proved ruinous to me. I killed my mother in obedience to him. Call *him* polluted, then. Stone *Apollo* to death!'

Tyndareus came straight back. 'Since you are so brazen and unrestrained, intending to offend me, I now resolve to see you dead. I will go today before the assembly of citizens and urge them — they'll not need much urging — to condemn you and your sister to death by stoning.' It didn't occur to the old king that this course of action would simply extend the chain of retribution he'd just been inveighing against.

He pointed at Electra. 'Indeed, she deserves death more than you, since she inflamed your rage against your mother. I know she was constantly sending you secret messages full of venom; dreams about Agamemnon, rubbish about Powers below the earth condemning the relationship with Aegisthus. You, girl,' and he swung round at her, 'you ignited the whole palace in one conflagration of hate. Publicly call your parents "murderous adulterers" once more and I'll see you banished to some distant city and confined in a dungeon. You'll never see the light of the sun again.'

And King Tyndareus wasn't done yet. 'Menelaus, I warn you: stick up for him and you'll have me for an enemy. It will cost you. Reckon the value of our kinship. You must refuse to save this man's life. Leave him to suffer death by public stoning, or never hope to set foot again on

Spartan soil. You have heard me. Don't reject your friends who reverence the gods and do right. Don't support this impious criminal. Servants, conduct me out.' And he hobbled away into the morning.

'Go, then!' cried Orestes to his departing back. 'I'll talk to my uncle uninterrupted by your sour old age.' He turned and refilled Menelaus' cup. 'Uncle, what's troubling you most?'

Menelaus didn't want to quarrel. 'I don't know what to do for the best,' he said. 'I'm worried and I want to think.'

'Listen first, then, to what I have to say.' Orestes was appealing for his life. 'Give me what my father gave to you. You'll repay your debt to him if you save me. This isn't about justice. You should help me with *more* than justice, as my father with more than justice gathered the army and marched off to Troy for you. He wasn't wrong to do this. Not for justice but for love he tried to heal the wrong committed by your wife. Help me now, repay like with like. My father in the sweat of battle sold his life for you, a true friend helping you get Helen back. So now, repay

45: Menelaus

me that same debt you incurred then. You need only work one day for me, not ten long years. Stand up today in the city and save our lives.'

Several good points here; but now Orestes went into the forbidden zone. 'May I ask you to remember that my elder sister, at your conniving interference, was sacrificed for you to win back your wife. I'm not asking you to kill your own daughter. Only to save Electra and me. For the sake of my lost sister Iphigeneia, I kneel to you. Yes, I have sunk that far. Swallowing shame, I'm begging for deliverance for our whole House. Help us in our need, Menelaus. You have the power.'

And once again, just as he'd done with Clytaemnestra at Aulis all those years ago, Menelaus replied with well-meaning half-promises. 'I'd help if I could, Orestes, but I've come here worn with voyaging and hardship, carrying my single spear with no fighting-men at my back. It's a feeble company of my surviving friends to tackle the citizens. I'll try to persuade Tyndareus to change his mind and get them to moderate their fury. Let's hope we can say the right things and carry our point. After all, a ship with mainsheet drawn too taut will find her deck awash; but pay out the sheet and she rights herself. When citizens are stirred to anger and violence, approach them gently, slack your sail to the storm and choose your moment. Then calm will probably return and when the sky clears you can ask for what you please and get it. The gods hate extremists. So in fact do most citizens. I'm off, to work out what I'm going to say.' And Menelaus too left the hall.

'You coward.' Only Electra heard her brother's low growl. 'Didn't you once command the navy? Yes. To win a woman; not to help your friends. Traitor! Running away, turning your back on us. Have you forgotten Agamemnon? Oh Father, you have no friend to support you. I am betrayed. My one hope for safety lay with Menelaus. There is no hope now. Argos will put us to death.'

A PAUSE: *By now, Menelaus prefers things calmed with words, not inflamed by deeds. But what of old King Tyndareus here? One minute he's making the case for exile versus execution, next minute taking offence and shouting for Orestes and Electra to be stoned to death! A marvellous example of hypocrisy and lack of insight. How do you feel in the presence of these two, Menelaus saying he's for the family, Tyndareus saying he's for the law? Do they remind you of anyone?*

CHAPTER 20

PYLADES

Just then, someone else burst into the emptying hall. 'Who's that?' Orestes was understandably jumpy. 'Oh, wonderful! You, Pylades, best of friends, back again. Come in, come here.' While Orestes could hardly contain his delight at seeing him — 'a sight more welcome than calm sea to sailors, a trusty friend in need' — Electra found wine and fresh pancakes for Pylades; then, never mind that it might be the last day of her life, went off to see to the household.

'I've been finding out what's going on,' Pylades told Orestes between mouthfuls. 'They're setting up an assembly in town. Yes, a crowd's gathering. They say they're sentencing you both to death. Now tell me, what's happening here? How are you?'

Orestes wasted no words. 'Disaster. I'm a dead man, Pylades.'

'Then you can dig a grave for me too. You're my dearest friend. And that includes my family. Yes, you are. And friends share everything.'

'It's Menelaus. He's betraying us. He's come, but he's useless. He's brought that abominable wife of his, or rather, she's brought him. Yes, that woman who sent thousands of Greeks to their deaths. They're staying in my house here — if I can call it mine. Their daughter too. I asked him not to stand aside and see me and my sister stoned to death, but he was far too cautious, like all treacherous friends. My grandfather Tyndareus has arrived as well, the one whose two daughters are so fair — and so chaste!' His sarcasm was bitter. 'He's furious, of course, at what I did. Secretly Menelaus favours him over our father, his own brother. He's scared of him; he daren't stand by us. He may be bold with women but he's no good with a spear. We're in danger, Pylades. This assembly you say is gathering: I'm charged with murder, the citizens are voting and the sentence will be death.'

'Well, escape, then,' cried Pylades, as Menelaus had before him. 'We'll take Electra and get away from here.' But even as he spoke, he knew they were besieged. Hadn't he just smuggled himself in through the armed guards thronging the streets. The palace was a citadel surrounded by hostile troops.

'We can't escape. But Pylades, how are things with you? Tell me, have you been home to Phocis these last few days?'

46: Pylades Rides from Phocis to Argos

'Yes. Theodore here lent me a good horse — you were too ill to remember. Like you, I don't know which way to turn. One disaster heaped upon another. It's my father. He's furious and he's banished me from home. It's because I helped you deal with your mother. He says I'm polluted. I'm in no legal danger here in Mycenae; Argos can't punish a Phocian subject. But the rabble's dangerous.'

'So my pollution has wounded you too.' A quarrel between Strophius and his son! Would the increase of his guilt never end?

'Yes, but I can put up with that. Unlike Menelaus, I believe that, given honest leadership, the citizens will make honest policies.'

Orestes was silent, deep in thought. 'Pylades, you've decided me,' he said, 'This is what I'll do. I'll go to the assembly in town myself and address the people. Now, today. I'll tell them I avenged my father. They loved him. If they set on me, that's better than lurking here in silence and dying a coward's death. If they kill me, at least I'll die honourably. With luck, they won't. I have a just cause and I'll stick to it. They might even pity me when they see how outraged I am by my father's murder. Yes, that's what I'll do. Should we tell my sister?'

'For heaven's sake don't,' said Pylades. 'It'd cause a scene and

waste time. Say nothing. No one else has heard your plan.' More secrets.
'Let's go.' They left the hall undetected and went first to Agamemnon's
grave. Orestes, still very weak, begged his father's protection, adding to
Pylades, 'Suppose the Furies drive me mad again?'

'Then I'll look after you. Put your arm over my shoulder. We'll
march straight through the city. I'll go first. Come on, I'm your pilot. I'd
be no friend if I didn't help you in such deep danger.'

'Friends are better than family,' said Orestes. And they set off
together to face death.

Electra, finding the dining hall deserted, went straight to the
kitchens. 'Laodameia, thank the gods you're here. Where's Orestes? Has
he gone mad again? Or been driven out of the palace?'

'No, he's walked off to face the crowd and stand trial.' (She knew.
They all knew. So much for secrets.) 'Oh Princess, today will decide
your life or your death.'

'For goodness sake what's he thinking?' cried Electra. 'Who's put
him up to it? Pylades, of course.'

The day dragged on. Much later, a young man burst in. 'Princess
Electra, I bring terrible news. Orestes, unhappy son of great King
Agamemnon, is doomed. The assembly has condemned your brother
and yourself to die.'

'To die! I knew it,' cried Electra. 'What happened? Tell me.'

'Orestes himself — unexpected, heart-rending — was there in the
assembly in Mycenae to stand trial for his life,' declared the messenger,
'he and his companion Pylades walking side by side. Orestes' head was
bowed, his frame shattered by illness, Pylades like a brother sharing his
pain with gentle concern, guiding and supporting him.'

'Well what *happened*? What did they say?'

'Orestes asked, "Do we die together, my sister and I, or separately?
Are we to be stoned, or must we take daggers and cut our own throats?"
But first the question was raised, "Should Orestes die, or not?" Several
people addressed the assembly.'

All Electra's exasperation failed to hurry the story out of the
messenger. Apparently the first to speak had been a minion of Aegisthus
who'd learnt to jump to the winning side; he was useless. Then a prince,
who urged the assembly to sentence neither of them to death but to
banish them; some shouted approval, others disagreed. Next, a man
stood up and spoke for Tyndareus; ignorant and full of bluster, he yelled

that they should both be stoned. A manual labourer followed, a shrewd and courageous man of integrity, well able to come to grips with the argument. He said that Agamemnon's son should be honoured for what he had done. His words seemed sensible to the judges, and there were no more speeches.'

It seemed the messenger had finished, but still he went on. 'Then Orestes himself stood up. He warned them that no man could leave his home and march to war if brave men could be cuckolded by stay-at-homes. He reminded them how he had dared to avenge his father by taking the life of a depraved and godless woman. "Men of Argos, if wives can kill husbands without guilt, then you'd better die today before the women make slaves of you. Wives lack encouragement, but not enterprise." It sounded plausible, but it didn't convince the assembly.

47: Orestes and Pylades

In the end Tyndareus' man won the day, demanding your death and his, Princess. Your royal birth did you no good at all. The only favour Orestes gained was that you wouldn't be stoned. He promised you would make an end of your life today, then he would fall upon his own sword. Menelaus, you ask? No, he said nothing at all.'

Pylades, weeping, had apparently brought Orestes back from the town, many friends following in tears. 'Distress to break your heart,' said the messenger. 'Prepare your dagger then, ill-starred Electra, or noose your rope; for Apollo has proved no saviour, but your destroyer.'

Into the servants' hall came the small crowd from the town, Pylades supporting his friend's halting steps with the steadfast care of a brother. 'Menelaus could have saved us,' lamented Electra. 'Sorrow succeeds sorrow and there is no permanence. I blame our ancestors. It's the curse on the House of Atreus which finally falls, cruel and implacable, on me, and on my father, and on my brother.'

'Oh be quiet Electra,' pleaded her brother, sitting down and rubbing his sore foot. 'Accept the facts. Endure what comes. For the gods' sakes stop harping on our miseries; it just sets everyone crying and makes us look like cowards.' But silencing his sister was not so easy.

'Our family is lost, vanquished and gone. Our prosperous home is destroyed by divine jealousy and by the malice of other people.'

'The point is, Electra, we've got to die today, whether by rope or sword, and we've got to do it ourselves.'

'Then you will have to kill me, not just anyone.'

'I've killed my mother. I'm not going to kill you too. You must do it yourself, my sister.' Softening, Orestes turned towards her with words of endearment and they hugged each other. 'We shall never have marriages, or children, or see the light of tomorrow.'

'Menelaus, that cowardly traitor to my father, didn't he put in one plea for your life?'

'No, he was there but he didn't show his face. All he thinks about is succession to the throne of Argos. He never meant to try to save us. But come on sister, we're different from him; we are royal and worthy of Agamemnon's line. Let the manner of our dying show our worth. We shall each die by our own sword. Pylades, be umpire of our rival deaths, wrap our dead bodies decently and bury us both in our father's grave. Good-bye. I'm going now to do what must be done.'

But he'd reckoned without Pylades. 'I absolutely refuse to accept all this. Come outside, both of you, in the open air.' He grabbed Orestes by the arm and beckoned Electra. Guards were everywhere, though at a distance. They couldn't escape, but they could sit down on the grass.

'Listen. If you die, then so do I,' said Pylades. 'You're in trouble. What would my life be worth without my friend? True, I didn't kill my own mother, but I helped you kill yours and I'll share the consequence.'

'Go home to your parents in Phocis,' cried Orestes. 'Find someone else to marry, have sons, inherit your kingdom. No, don't die with us. Best of friends, this is good-bye.'

Ignoring him, Pylades stuck to his line. 'I'm not saving my own life by leaving you. I shared the killing and I'll not retract. My duty is to perish with you both. I meant to marry Electra, so in my eyes she is my wife already. We'll all die together. But first, wait. Let's think. What about Menelaus? Doesn't he get punished at all?'

'I'd die content if he did!' The desire for vengeance had not left Orestes.

'Well then, why don't we kill Helen? That would send Menelaus raving mad. She's here now, hiding in your house, probably making a list of all the valuables. Revenge, my friend. We've nothing to lose.'

Orestes hadn't thought of that: inside the palace they were still free. 'How on earth? She's got her Trojan bodyguards there.'

'We can deal with them. We go into the palace together, ostensibly to kill ourselves — yes, me too — weeping about our fate. Secretly she'll be shedding tears of joy. Swords hidden in our clothes, we deal with her guards. Then we kill her. Satisfaction all round, since she's hated by everyone. You'll no longer be called a matricide. You'll be *the man who got rid of Helen, killer of thousands.*'

Orestes was deeply moved. 'Pylades you are a true friend. You helped kill Aegisthus, you stood at my side in danger. Now again you point to vengeance on my enemies. What more can I say.'

'Well, gods forbid that Menelaus thrives while your father and you and your sister all die.' (And your mother too? No, perhaps best leave her out, thought Pylades.) 'And gods forbid that he and Helen, who owe their lives to Agamemnon, should possess your house. If we fail to kill her we'll burn it down and die too, a noble death. Or perhaps we'll escape? Victory!'

'I want revenge, yes,' said Orestes. 'If only we could kill her without being killed ourselves.'

'Listen,' said Electra quietly. 'I'm thinking of a way to save the three of us. Come here, Pylades.' They drew into a huddle on the grass. 'What about Hermione? Right now she's at Clytaemnestra's grave. She's only just gone.' Her voice dropped to a whisper; not only walls have ears. 'When she comes back, we can seize her as a hostage. I know how to do that. Then when Helen's dead, if Menelaus threatens us you can draw your sword, Orestes, hold it tight against his daughter's throat and tell him you'll kill her. He'll have to promise you your life or lose his daughter. He's no fighter; he'll come round quickly enough. That's it.'

'Pylades,' said Orestes, impressed, 'this is the wife you would die for. Or the rich blessing you may yet live to win.'

'Gods grant I may bring you to my Phocian home, Electra, and honour you with wedding-feast, song and dance' … a proposal from Pylades.

Now Orestes took the lead, staring towards the road. 'The daughter gets back soon, you say? Electra, you stay out here and meet her. If Menelaus comes first, bang on the door or shout into the hall. Pylades, we'll go in now, swords ready. *O my Father, I need your help,*' he cried. '*Deserted by Menelaus, I intend to take his wife and kill her. Help us. Save your children's lives.*'

Electra chimed in, sending prayers to her beloved Agamemnon. '*Father, dwelling in the shadowy halls of night, I and your son Orestes call upon you. May Zeus hear our prayers. United in one perilous struggle, we live — or pay our debt for our loyalty to you, and die.*'

'Come on now, let's get on with it,' cried Pylades. He jumped to his feet, pulled Orestes to his and they went into the house.

A PAUSE: *Fraught with tension the three of them sit on the grass and plot. It's kidnap and extortion now, as well as murder. Orestes needs the solid, practical, self-sacrificing friendship of Pylades as well as the tricky cleverness of Electra if they are to save their lives. What do you think of the argument that 'doing evil that good may come' is worth it, the end justifying the means? What happens when personal integrity challenges public image? Have you come across such a conundrum in your own life? What happened?*

* * * * *

CHAPTER 21

HERMIONE AND HELEN

Electra, left outside, summoned her friends from the kitchens and told them the whole plan. The women were glad to keep watch. They loved Electra who, for all her waspish ways, was a truth-teller and would be a sound employer, unlike some of the rulers in Mycenae. 'Post yourselves, some near the road, others here along the path. Watch out for anyone from the city. Mind the guards.' They were tense and jumpy, immensely upset by the morning's events and expecting the worst. 'I'm going to listen.' Electra climbed the steps, put her ear to the keyhole of the great front door and paused before sending a half-whispered shout in through it. 'Orestes, the coast's clear. Why are you taking so long? Haven't you done it yet?' Silence.

Hopeless, she thought. Are their swords blunted by Helen's beauty? At any moment some fully armed Greek will burst in to the rescue. Only then did she hear a shriek from indoors: Helen, attacked, running away,

48: Hermione

crying out for Menelaus. 'Destroy her, both of you. Go on, do it,' called Electra, loud as she dared.

And at that moment the message came: Hermione's coming. 'We'll capture her; she'll be a fine catch. Don't let on, you women.' Suitably arranging her features, Electra crossed the grass to meet her cousin. 'Oh, Hermione, you're back. I've been thinking of you, hanging the flowers on Clytaemnestra's grave. Did you remember to pour the wine for the gods of earth?'

'I did. But I heard shouting from indoors. It scared me.' Hermione looked pale.

'Well, what's happening to us makes everyone cry. You won't have heard. The city's condemned Orestes and myself to death — yes us, your cousins. It's a hard necessity but it's been decreed. That explains the cry you heard: Orestes, in despair, was with your mother, pleading for his life and mine.' She paused. 'Hermione my dear cousin, would you do something for us? Would you join us in begging Helen to ask your father to stand by us, not see us killed? My own mother brought you up herself. Take pity on us, help us in our misery. Go in, go to your mother. Plead for us. You hold Orestes' life and mine in your hand.'

'Of course, I'll go as quickly as I can. You shall be saved if it's in my power.' Hermione hurried in. Electra stayed by the door, listening. That was the young woman's voice inside, raised in fear: 'What's happening? What do you want?'

'Keep quiet!' That was Orestes. 'You're coming in here for our safety, not your own.' And so Hermione, on her unsuspecting way to find her mother, walked straight into the trap and was captured in her turn.

* * * * *

Though Laodameia, no longer able to play much active part in the life of the household, mostly stayed in her room nowadays, she was held in affection and respect by all. And she kept her ear to the ground. She soon heard of Helen's fate. The gossip was that she had been murdered that afternoon — 'and quite right too.' But had she? 'They killed her, then she vanished,' said one informant (just as Iphigeneia's poor body was purported to have done so many years before, thought Laodameia.) 'No, no, they didn't do it; they turned to catch her daughter and Helen simply disappeared,' claimed another. 'Poor Menelaus,' murmured someone else, pleased anyway: 'all that misery and hardship for nothing. His wife home from Troy after all this time, dead, for nothing. The war against Troy, for nothing!'

Pylades had dealt with the bodyguards. Electra had put Hermione into a small room high in the house (she couldn't escape; her gaolers were women Electra had detailed with care) and gone to join her brother in the palace. But Orestes had set out along the corridors to find Laodameia. This was goodbye. She was in her room, wretched more at the news of his impending death than at any rumoured loss of Helen. Would she always be tormented by her feelings for this boy, wondered the old nurse. He hasn't stopped short of murder, as I well know. But whatever he does, I love him.

Orestes seemed diminished. 'I'm not afraid of Menelaus,' he told her. 'Let him come. If he still won't guarantee safety for me and my sister and my friend, well, we've got Hermione now and we'll play our trump card.'

'Oh, dear boy, yet more terror in the House of Atreus? Yet another fight between you and your relatives? Just as you were getting so much better too.' She broke off. 'Isn't that smoke? Oh look, a huge bonfire outside.' A pyre for Helen? No. The children were getting ready to fire the palace. 'Menelaus will be here soon, won't he? He knows what's happening. He'll certainly have no mercy to spare for you, defeated and desperate as you are, Orestes. You've barred the gates against him, haven't you, barricaded the house?'

There was nothing to say. They hugged. 'Goodbye, dear nurse, my faithful friend. You must leave the house. Go now, the back way. I shall not see you again.'

'Goodbye my dearest boy. The gods be with you. My heart is broken.' Laodameia went down to the kitchens, he up on to the roof and evening came upon them.

Electra's plan worked. Menelaus came into the grounds unimpeded in the gathering dark and hammered on the palace doors. 'Open up, mother-murderer. I know you've killed my wife. Slaves, open up!'

Orestes, with Pylades looking over his shoulder, leant from the battlements above and yelled down at his uncle. 'Go away Menelaus! You can't come in.'

'What have you done to Helen? They say she's disappeared; not dead but vanished. That's absurd. You've killed her.' Sad, pitiable Helen.

Now Menelaus, registering the lighted torches on the roof, saw that between the mother-killer and his accomplice was held a struggling young woman. Hermione! My child, held prisoner, with a sword's edge at her throat. 'At least I'm in time to save my daughter from your bloody hands. You'll pay for this. You've murdered Helen. Will you kill Hermione now? Haven't you killed enough?'

Orestes shouted back, 'I'm the son who avenged his father. You failed me in my time of need and betrayed me to death. You deserve all you get. We'll set fire to the house, destroy our own ancestral home so you can't have it, and I'll cut her throat over the flames. In fact I'm doing it, now.' And he raised his sword.

As predicted, Menelaus gave in. 'No, no, no! Stop, don't do it.' His shoulders slumped. 'You have me trapped. What do you want me to do?'

'Call the assembly and persuade the citizens to spare our lives. If you still won't guarantee safety for me and my sister and Pylades my ally, you'll see your daughter, like your wife, dead before your eyes.'

'So you *did* murder Helen?'

'I wish I had achieved that,' Orestes told him. 'I deny it with extreme regret. The gods baffled me.'

'Are you laughing at me? And now you're going to kill Hermione, my child, adding blood to blood. You've done enough. Restore my wife's body. I must bury her. O God, I brought her home for you to kill.'

'I wish I had,' repeated Orestes.

'Now for action,' cried Electra, appearing on the roof. 'Set this house on fire. You Pylades my friend, make a bonfire of these walls and battlements.'

It was at that moment, with the three friends on the battlements holding Hermione prisoner and everyone yelling with rage or fear or triumph, that Theodore appeared from the stables. Laodameia had sent for him and then she'd come round outside from the kitchen entrance. The women were huddled around her, and Menelaus was on the step outside the great palace door.

Theodore strode out and stood on the grass where the three friends had laid their plot. He called up to the battlements in a voice that would have summoned a herd of horses, and everyone on the terraces and those still inside the house could make out what he said.

'Calm down, all of you. Orestes, take your sword from that girl's throat. You, Menelaus — you think he's killed Helen and so he's taken a hold over you. But it hasn't worked. Your wife Helen's not dead. No one's killed her. She's in the stables being looked after by Philip. As your relation she'll have a lot of explaining to do.' Everyone was listening intently.

'And it's high time you chose another wife. Your Helen's charm is what caused the war and all those deaths. A poet I know said that war had "*purged the bloated earth of its superfluous welter of mortality.*" But it wasn't good.' So much for Helen and the victory over Troy.

'Orestes: Hermione is to be given to you yourself as your wife when you return home at last; so sheath your sword. Your sister Electra you must give to Pylades; she's the wife you promised him, and a life of bliss awaits him in the years to come.' Everyone listened to Theodore as to an Oracle. 'Menelaus, the throne of Argos goes to Orestes; you have to agree. You yourself must go to Sparta and be king there after Tyndareus. Keep it as your lost wife's dowry, making up for the griefs and cares she plagued you with.

49 Laodameia the Poet

'Laodameia, my friend, come over here on the grass.' Gently Theodore took her hand. 'You must write all this down and keep it safe. You know more than anyone here. You're a poetess as well as a faithful nurse and you're going to win the poet's crown. You'll see peace in your time, and greet your friends with blessings once more.

'Lastly, I know people in the city who will put things right, Orestes. The assembly will understand that it was because of Apollo that you shed your mother's blood. Even so, you must leave this place. Make for Athens. The Furies are tracking you down, wanting to fill you with horror and despair. They've got snakes in their hair and they will hurt you. It's retribution.' Snakes again! 'Zephyra is ready. She will look after you. So too will you look after her. The Goddess Athene will be at your side. Go in peace.'

A PAUSE: *Theodore becomes the beloved leader, teacher, friend. Some people find an outer leader such as he; they learn from him and may or may not move on. Some find the inner leader, inner friend, the guardian within or the angel out ahead. This guide will never leave us, always love us. If you have never found such a leader, inner or outer, ask yourself again, Who or what is my god? A person? Or peace, security, stability? — justice, mercy, love? Or . . . ?*

* * * * *

PART THREE

ATHENE AND THE FURIES

CHAPTER 22

GODS AND GHOSTS

Driven out from Argos, Orestes headed not directly for Athens, but for Phocis. Theodore had secretly made Zephyra ready for him and he rode alone with his horse, Pylades having gone with Electra in the chariot drawn by its own pair. He felt stronger physically, but his mind was troubled. He was haunted by the idea that there were things chasing him, angry female figures half-seen in the twilight, driving him on. He conceived a belief that if he looked at anyone his glance would kill them, so he rode with his head down, avoiding everyone. And they avoided him.

50: Zephyra, Best of Horses

Bereft once more of Laodameia and missing Theodore's support, he longed to find Demetrius for some much-needed human contact. However, it would not be wise to present himself to King Strophius. Skirting the palace, he decided instead to seek the benison of the gods. He and Zephyra found their way to nearby Delphi, climbing again to Apollo's temple high in Mount Parnassus. Now, having seen his horse safely stabled, he stood on the edge of the gathering outside the doors. Despite the things he'd said about Apollo, might he not after all be a friend? Long ago Orestes had met the Pythoness, the Oracle who spoke for the god; and now she was standing here again, making her obeisance to Mother Earth, honouring tradition and praying before entering the temple.

'*Apollo speaks for Father Zeus,*' she proclaimed and the crowd listened, entranced. '*I honour the nymphs who live in the deep, rocky hollows. I love the haunt of birds where spirits drift and hover. I revere great Dionysus who rules the land, marshalling his wild women. Pallas Athene herself is honoured at our temple and crowns our legends. Come forward, draw your lots and enter my sanctuary, where Apollo will speak in his temple.*'

Orestes, gaining admission, moved in through the portals with the rest; but keeping to the side and seeing a little door in the wall, he slipped through it and found himself in the sanctuary. Seeing a seat near the big, curtained stone at its centre (the Navel Stone; he remembered its name) he sat down alone and listened. The Oracle processed through the temple among the people and came alone into this holy of holies.

To the crowd's shock, with a loud shriek the priestess immediately shot out again. Falling to her knees before them in a most un-Oracle-like way, Orestes heard her cry, 'Dread sends me reeling from the Navel Stone.' She could hardly speak for terror, but she struggled to compose herself. 'There's a man there in the vault, an abomination to Apollo, sitting by the Stone where suppliants sit for purging. His hands are dripping blood. His sword is drawn. He's holding an olive branch. That's good, but there in a ring around him is an appalling company: women, sleeping, nestling against the benches. Gorgons I'd call them, but no wings.' The Pythoness shuddered, cringing with horror. 'Dressed in black, repulsive, gasping, oozing snakes — ugh! — they're the Furies. This is far beyond me. Over to Apollo. The mighty power must purge his own temple.' And the Oracle herself fled from the building.

Orestes, hearing this and sensing if not seeing the sleeping Furies, turned to the Navel Stone at the sacred heart of the sanctum and bowed, eyes tight shut, hands over his face. And it was as if the curtain around it lifted and Apollo himself was standing there, immensely tall, rising over him as he stood in prayer, surrounded by the Furies all sound asleep.

As clearly as if he were in the stable at Mycenae, Orestes heard in his head the voice of Theodore, his trusted friend. Theodore had overseen his return to health, had understood his dilemma, had never denied his hurt and guilt and loss. He had given him more than the best horse to be his friend: he'd spoken with an inner authority that brought a glimmer of hope. And now, needing no Oracle, it was Theodore's voice that spoke for the god.

51: With Apollo and the Sleeping Furies © Tricia Newell

'I will never fail you, Orestes. I am your inner guardian. Whether I'm standing by your side or worlds away I will show no mercy to your enemies. I have begun by sending these Furies to sleep. But they will awaken, and they'll drive you on and on, over the mountains and over the seas, through the cities, for ever as it seems. Never surrender, never resent the stress, never yield.' Yes, here by the Navel Stone in Delphi Apollo was speaking with Theodore's voice. 'You, Orestes, must go to the citadel of Athene, my sister. Kneel and embrace her ancient idol in your arms. Honest judges will hear your case. Use words and magic spells, and the master-stroke will be devised that sets you free. No more torment, ever. *After all, it was I, Apollo, who persuaded you to take your mother's life.* What do you say?'

Strength flowed through Orestes. Whatever he must face, he now knew what he had to do. 'Lord Apollo, you well know the rules of justice. I see you know compassion, too.'

52: Orestes and Zephyra

'Remember that,' came the voice in his head. 'Here to go with you is Hermes.' Briefly Orestes glimpsed the messenger god, winged and sandalled among the shadows; and he remembered his horse Zephyra, waiting for him in her temporary shelter here in Delphi. 'Guard and shepherd this man. He is my suppliant, and outlaws too have rights that Zeus reveres.' Both Apollo and Hermes vanished but they left a spark of hope. Apollo was supporting him and Hermes was to be his leader. His friend Theodore, though absent, was there for him and so was Zephyra.

Faintly an echo followed: 'Lead him back to the world of men with all good speed and let no fear overcome him.'

But fear immediately overcame Orestes despite Apollo's words. He would have left the temple on the instant, but right beside him at the Navel Stone there loomed a shrouded figure. 'I am your Mother,' it said.

'You can't be, you're dead!' he gasped. 'You're — a ghost.'

Clytaemnestra's ghost ignored him and hovered over the sleeping Furies, hissing at them. 'Wake up! You're useless. I'm stripped of honour, withered by guilt from the outraged dead, and it's all your fault. You're asleep. How *could* you? I suffered terribly too, from family members I loved. No one remembers, no one tries to avenge *me*. Instead, I've been slaughtered by his matricidal hand: this man here.' She swung round to glare at Orestes with her ghastly face. 'See these gashes? You made them.' To the snoring Gorgons again, 'Awake, my Furies, hear me. Remember the libations I poured for you? You certainly lapped the honey I soothed you with, I the Queen, pleading for vengeance. You're letting him get away with it. Look out! Free as a fawn he'll escape and flee far away.'

The Furies uttered a sharp moan but slept on, mumbling in their sleep, promising to hunt Orestes down, while Clytaemnestra's ghost screeched at them, 'Well, what are you doing? Get up, stop him, wither him, waste him, burn him out … ' She faded from sight.

Only now did the Furies wake up, aghast to think they might have let go of their prey, venting their fury with Apollo (to them a mere stripling of a god) for having the power to send them to sleep. 'You, Apollo, you insisted on this crime and the guilt is yours. You made him do it, putting men before women, destroying the old dominions of the Fates. You commanded the man to kill his mother. Now you've taken his part, the godless one, the matricide, and let him escape. This isn't justice; this man will go on killing. There are stains on the hearth. Where is the justice for *her*?'

Orestes tried to run from the sanctuary, from the temple and away, but again, too late. He could only slip behind the curtain. What would Apollo say, what would he think? Surely these Furies, these Gorgons of remorse, were right to support Clytaemnestra, for no one else had done that. Again he heard Theodore his wise mentor: 'That's not your responsibility, Orestes. Drive them out. Fast! Apollo's here for sure, in full armour, brandishing his bow for you, shouting at them to get out

53: The Furies Remain

of his temple. They have no right to be in these halls. Come out from behind that curtain and help the god to strike his arrow of lightning in their faces.'

Orestes threw the curtain aside and faced the hissing snakes. They closed in on him but now he was undaunted. 'You revolt the gods,' he cried, stepping towards them. 'Do not desecrate Apollo's shrine. Out, you flock without a herdsman. Out! This god will never shepherd you with love. Apollo *commanded* me to avenge my father. What of it? He ordered me to come to his temple here to be purged. You are not fit to approach this house. Yes, you drive matricides from their homes. But what of the wife who strikes her husband down? Some atrocious crimes stir your rage, but others lull you to sleep. You didn't even try to punish Clytaemnestra, not a glance in anger to avenge Agamemnon. Your man-hunt of me is unjust. I know that Athene, sister to Apollo, will oversee my trial.'

'Don't you try to cut our power with your logic. We're hot on the trail. We shall never let you go free, never,' cried the Furies, fully awake now. 'We'll hound you to death. Serves you right.'

'And I,' cried Orestes, 'am the suppliant of Apollo and he will defend and save me. He will not fail the outcast.' And he slipped from the grasp of the Furies on a tide of hope and trust. Leaving them confused and angry, groping around the Navel Stone, he ran from the temple.

As he went, Theodore's voice within was telling him, 'You are exiled from Argos. Now you must depart from Delphi too. For one whole year you shall wander the land till you find yourself in Arcadia, where for a time you will have your home. It is a land of mountains, and your name Orestes means *Mountaineer.* From there you must make your way to Athens and stand trial, arraigned by the Furies for your mother's blood. On Ares' Hill the gods will dispute your case. A trustworthy jury set up by Athene will cast the votes and you will leave their court absolved.'

FIRST PAUSE: *Here we meet the Furies face to face, the snaky hair and the Gorgon glance that turns people to stone. The Delphic Oracle avoided that fate, but was still driven from her own temple by goddesses trying to dispatch the god Apollo. Isn't this what happens when churches and mosques and synagogues and temples make war, each on their own idea of the other? Since in truth they're all following their own path up the same mountain, might they not honour and encourage each other instead? Have you come across religious prejudice? How does it feel to you?*

And so Apollo vanished. Orestes found the stable where he had left Zephyra. She whinnied gently to him, pawing the ground as if she couldn't wait to be off. However, the warm and strengthening feeling of Theodore, that wise lover of horses and people, soon faded. He remembered the tale Demetrius had told of how he, Orestes, had been killed in that fictitious chariot race, tangled in the reins and dragged by the young horses. He wished he had been; to have been cut down honourably in his youth before he had had a chance to exact vengeance on anyone seemed vastly preferable to his present guilt. Oh to be dead with his innocence intact.

His steed, unlike himself, had been fed, watered and rested. He paid what was due for her care, climbed on to her silky warm back (once, he would have vaulted up) and rode alone out of Delphi. He scarcely knew which road to take, but the mare seemed sure of her direction and trotted happily through the spring sunshine, cavorting a little now and then from sheer high spirits. She was his only friend now and he was glad of her beyond measure.

54: A pillow for Orestes

The next months were a blur of shame. He rode, he thirsted, he worried, he wrestled with darts of guilt that would have felled one far less aware than he. Remorse. How could he have done it? And dread; the Furies were after him, there was no doubt about it. He heard them in daylight; he almost saw them by night, though Zephyra, untroubled, grazed in peace.

Occasionally, to try to drown their voices, he would put up in a hostel, leaving early next day; more often he slept rough on the rocky ground, his back against his horse or his head pillowed against her warm flank. By day he walked beside her, heart failing, hands hanging down; or he rode, too exhausted to walk, slumping along on her faithful back, ever deeper into distress. He spoke to no one, wandering without aim through the heat of summer, by the coast, in the mountains, far inland, anywhere she would take him. The Furies were ever at her heels, their snaky locks hissing at him, 'Serves you right.'

55: Orestes and the Furies in the Outlands © Tricia Newell

Sometimes Orestes wondered if Hermes had transformed himself into this steadfast bay mare, for he saw nothing otherwise of the divine helper he had been promised. His care of his one friend was tender and consistent, through the heat of summer and all the more in the cold winter. He took little thought for his own comfort, only hers; but Zephyra probably saved his life with her gentle loyalty and her healthy disregard for his distress. She kept him warm at night and by day she trotted or plodded indefatigably along, showing him the way. In the dark days towards mid-winter they reached Arcadia, the state next to Argos, as Theodore had foretold. There they stayed a while. Orestes remembered the promise that one day he would make his home in Arcadia, and he was glad.

Now at last things began to improve. Spring was coming, days were getting longer, the nightly cold less intense. Life was returning as he and Zephyra set out for Athens.

ANOTHER PAUSE: *Orestes probably owes his life to Zephyra, as Theodore will have known when he sent them off together. How do you feel towards animals? Has an animal befriended you, as Zephyra did Orestes, and have you ever owed a great deal to an animal?*

* * * * *

CHAPTER 23

PALLAS ATHENE

56: Pallas Athene before the Acropolis

And so it was that by the beginning of spring Orestes came at last into the great city, found a good stable for the mare and went straight to the Acropolis. There he sank exhausted to his knees at the ancient shrine of Pallas Athene, most urbane and civilized of deities (apparently left-handed, and very unlike Artemis, that goddess of the outdoors who had demanded the life of his sister). Athene had not been born but had sprung fully armed from the head of Zeus; or so it was said. Child of the father, no mother in sight, she was a good friend to her brother Apollo and full of wisdom and justice.

As he knelt at the feet of her statue everything changed for Orestes. Some new life within him — could it be from Hermes? — made him throw his arms around the knees of the image, bury his face against the hard stone and pray to her with intense passion. '*I have done enough. By coast and by mountain I have obeyed Apollo and struggled to reach your house. I will wander no more. Great Goddess, receive me kindly, for, yes, I am cursed and an outcast. However, I am not asking you to purge me, because I am already innocent. A year in the outlands, wandering the beaten paths of men, has knocked all guilt out of me. My hands are clean, I'm harmless now and I shall not murder anyone else. My fate is yours. I await the consummation of my trial.*'

At that moment the Furies, who had followed his sandy footprints, burst upon the shrine hissing and shrieking. They didn't at first spot their prey, twined as he was around the knees of Athene's statue. They clustered together conferring. 'We're exhausted,' they said. 'Our lungs are bursting, keeping track of him. We have hurdled the waves without any wings, leaving ships behind us. Have we missed him? No, he's here somewhere, cowering like a hare. Makes us laugh. Let's scour the place before he escapes. We're for Clytaemnestra. We won't let this matricide dodge free.'

57: Orestes at Athene's Feet © Tricia Newell

Horrified, he hid his face against the stone figure. Then, unexpectedly, it was as if Theodore's voice spoke within him. 'Enough! Buck your ideas up, Orestes. Have courage. Stand straight and tall and face the Furies.' And he did.

'There he is,' they shouted. 'Look at him, clutching the knees of power again, currying favour with the gods. 'So, he wants to go on trial for his crimes does he!' Contempt oozed in their voices. 'Never. With us it's an eye for an eye and a tooth for a tooth.' Hideous fingers waggled at him. 'You'll pay agony for mother-killing agony, you and the rest. All mortals who outraged a goddess or a guest or a loving mother will be paid back in kind. You'll go to Hades.'

Orestes stood up. 'My hands are washed clean,' he said, taking a step towards them. 'It's Apollo my master who compels me to speak. I've done my bit and I've done enough. Now, with pure and reverent lips, I call upon the Queen of this land to help me. Come, Athene,' and he raised his voice, 'for I am on your side, your devotee for ever. Where are you now? Come, you too are a god, you can hear me from afar. Set me free.'

The Furies kept trying, threatening that neither Apollo's nor Athene's strength would be able to save him. 'No more joy for you. You're just a husk, a wraith,' they hissed, snaky locks writhing in the air. 'We have rights over you. No one will receive you, since we hate you. If they do invite you into their houses, you will sit at a separate table and drink from a separate cup. We conspire and if you're guilty we rise in flames against you to the end.' But Orestes, remembering how Theodore had stood up to Menelaus and everyone, stared them out in silence, sticking to his prayer despite all.

Apollo's Oracle had been a pushover for the Furies, but now they began to doubt their power. They called upon their own goddess. '*Mother Night, hear us. Avenge the blinded dead. That whelp Apollo is spurning the rights the Fates spun for us, tearing this dithering victim from our grasp. But we can't be tried. No god can be our judge.*' And the snaky tentacles reached towards Orestes. '*The centre, our ancient power, holds. We are the skilled, and not without our pride. Beneath the earth our strict battalions form their lines, going in groups through the mist and the sun-starved night.*'

And all at once there stood Athene herself, armed for combat with her helmet, her spear and the snake-skin aegis she wore around her as a shield. Orestes didn't know it, but he would henceforth be 'under her aegis', protected by the goddess. Seeing the Furies at her shrine, she unfurled this scarf-like aegis with its Gorgon portrait upon it. Orestes threw himself down at her feet.

'Who called me? Athene asked. 'I have come home from the wars with unflagging pace, flying wingless, my racing spirit in her prime. Some new companions on the land? This stranger, this young man at my feet, yes, I know that you called. But whoever are you others? I do not fear you, but I wonder who you are? You certainly don't look like people born of the sown seed. Nor goddesses, no. Nor mortals either, by the look of you. Your features are … but wait, I must mind my manners here. You've done nothing wrong. I mustn't offend your rights or violate tradition.'

'We'll tell you who we are,' they said, surprised at being acknowledged. '*You* are just a young daughter of Zeus; but we are the everlasting children of Night. Deep in the halls of Earth they call us the Furies.'

58: The Goddess Athene

'Now I know your birth, your rightful name. But I don't know what you do, your powers. I can accept the facts; just tell them clearly.' Athene was paying close attention.

'You will learn quickly. We find the murderers, destroyers of life. We drive them from their houses, hound them with remorse so that there is no joy for them at all. This man' — and even in Athene's presence they hissed at Orestes — 'he murdered his mother and then said there was justice in what he had done. We have shrieked him on through this year of joyless flight.'

'Murder? Why did he do it? Was he forced? Did he fear someone's anger?' Athene really wanted to know. 'There are two sides to this and I'm only hearing yours. What made him do it? I know you want justice, but I think you're set on the word rather than the act.'

Orestes, lying at her feet with his eyes closed, realised to his astonishment that they were listening to her. 'Teach us. You're showing us respect, so we respect you. Why don't you examine him yourself. You obviously have a genius for refinements. You'll judge him fairly. We'll turn responsibility over to you to reach a just verdict.' The Furies did not mention Iphigeneia, nor give Clytaemnestra's point of view.

59: The Sword of Justice © Tricia Newell

Athene turned to Orestes. 'Your turn, stranger. What do you say to all this? Stand up, tell us where you're from, your birth, your fortunes. Then defend yourself against their charge. Are you a suppliant for purging, which is sacred? Is that what's brought you here to my hearth?'

'Queen Athene, let me answer your questions,' he replied. 'I am called Orestes. No, I haven't come for purging. I pose no threat of pollution; sweep it from your mind. Look. Not a stain on these hands that touch your idol. I have been cleansed. I was born in Argos. My father was Agamemnon, commander of the men-of-war fighting in Troy in your name. What an ignoble death he died when he came home! My blackhearted mother snared him in her net and cut him down. But I came back, having survived years of exile.

'And yes, I killed the one who bore me, I won't deny it. I killed her in revenge. I loved my father fiercely. And Apollo shares the guilt. He told me to do it, warned me of the pains I'd feel unless I acted to bring the guilty down. Was it not to obey the god? Judge us now. My fate is in your hands. Stand or fall, I shall accept your verdict.'

Athene was stumped. 'This is too large a matter even for me, let alone for mortal men to judge. I can't decide murder cases. Murder whets the passions. But you, a cleansed suppliant, so long as your wildness has really been tamed, would bring no harm to my house. If you are found innocent, I'll adopt you for my city.

'However,' and she indicated the Furies, 'these others have their rights too and that's hard to dismiss. If they fail to win their day in court, the venom of their pride will spread and their everlasting plagues will blight our land and our future.' So: a crisis either way. She too was in a double bind. 'Embrace the one? Expel the other? It defeats me.' She pondered a long moment.

At last she swept her mighty sword into the air. 'This is what we will do. It's up to us, I will appoint judges who can deal with murder. I shall swear them in and found a tribunal here for all time to come. Now you Furies — now Orestes: you're the contestants. Gather each your proofs, summon your trusted witnesses, choose your defenders; they will be under oath to help your cause. And I will pick twelve of the finest men of Athens to be both judge and jury. We will return and decide the issue truly and fairly, bound to our oaths, our spirits bent on justice.' Athene wasted no words.

'I will set up the tribunal on the Areopagus nearby, the Crag of Ares.

60: Reconstruction of the Acropolis and Areopagus in Athens, 1846
painting by Leo von Klenze (Museum: Neue Pinakothek)

You, the suppliant, will be summoned before the court. Till then, go and rest.' Her voice grew fainter as she left her shrine and vanished.

The Furies gathered in a huddle. Orestes, hiding behind Athene's statue, heard them talking angrily, churning their case among themselves. Realising they had given away their power, they had plenty to be furious about. 'If his outrage against his mother wins the day, all the old laws will go. This man's matricide will free everyone to kill their parents, for ever. No hope for the mother now, nor the sobbing father. No longer any use calling on us for fairness. The house of just retribution will fall. We are the Furies, but our rage has always sought out the crimes of men. Now it will dissolve, sweep the world and let loose its lethal tide on anyone. Anyone who, groping to cure his own torments, tries to pass them on to his neighbour, blaming him, saying it's his fault and serve him right. But, poor wretch, it comes back on himself with a vengeance. It helps, at such times, *to suffer into truth*.'

As they warmed to their somewhat incoherent theme Orestes, out of sight and listening carefully to every word, picked up one phrase: *suffer into truth*. Yes, with Zephyra's faithful support, wasn't that just what he had been doing this long year.

'So what now?' muttered the Furies, snaky heads entwined. 'Is there one city left that still reveres our ancient rights? One city that leads neither a life of anarchy nor one enslaved by tyrants? Worships neither revolution nor despotism? We Furies are pleading for *measure*.'

'Measure? What's come over them?' thought Orestes. They went on: 'The laws of the gods may veer from north to south, but the watchman must stand guard upon the heart and strike the balance. In the *middle* lies the power.' Surely they were changing before his eyes, which widened again at what they said next. 'We love the spirit's great good health. Our prayers call down prosperity and peace.' Well, thought Orestes, you could have fooled me. 'Violence comes from the overthrow of *reverence*. Do right, all you people. Revere the altar.' Really? Surely they didn't incur much reverence. They'd hardly want an altar of their own? 'Honour your parents,' they went on. 'Put them first with reverence. Welcome the stranger-guest to your house, seeing to his needs and respecting his sacred rights. Be just, not because you must, but because you want to; then joy will be yours.' The more oddly mollified they seemed, the more Orestes' astonishment grew. Even the snakes were spitting a little less.

However, these Gorgons were still not above a bit of revenge. 'If you are reckless, if you murder and maraud and steal, we will harry you and you will be sucked down in sheer whirlpools, the gods' laughter breaking over your hot hearts.' No, they're still the same after all. They were screeching now. 'If you've boasted, if you've lived for nothing but yourself and your golden wealth, you will crash on the reef of the law and drown unwept, unseen.' They began to dwindle, grow fainter, more attenuated. '*Terror* will hunt the godless day and night. Their destined end awaits them … ' Their voices grew fainter till they could be seen and heard no more.

Free to leave the shrine, Orestes made his way straight back to the stable and, standing knee-deep in new straw, hugged his horse, weeping tears of relief and dread into her silky dark mane. 'Dear Zephyra, my fate lies ahead of me, but I feel the gods are on my side,' he whispered as he brushed her lovely coat and checked her hooves. 'You seem happy here. Soon I shall be summoned and my case will be heard and judged. I shall make provision for you now with these kind Athenian people, in case it goes against me.' She blew gently at her hay in reply. 'O best of horses, you too have suffered on our wanderings and no longer look so young.

This evening I will bring you fresh wheat if I can find it, and a measure of wine to drink.'

61: Zephyra

A PAUSE: *At last we meet the Goddess Athene, who brings redemption into this story. While the Furies and Apollo again fall to squabbling with each other, Athene brings in justice and a jury trial. She gives both the Furies and Orestes a fair chance, insisting on hearing both sides equally. The Furies fail altogether to present Clytaemnestra's case, mentioning Iphigeneia not at all. It is because Orestes takes his own part, showing how he has 'suffered into truth' in the Furies' phrase, that Apollo and Athene defend him. This calling upon the gods for help is what saved him. Is this something that has meaning for you?*

CHAPTER 24

THE TRIAL

That night Orestes slept better than he had for what seemed years. He was in the hands of the gods. His fate was relinquished entirely to the heavens. He had *suffered into truth* and there was nothing more to be done.

When the summons arrived he was ready. He made his way to the so-called Crag of Ares, with the Areopagus set on its rocky top. Here the tribunal was held in the open air. Pallas Athene entered in procession, her herald before her and twelve good citizens behind, men she had chosen to be judge and jury, each carrying a ballot-stone for the vote. 'Call for order, herald; marshal our good people with your trumpet.' And he did, straining his instrument to full pitch with an ear-stabbing blast, making everyone jump. The jury took their positions. Athene sent Orestes to stand by the Stone of Outrage, as far as possible from the Stone of Unmercifulness to which the Furies were directed.

62: Athene, Goddess of Justice and Wisdom © Tricia Newell

The goddess, with the balance of justice in her hand and the wise owl on her shoulder, took her seat between two pillars. Behind them stood the urns into which the ballots would be cast.

'Silence!' she cried. 'People of my city, silence is best, until everyone has taken his place at this court of judgement. Silence — you too, Furies — so that you can learn my everlasting laws and well observe our verdict.'

The great arena was filling fast. Everyone had heard about the prince of Argos who had murdered his mother the queen and her lover. Each had an opinion about it. 'Matricide. That'll be death for him,' they whispered, despite Athene's injunction. 'But he may go free. You'll have heard what his mother did? Yes, Clytaemnestra. She killed his father, murdered the great Agamemnon. Guilty as Hades, that one.'

63: Apollo, God of Light and Knowledge © Tricia Newell

A hush fell over the gathering, for a light was filling the immense arena. And there stood Apollo, his presence bright before Athene's court in her own city, standing huge and golden behind Orestes. A reverential hush fell on each of the twelve good men and true, amazed to be in the presence of yet another god.

'Lord Apollo. What part have you in this? Tell us.' Athene's voice was stern, goddess to brother god.

'I come as a witness.' Apollo spoke with great seriousness. 'This man, this suppliant, came to Delphi and sought my advice. I am his champion, for I share responsibility for his mother's execution. I am the one who purged his bloody hands as he wandered in the outlands. Begin the trial. You, Athene, know the rules. Now, turn them into Justice.'

Accepting Apollo's invitation, Athene turned to the Furies. 'The trial begins. Which of you speaks for the rest? You? Right, yours is the first word. The prosecution opens. From start to finish, set the facts before us and make them clear.'

The Speaker for the Furies was dark and fierce, snakes hissing. 'We will be brief. Orestes, answer count for count, charge for charge. First, tell us, did you kill your mother?'

'I killed her. I don't deny it.'

'Ha! Got you already. First round to us.'

'You exult before your man is on his back,' returned Orestes with commendable swiftness.

'Secondly, then, tell us, how did you kill her?'

'I drew my sword — and I cut her throat.'

'And our third question. Who put you up to it? Who led you on?'

'This God told me to. Apollo is my witness.'

'How did you know it was he? Did his Oracle speak for him? Did she drive you on to matricide?'

'Yes. The Pythoness gave me Apollo's command. And to this hour I have no regrets.' With Theodore's help Orestes had been struggling to put the remorse and guilt and shame of his actions behind him — a huge task. Now he was prepared to defend himself, not only against these Furies but also against himself. 'I trust that my father, King Agamemnon of Argos, will also help me from the grave.'

'So you're trusting to corpses now? If the verdict goes against you, you'll change your story quickly enough,' hissed his opponent. 'You made your mother a corpse, that's certain.'

'My mother committed two deadly crimes: she killed her husband, and that meant she also killed my father. You never drove *her* into exile. Why not? Those murders set her free to live with her paramour. She lived on in her own right as ruler of Argos. Yet I live on for trial. Is that fair?'

The Furies' case was becoming thinner. 'She killed Agamemnon,' said their Speaker, 'but he was not her blood-relative, only her husband.'

Orestes tried to argue that neither did his mother's blood run in his own veins, but they came back with 'Are you disclaiming your own mother's kinship? How else could she carry you in her body? Murderer! She gave you life.'

Orestes, somewhat daunted by the obvious truth of this, turned to Apollo. 'Advise me, show me the way, Apollo, I pray. Was it just, that I struck her down? I did strike her, I don't deny it, but I did this bloody work at your command, and *I have suffered into truth*. What do I say to the judges?'

Now the God Apollo himself spoke. 'I tell you and your high court, Athene: yes, it was just. Seer that I am, I never lie. My Oracle never deceives anyone; she speaks only words that Zeus, our omnipotent Olympian Father, commands. This is the Justice of Zeus.'

'Are you telling me,' snapped the Speaker of the Furies, 'that Zeus himself gave that command to your Oracle at Delphi, actually charged this man to avenge his father's death and spurn his mother's rights?' There was horror in her voice.

'Orestes' deed was different from Clytaemnestra's,' pronounced Apollo. 'That noble man Agamemnon was murdered by his wife, slaughtered at a woman's hand. He should have died in battle, covered in praise, his sceptre the gift of a god. There should have been fighting, swords, arrows whipping in. He should have been honoured in his death. Let me tell you, Athene. You judges poised to cast your lots, listen to what happened to Agamemnon. He arrived home victorious from the long war in Troy; home to his wife's loyal, waiting arms and a welcome bath. There she netted him and killed him. That's the kind of woman she was. What an outrage! Such a death for the lord of the squadrons. Judges remember, before you reach your verdict, it was that magnificent man who was murdered.'

The Furies were having none of it. 'You say Zeus sets more store by a father's death than a mother's? Well, Zeus shackled his own father, Chronos, when he was old. Doesn't that contradict you?'

'That's beside the point,' murmured the jury members. But the Furies, though charged by her, had completely forgotten Clytaemnestra's case. What, they might have asked, of Agamemnon's own murder of his daughter? What of Princess Iphigeneia? There was no one left to speak for her. No one in Athens knew what had happened to her. She didn't matter. Her disappearance had long been forgotten.

'You Furies are disgusting.' Apollo, glaring at them, became fanatical. 'You grotesque, loathsome creatures! The gods detest you. Women. Ugh! Once a *man's* dead, he's dead. That's it. No returning. No spell sung over the grave can sing him back. Not even Zeus can do that.'

The Furies tried their best. 'So you'd force this son's acquittal, would you? So much for Justice. Look at him there with Apollo. This man can spill his mother's blood then settle into his father's halls in Argos, can he? I tell you, he will never be able to use the public altars. Could the holy water of his kinsmen touch his hands again?' The Speaker's voice rose to a screech. 'What will you have done if you let Orestes go?'

Apollo rounded on the Speaker with another belief. 'Here is the truth. The woman you call the mother of the child is not the parent, just a nurse to the new-sown seed that grows inside her. The man is the source of life. It's his child. She is just a fertile field keeping the shoot alive.'

He flung out his arm towards Athene. 'Look. Here's proof the father can produce offspring without a mother. Here she stands, our living witness. Child sprung full-blown from Olympian Zeus, you were never bred in the darkness of the womb. No goddess could have conceived you, Athene. I will raise your battlements to glory. I sent this suppliant to your hearth that he might be your trusted supporter for ever. In him you win a new ally. Dear Goddess, he and his descendants will venerate you for all posterity.'

Athene had heard enough. 'It is time to vote. 'Judges, soon you must cast your lots, honest as conscience may decide. Furies, have you more to say?'

The Furies conceded again. Riddled with superstitions about sacrifice and oracles and rites, they still made no defence of Clytaemnestra, nor spoke for Iphigeneia. 'No. We've shot all our bolts,' said their Speaker, awed by the goddess. 'We wait to hear how this court will decide.'

Athene spoke and a great hush filled the Areopagus. 'This is the first time a murder has been tried in a court of law. Till now, only revenge has punished bloodshed. Instead, now and for ever, this will be the court where judges reign and juries decide. Here from the heights of the Crag of Ares, instead of retribution, the twin powers of *terror* and *reverence* will protect the people from injustice, through the day and through the mild night.'

Terror and reverence. Surely, thought Orestes, she's repeating what the Furies themselves said when she left them at her shrine in the Acropolis. Athene was still speaking. 'Revere the ancient rights. Don't try to make new ones. If tradition works, leave it alone. Foul a clear well and you will suffer thirst. Neither anarchy nor tyranny shall rule our city, my people. Worship the *mean*, I urge you; shore it up with reverence.'

The mean? The Furies had said that too, hadn't they? They'd pleaded for *measure*. He remembered their words: in the *middle* lies the power. But Athene had come back to reverence — and terror. 'The stronger your *reverence* for the just,' she went on, 'the stronger our country's wall and the city's safety. But never banish *terror* outright from the gates; terror of injustice. For this court will be swift to fury, rising above you as you sleep, our night watch always wakeful, the guardian of our land.' Never can she have sounded more godlike, thought Orestes, gazing into the eyes of the great bird perched on her right shoulder. 'I am founding this majestic court of law here and now,' Athene told the people. 'So rise to your future. Each man must cast his lot and judge the case, revering his oath. Now I have finished.'

Apollo wasn't listening. While his divine sister was taking this stupendous action, he too was instructing the men of the jury in the ways of justice. 'When you drop your pebbles into the urns to cast your lots, my friends, observe strictly the oath you have sworn. The truth … You have heard what you have heard.' Orestes, his life hanging in the balance, watched beyond feeling as the jurors moved towards the two great urns to cast their lots and determine his fate — life or death.

'Get it wrong, you men, and we ruin you,' yelled the Furies.

'Vote for my side or else,' threatened Apollo. They were double binding the jurors, just as the members of the family of Atreus had been bound. The twelve men filed through, and the twelve stones clanged hollowly into the echoing urns.

A PAUSE: *As public prosecutor of Orestes, Athene does not have all the facts. The court doesn't know Clytaemnestra's case because the Furies don't tell it. By handing Athene the power to decide, they betray their client. Is she not worth defending? The Furies themselves are the failure here. Representing the feminine principle, they cave in at the start, weak and unable to defend themselves. Do they deserve to win the case? The male playwrights who brought us the story are saying that if women can't defend themselves they deserve to lose. What do you feel about this? What should have been the feminine case?*

* * * * *

CHAPTER 25

THE VERDICT

As the stones were counted, the Furies turned on Apollo, claws out. The quarrel was theirs, after all. 'You and your Oracles! You're a young god, Apollo, out of your depth. How dare you try to seduce the ancient goddesses with your threats? So you'd ride us down, would you, for all our years. Believe us, if we lose this trial, we'll crush the land.'

Apollo's golden purity stood out against their hissing darkness. 'Among the gods, young and old, you go disgraced,' he declared. 'I will triumph over you. Spew your venom, then be quiet.'

That was enough quarrelling for Athene. 'Silence! I shall render the final judgement. Orestes, know this.' And she raised her arm, her hand clenched as if she too held a ballot-stone. 'I will give the casting vote. If the numbers are equal, I will throw in my lot for you. Citizens of Athens, in years to come, know this: if the votes are balanced, the defendant shall always be *acquitted*. Clemency shall always take precedence over harshness.

'It is true,' she affirmed to the court, 'I honour the male with all my heart. I am my Father's child. No mother gave me birth. I cannot set more store by this woman's death than by her husband's. After all, she had killed him, guardian of their House. If the pebbles fall equally, Orestes wins. Now, shake the lots from the urns, you tellers — quickly, quickly.' And the men came forward to empty the great pots and count the ballot-stones.

Silently Orestes prayed, *O God of the light, Apollo, will it be the noose or the new day?* Silently the Furies prayed, *O Night, dark Mother, are you watching now? Do we go down? Or forge ahead in power?* Apollo spoke. 'Count the pebbles fairly, friends. Honour justice. An error with one stone could mean disaster — or the restoring of a house to greatness.'

Solemnly they counted them, wrote down the tally and handed it to Athene. She read, lifted her arm again and proclaimed, 'The lots are equal. I cast my vote. The man goes free, cleared of the charge of blood.'

'O Pallas Athene you save my House!' cried Orestes. 'Your vote reclaims my fatherland. The man of Argos lives again on the great estates of his fathers, thanks to Athene, and to Apollo, and to Zeus, Lord of all fulfilment, who saved me. And now I journey home.'

Orestes' words rose towards kingship. 'But first to you, Athene, and your assembled host, I swear by my future that no man of Argos shall ever make war on Athens. Even if we must rise from the grave, we will deal with those who break this oath. All those who keep it, who uphold your rights for ever, Athene, we bless with all the kindness of our heart. Now farewell, you and the people of your city. I wish you good wrestling with a grip no foe can break, a spear to bring you triumph and a saving hope.'

FIRST PAUSE: *Now the course of history is changed. Athene, acting out of wisdom, does something new, huge and culture-changing. Now, not only Orestes but the whole world can begin to move on. For the law of retribution starts to give place to the laws of justice and clemency. Athene declares that, if the vote be equal, she herself will decide the case; and she will support Orestes, the defendant, with her casting vote. From henceforth clemency shall prevail (meaning it is expedient to treat people decently — mercy itself comes later). It is said that her stance here has affected jury trial ever since. How would you have voted in Orestes' trial?*

So Orestes left the court on the Hill of Ares content, and Apollo followed. Only the Furies remained, reeling in wild confusion around Athene, and many of the crowd stayed on to see what would happen.

'*You*! You young gods, you have ridden down the ancient laws.' The voice of the Furies' Speaker was choked with rage and misery. 'If we can no longer poison the land, or curse it or burn it sterile, what *can* we do? It's unbearable to be mortified by Athens — we, the daughters of Night, our power stripped from us.'

Once again Athene, goddess of wisdom and justice, came into her own. She did something else that was new: *she gave the enemy a way out with honour.* Earlier she had listened with great care to the Furies' case. Now she turned towards them, asking, 'And you, what can I do to merit your respect?' The little owl, alighting on her shoulder and settling her feathers, blinked the huge eyes that could see so well in the dark.

64: Athene and her Owl

'Listen to me,' she went on. 'Lift your heavy spirits, Goddesses. You were not defeated. The vote was tied, a verdict fairly reached with no disgrace to you. Apollo, who is the light of Zeus himself, bore witness that Orestes certainly did the deed but should not suffer harm. Before you vent your anger and hurt the land, be calm. Consider: I promise you your seat in the depths of earth — yours by all rights. I promise that you shall be stationed each with a glistening throne, each covered with praise. My people will revere you.

'It's a disgrace.' The Furies' indignation was far from spent. 'That the proud heart of the past should be driven under the earth, condemned like so much filth. Night, dear Mother Night! All's lost, our ancient powers torn away by the cunning, ruthless hands of these gods, so hard to wrestle down. They obliterate us all.'

Athene heard them. 'Of course you're angry. You are older. I am young, yes, but I put my trust in Zeus (I am the only god who knows where he keeps his lightning-bolt, should I need it.) You too are goddesses. You have your power; but not power to turn on the world of men and ravage it past cure. So please do not blight the land and its harvest. Lull asleep the salty wave of your anger. You are held in awe. Be proud, live with reverence, live with me. This land is rich. Stay, and you will come to love it, I promise you. Through all my citizens, respect will flow to you.

'This is what I propose,' she went on. 'You shall be throned in honour in my ancient temple, the House of Erechtheus near the Acropolis, which I shall give to you for your own. Men and women in great numbers will process by in solemn file to honour you. But never create war *in this land*. Let our wars rage on abroad with all their force to bring us fame. But my curse is on civil war, the bird that fights at home.

The Furies took a lot of mollifying. At last their Speaker said, 'So where is this temple, then, this home you say is ours?'

'It's where all the pain and anguish end. Accept it. You shall be honoured there and be so powerful that no house can thrive without you. Whoever reveres us will have good fortune.' *Us*? Athene was not only bestowing power upon the Furies, but linking herself and the other gods with them. The magic of the goddess was working, the hate and fury slipping away.

'Tell us, then,' said the Speaker, 'what spell shall we sing to bind the land to us too, for ever?'

'Goddesses,' replied Athene, 'you can bestow this blessing. *Not conquest, not war, but peace shall rise from earth and water. This land shall be blessed by sky and wind and sun, with cattle in the fields, with fish in the sea and birds in the air. The city will be filled with untiring power. The citizens will thrive the more as they worship you in your own temple.*'

She swung round to face those who had stayed to hear her; and there were still many about though the sun had set. 'Do you understand, people of Athens? These goddesses are kind. Now in your presence I shall re-name them. They were once called the Furies. Now, I shall know them as the *Eumenides*, the Kindly Ones. They will deal with mortals clearly, once for all. To some they will deliver songs, to others a life of blinding tears. The Eumenides shall work their will.'

'*Rejoice, people of Athens,*' sang the Eumenides, looking kinder as they sang, all the snakes asleep. '*You are loved both by Zeus and by Athene, the loving goddess. Nestling under her wings and blessed by the Father, you will achieve humanity at last.*'

Athene led the Eumenides in procession from the Areopagus to their new temple by the holy light of the torches. 'You citizens, treat them with compassion, compassionate as they will be to you. For they are the Well-Meaning Ones. Now, let the torch move on.'

'*O Venerable Eumenides,*' sang the citizens, '*bless the land with your kindly hearts, sing your blessings out, carry the dancing on and on. This peace between Athene's people and their guests must never end.*'

Meanwhile, Orestes went to the stable, settled his account, thanked the kind grooms and threw his arms around his horse's neck. This time his tears were of joy. His farewells were few and he started out for Mycenae then and there. How different was this ride from the last. Zephyra, sensing the air of home, turned her head Westward towards Argos and, fed on good barley, would not be slowed till dusk. Well on their way they found lodgings and set off early the next day, coming to Mycenae that same evening.

ANOTHER PAUSE: *Because they are listened to, heard and respected by Athene, the Furies become the kindly Eumenides, honoured in their own temple. How do you feel about this? Are there any Furies around for you who might be dealt with in some similar way? What would happen?*

* * * * *

PART FOUR

RESTITUTION

CHAPTER 26

A TEMPLE IN TAURIS

Alone in the morning light, seated on a low wall running around a temple precinct, a priestess was thinking aloud. Dressed in temple robes, gazing out to sea cheek in hand, she radiated unhappiness. 'How did I come to be in this awful place,' she asked the seagulls, 'Why can't I remember? I'm a foreigner, an exile, almost a slave, doing this horrible job.' And she tried to answer herself, attempting for the hundredth time to work out the puzzle of her origin.

65: On the Sea Wall

'Where did I come from? Why such misery? Why have I forgotten? Well, I know my great-great-grandfather was a proud and tormented man and when his son married, he brought his royal bride on flying horses. And I know that their son was my grandfather, and his two sons were kings. So who am I? I haven't been here so very long, surely? Oh I am sick at heart. I know the world is not all like this.

The priestess rose wearily to her feet and stared out to sea. 'It's about Artemis,' she told the gulls, in a murmur lest even the sand-dunes had ears. 'Artemis of *Greece*. When people speak of her, I feel rescued and warm and safe. But there's an ugly Artemis here in this barbarous land whose rites are horrible. She delights in being worshipped and the ignorant people here honour her with bloody sacrifice. The stink of a horrid sanctity hangs around this temple. How I detest it.

'Yet, though I hide my terror deep, I also believe her threats. Her sanctuary here is drenched with the blood of animals — the occasional human too, sacrificed at her inmost altars with dark rites I dread. Thank the gods, there are other people to take care of those unspeakable killings. I only have to cleanse and consecrate the victims and touch their hair. But oh, it disgusts me and I hate it all.'

One recent evening she had contemplated swimming out into the Friendless Sea and putting an end to her existence. But the goddess had spoken in her head. 'Do not do it. Going to the Deadlands is no escape, for I am there also. Die before you die; there is no chance afterwards.' She had dragged herself back into the temple and slept.

Slowly now she left the wall and the sea and moved towards the great door. 'I'll go and find my companions.' Serving as priestess in the temple, she was helped and befriended by several young women whom King Thoas had carried off from Greece in a recent war. Snatched from husbands and children, parents and lovers, they too were enslaved here in Tauris. 'At least he's given them the task of looking after me. A blessing, that we all live together in the temple.'

Appointed to wait upon the priestess, who seemed to be a young woman without a past, these friends in their own exile were happy to look after a fellow slave. They had to spend long hours in the temple performing the necessary rituals, but that left time both for singing and for talking together. They would often chant for her of their homeland, and tell the priestess stories which brought her great comfort. They could tell she was Greek by the way she spoke. 'She's special. I bet she's really a princess as well as a priestess,' declared the youngest. 'She came long ago, on a horrible ship just like ours. But she doesn't seem to remember anything about Greece.'

They were glad to see her that morning, though sorry that she was red-eyed and downcast. 'Oh there you are. I've been out by the sea, my heart dancing with tears, but there's no lyre playing, no joy in the dance; its music is fit only for the dead. I'm so sad, dear maidens, I haven't stopped crying since I woke up.'

'Dear Princess, whatever's happened?' They clustered round. 'Tell us. We are Greek, you trust us; we're sure you're a king's daughter. What would you have us do for you?'

'Oh, friends, what would I do without you? Last night I had a horrible nightmare and under the morning sky just now I decided to face it. Here it is, my dark dream (as if telling it could really make it better). I dreamt that I was in Greece — I knew in the dream it was Greece — far away over distant seas, in a palace with you, my maidens, all sleeping around me. There was an earthquake and the whole great house fell down. We all escaped unhurt, but just one pillar of the house was left standing. And that pillar — that pillar spoke! It seemed like a man. In the dream I had to wash it — wash *him* — down, make him clean as if for the ritual here, where my job is to make unknown men ready for death. And I did it, my eyes streaming with tears.

'Oh dear friends, this is what I make of this dream. I knew him. I can't remember anything else, but I seemed to remember him. Someone I knew in Greece, though I've never seen that man. The one pillar left standing must mean the eldest son of the house, mustn't it? And he is dead. He is the pillar I washed with my tears. After all,' she sobbed, 'everyone I weep for is on their way to the tomb. So my tears can still be for him, although I am here on this bleak shore beyond the Friendless Sea and he is no more. Oh my dear friends, who is he —who was he, I mean?' She broke off and looked around the temple. 'Shh! Artemis is near. I'd better stop now. I won't say anything more.'

To keep themselves happy the women often sang Greek songs in the temple — to Artemis of course, for anything else would have been frowned upon by the pious King Thoas. But, though they all secretly loathed the barbarous goddess familiar to the Taureans, they loved and worshipped their own Greek Artemis. They sang to her now. '*Moon Goddess, huntress of the woods, helper of young maidens and of women, we pray that you will help your priestess with her terrifying dream. And help her to remember.'*

66: The Image of the Goddess Artemis

They were inspired in their singing by the loveliest thing in this dark and ugly temple: a carved Image which had apparently fallen from heaven straight into a shrine on the altar itself. Beautiful, small and precious, this Image was leaning on a low plinth. It was kept well away from the ritual sacrifices, which were held in a separate sanctuary. The eyes seemed to be gazing away over the sea to far distant Greece.

King Thoas was well aware of its value, both in coinage and in the useful reverence it evoked in the people. It belonged in his temple and here it should stay. Fortunately I have that Greek priestess to look after it, thought the King. She does a good job. Luckily, she remembers nothing; I took care of that. A blow on the head, sustained during the capture, had concussed the girl and he had followed it up in other little ways. If kept secret, opium had its uses and the strange princess' memory was kept permanently dulled.

But now the morning sun shone gently in at the door and a beam fell upon the little Image. '*Peace comes from you, Artemis,*' sang the women. '*We are the handmaids of your handmaid from Greece, she who holds the keys to your temple. Hers was once our land too, far away over the Western sea. We remember the horses and the towers, the wells and the garden trees, and the seats where our mothers and fathers sat. May peace come upon all of us who dwelt beyond the Clashing Rocks that grind in the swell of the Friendless Sea.*'

Finishing their invocation, they turned to the priestess. 'What would you like us to do?'

'Dear friends, I'd like us to make a funeral rite fit for the dead prince of my dream. I'll sing the first lament for him myself.' Her song was a plaintive one, praying for rest for him, asking his forgiveness that she could not be there for this dream-prince's funeral, nor pour libations at his tomb, nor cut locks from her hair in the proper Greek way. Half-images came and went in her mind; somehow she knew what those rituals should be. '*Instead,*' she finished, '*we pour a cup of love to you, as to one dead, from one who is so far from what to both you and to us was home.*'

'You and *us*?' she said to her friends. 'Why did I say that? How do I know what my home was. If I did have a home in Greece, everyone there must believe I've been butchered by my captors — that I lie in a tomb somewhere. If they thought I'd been married, say, and taken to a far land, wouldn't they wonder why I hadn't come home to visit them? They'd have come to look for me. And if they thought I'd been enslaved like this, surely they'd be here by now. It's been years and years. No, they must have long decided I'm dead. That's why no one comes.'

'That's terrible,' said a woman named Larysa. 'It sounds as if your family has forgotten you, just as you're struggling to remember them.'

'I wish I hadn't been born,' cried the priestess. 'I do know that all my life there's been the sense of an evil spirit around; one huge battle, right from the beginning. Boys learn to read and write, but I only learnt sewing and quarrelling. They did something terrible to me, I don't know what. And now, far beyond the seas of home, estranged for ever from the land I can't remember, I am unloved by any man. I have no child, no place to go. I am helpless. I sit and stare out over this dull, barren shore. Everything's gone. My friends, we shall never, you or I, dance or sing or sew our tapestries there again. Instead, we shall help to sacrifice friendless men and our ears will ring with the cries of strangers dying unheard. Oh, the horror of their tears.'

All her friends could do was sing for her. '*Peace be to all of us who live exiled from our homeland, far beyond the Clashing Rocks that open into the waves of the Friendless Sea; peace ...*'

A PAUSE: *It is said, 'Behind every languor there lies a rancour'. Helplessness can lead to depression which is masking a hidden rage. There is nothing the priestess can do, and she is undoubtedly depressed. Is helplessness something you have experienced significantly, or do you know someone who has? What has the reaction been? What other reactions might there be?*

* * * * *

CHAPTER 27

BEYOND THE CLASHING ROCKS

67: Map: from Greece and the Aegean to Tauris over the Friendless Sea

To reach the further great sea that lies North Eastward from Greece, a ship must navigate channels between rocky islands and negotiate narrows that freeze the blood of sailors with terror of shipwreck. The only way into that far sea lies between the Clashing Rocks. It was said that those mighty cliffs would allow no ship to pass between them. Whether randomly or with intent, as soon as any living thing tried to fly, swim, row or sail through they clashed together, but slowly, so that there was a chance, if the oarsmen were swift, that a galley might escape being crushed.

68: Approaching the Clashing Rocks

Some time had passed since the return of Orestes with his horse
Zephyra from Athens to Mycenae. Although oarsmen from Greece
would rarely venture so far, the galley on which he and Pylades had now
taken passage had safely run the gauntlet of the Clashing Rocks, thanks
to the skill and courage of the crew. Beyond that terror she was sailing
as far again over the high seas, a fair wind carrying her on her journey
towards the distant country to which they were bound.

Orestes was in a state. He had not been himself for some time and
Pylades, who knew the signs, considered that his friend still became

too easily shaken and distraught. Electra had not been having a calming effect on her brother. He'd spent a lot of time visiting Laodameia, or in the stables with Theodore, or with Zephyra on long, lonely rides.

He had confided to Pylades that the Furies, although placated by Athene, had not altogether given him up. They still troubled his sleep and haunted his leisure and he longed to be rid of them for good; especially since Hermione, now staying in Arcadia, had consented to marry him. They suited each other well despite the age difference, cousins or not, and Orestes seemed content to plan for a double wedding, with Electra soon to be married to Pylades. All Theodore's stipulations were being acted upon.

O Apollo, this ship! Where have you brought me? What's this new trap? A fair wind was sending the galley scudding North-Eastward over a blue sea, under sail so the rowers could take a much needed rest after the terror of the narrows. Orestes, alone in the prow, leaned on the gunwale. He was talking to the god, but in his mind was his friend and mentor, Theodore. He was deeply grateful that the head groom had brought order to the House of Atreus. Everyone, even Electra, had turned naturally towards Theodore. He had somehow engineered peace between the town and the palace; he'd quietly re-ordered the household and sent the family members on their various ways. Laodameia now had plenty of time to record her stories and poems; loved by everyone, she was supporting both Electra and most of the women in the servants' hall as no one else could. An unexpected peace had broken out in the light of the wisdom that seemed to be dawning with Theodore in Mycenae.

Orestes had been slowly getting stronger. He'd spent a lot of time in the stables and confided in Theodore with huge relief. To the rustle of straw and the crunch of the horses quietly munching their oats, he told him, 'I killed my mother and avenged my father because Apollo told me to. I wandered homeless with my beloved horse — yes, stop shoving at me with your nose, Zephyra, I've got some carrots for you — hunted by the Furies, till I got to Athens. There I was exonerated. Yet still it's not over. They won't leave me alone. Where do I go now?' And Theodore had listened.

The upshot was that Orestes had ridden north yet again to the temple in Delphi and implored Apollo: *What can I do to end these miseries once and for all?* And the Oracle had told him to leave home again. Gazing down into the restless sea, he remembered her words.

'Orestes, you must go and look for … ' What? Some distant country called Tauris, where Artemis apparently had an altar. He'd ridden back to Argos and explained to Theodore how, in this foreign place, he was to seize a divine Image which had apparently fallen from heaven into a shrine in some far temple. 'Then, never mind the danger, I'm to bring it back to Greece. *If this were done, Orestes, you would have peace from all your wretchedness.* Apollo's own words.'

'Sounds as if you'll have to go, then,' said Theodore mildly. 'Wouldn't Pylades go with you? You could delay the weddings and both of you get married when you come home.' He did not seem to think Orestes should disobey the god, despite what had happened last time. 'Seems you have another quest ahead of you.'

Now, land had been sighted. Tauris lay on a huge, diamond-shaped peninsula projecting from Asia into the Friendless Sea. They made landfall on a desolate strip of coast, the captain anchored the ship in a deserted cove and the two passengers and many of the crew went ashore. Exploring beyond the headland Orestes and Pylades came upon a great temple down near the sea, a barbaric looking place. No one seemed to be about. The doors stood open in the heat of the afternoon and they peered into the dark recesses.

'Watch out; someone'll come. Do let's go.' Orestes, having seen enough, was backing away from the temple. 'This can't really be the sanctuary we sailed from Argos to find.'

'Well, I think it is,' replied Pylades. 'I'm sure there's something holy here, maybe hidden in that shrine on the altar? Human blood has been shed in this place, probably of Greek men. I can smell it. Over there, hanging — look — property stolen from slaughtered victims.' Pylades was noting a bloodstained sanctuary with a slimy floor and some nasty-looking things dangling from the roof. 'Quick pickings, when they catch their strangers. You're right, we do need to be careful, searching here.'

But he continued to poke around, while Orestes went outside and thought. Preposterous to suppose they'd made landfall at the right temple straight away. Surely not? This couldn't really be it? Well, Theodore, I have sailed into foreign seas where no Greeks live. I have done Apollo's will. But I don't find anything remotely divine in this horrid place.

Now what? He jumped to his feet as Pylades emerged from the doors and grabbed him by the arm. 'Come back in for a moment. I bet it's your precious Image.' There was excitement in his whisper.

'No,' said Orestes. 'Let's get away. Back to the galley quick, before something awful happens. My head's so muddled, I'm terrified of going mad again.'

'You're *not* going mad again, my friend. And we can't run for it,' returned Pylades. 'That's not like us. It would insult the gods and it wouldn't work. But I think what we're looking for is here. Tell you what; we'll clear off now and find a cave or something, well away from the ship in case she's been spotted by some chieftain. Then this evening after dark we'll take the risk; we'll come back here, break in (it'll certainly be locked) and steal whatever's in that shrine. Look at the ceiling. A thin person could squeeze between those beams, couldn't he?'

Orestes gave in. 'Danger brings a glint to your eyes, Pylades. You're right. Fear would get us nowhere and we haven't come all this way just to chicken out. Apollo will see that we succeed. It's he who's put us up to it, after all.' What would Theodore suggest, he asked himself. Well, no doubt about that. They hurried away along the shore to find some sheltering cave and await the setting sun.

FIRST PAUSE: *Suffering is finding vent in action as Orestes deliberately faces the Clashing Rocks, of terrifying repute. (After a dove was sent through, losing only some tail-feathers in the process, the hero Jason did manage this feat, and with such panache that the rocks stopped their clashing altogether. However, that epic voyage was still to come.) Have you, like Orestes, ever had to face danger with your eyes wide open? What happened for you?*

* * * * *

A little later, one by one, the friends of the priestess gathered again at the temple, whispering together their love and loyalty. '*O Artemis,*' they prayed, '*what of your priestess, our princess, daughter of a King? Exiled here without any memory, yet her dream tells that she's the child of a great Greek palace and is now bereft ... someone she seemed to know is dead.*'

In came the priestess to begin the funeral rite for the last survivor of her dream-palace. '*O unknown spirit who carries the dead on dark wings,*' she prayed, '*I bring drink-offerings and the cup that offers comfort. I bring the milk of mountain cattle, the hallowed gleam of wine, the toil of murmuring bees. By these shall you have rest — you, the last pillar of the house. Not by my tears, for you have no tomb here, where I and my friends could weep. We are far from home, where everyone thinks that I too, O God, lie butchered.'*

'*Woe, woe,*' sang the women again. '*Sorrow on sore sorrow has afflicted the house of her dream where an evil path has been carved. But now, let there be peace and rest.*'

69: By the Friendless Sea

Knocking was heard at the temple doors. Larysa, who had been leading the singing, cried, 'Someone's coming!' She held up her hand. 'Wait!' The ritual was broken off, the song silenced. 'Who are you?' she called as the great doors clanged open.

'Larysa, girl, is that you there? It's only me, your friendly herdsman from along the shore. Where's the priestess? I must see her. Oh there you are; get up off your knees, Priestess, listen to me! I've got wonderful news for you.'

'What news? You're interrupting my obsequies.' She rose to her feet. 'You can come outside to talk.' She led him back through the doors and out into the light, the women following.

'Some days ago we'd news of a galley getting through the Clashing

70: The Clashing Rocks

Rocks, heading our way. Well, that same ship made landfall here last night, came safely into our haven.' The herdsman was bursting to tell his story. 'Two young men have washed up in our care. They'll be good slaughter for the altar-stone in the sanctuary of Artemis.'

'Right, then. We'll sacrifice them. Quick as you can, you others, find all that's needed. What country are they from? You don't know? Well, can't you tell from their clothes?'

'They're Greeks, that's all I know.'

'Greeks! What — no name? Didn't you get any clue?'

'One called the other *Pylades*.'

'And who was the man who spoke. What was his name?'

'None of us heard it; I don't think they said it. They were down on the beach at the edge of the surf.'

'But you're herders. What were you doing by the sea? Oh, washing the cattle, I see. All these years, but we've never before sacrificed anyone Greek at this altar. How did you spot these men? How capture them? I want to know everything.'

'We'd driven the cattle down where the tide comes in through the narrows — you know, where there's a bay with hiding places in the cliff. One of my own lads spotted these two Greeks and he tiptoed back whispering, "God save us! Two glorious young men from another world are sitting there by the waves." A different chap, a bit pious, raised his hands to heaven and prayed to Poseidon. He thought they must be sons of Zeus himself, perhaps the Heavenly Twins. But someone else said, "Rubbish, they're shipwrecked sailors skulking on the shore." As you know well, Lady, we slay all strangers. They'll be a good sacrifice to please Artemis — please the people.

The herdsman's tone changed. 'But one of these men begins behaving very odd, waving his arms, groaning. Suddenly he shrieks and goes stark raving mad, yelling and shouting to this Pylades, scared stiff of something. But there's nothing there at all,' declared the herdsman, 'He were sick, turning the barking dogs and mooing cows into some sort of demons, all in his head. We wondered if the fit would kill him. Then, of a sudden his sword shines out and he leaps like a lion on our cows. Thinking he's fighting his enemies he stabs our cattle. When we see them hurt and falling over we springs to arms, blows the horn for help. That pair was too strong, too nobly born, for lads like us to tackle.

'Well, a bunch of us soon gathered. Next, he stopped his mad whirling and fell over, quite weak. When we saw that, of course we pelted him with stones. His comrade watched us come, but knelt and cared for him, holding his cloak above him like a shield. It was really cool, how he warded off every stone, but still cared for his battered friend.

'Then the fallen man gets up, calm and grave now. Seeing the danger, he groans. We stood above and pelted him some more till he gave a fearful battle-cry, "Ho, Pylades!" Then those two swords come flashing up the gulley between the rocks. I tell you, we ran for it. But more of our supporters come charging down from the trees and turned on the two of them, throwing stone after stone. But you wouldn't believe it, not one landed on 'em, like the goddess was keeping her prey unhurt. However, at last we grabbed 'em, so tired they could scarce stand up, and took 'em to the King. And he straight off sent them to you, to touch with your holy water — and then, kill 'em!'

The herdsman's story was avidly followed by every woman present. Two glorious young men? From their own beloved Greece? Who were they? Why here?

'So, Priestess,' finished the herdsman, 'sacrifice these two young chiefs to Artemis. That'll pay Greece back for letting you be taken as a slave.' All the local people had some idea of the Greek origin of their favourite priestess and her more recent friends.

But Larysa cut in. 'Amazing.' she said. 'Why should someone so mad, whoever he be, sail from Greece through the Clashing Rocks and out over the Friendless Sea? Why come all this way?' Silently Larysa was wondering, Might they have news of our families?

The priestess stood up. 'It's all right, my friend,' she said to the herdsman. 'Bring them here and I shall see that the will of the goddess is done.' As he left, she turned to the women. 'I used not to be so vengeful towards shipwrecked men. Certainly I'm angry at not being rescued by the Greeks, but what's happened to my suffering heart? Before my dream, I used to imagine our homeland and dreaded that my hand should accidentally fall on one of my own family, or on a friend. But now, I think my dream was about the last of my own kinsmen. And he is dead.

'So you two men, whoever you are, it's a cruel woman who waits for you here. I'll be shedding no tears for you; I suffer too much myself to mourn anyone else's torment. After all, the gods have never yet sent a ship past the Clashing Rocks to bring us any messages from Greece. This land of murderers has given its own lusts to its god. *Evil does not dwell in heaven.*' She swung on her heel and walked out to the old sea wall, followed by her friends.

Her spirits rose a little when Larysa, having made sure the temple doors were safely closed, joined them and said, 'Princess, everyone. Listen. You heard him say this ship burst through the Clashing Rocks and has arrived here? Well, surely it's a miracle that's swept them across the Friendless Sea? How else have they come all this way? Why here? We know the waves are said to be daughters of Poseidon, the old Sea King. They've guided this galley safely into our star-lit anchorage instead of wrecking her on the rocks round Tauris. Why?'

The priestess pondered. Slowly she responded, 'Yes. Surely the gods must have been looking after these two young men?' There is one hope for my soul, she thought. 'O my friends, could this ship from Greece, so bravely crossing the sea, be bringing peace and a ransom to heal our sick captivity? For us to see you again, our home … see the old walls I'm told are standing on the hill.' She broke off, lost in a dream. 'Come! Carry me away on wings over the sea.'

ANOTHER PAUSE: *If you had been listening to the herdsman's story, what feelings might you have experienced? Hatred, of invaders gate-crashing your shores? Rage, that no one had come before this? Fear, of the invaders? Dread, for the two young men? Curiosity — who might these Greeks really be? Hope, for ransom and rescue? Gratitude, to the herdsman for trying so hard and now bringing the story? Joy, that fellow countrymen were here? Worship, of the god Poseidon for their safe passage, or of Artemis, about to get her sacrifice? Or something quite different?*

* * * * *

CHAPTER 28

THE IMAGE OF ARTEMIS

As the priestess returned to the temple precinct, a group of men appeared round the headland and Larysa hurried away with some of the women to meet them. They soon returned with some burly local guards clutching two tightly-bound prisoners. So the messenger, that herdsman of the mountains — his story was true.

'You, my friends, are bringing the first Greeks ever to this sanctuary,' declared the priestess. 'A strange offering, this, to lay before the goddess. However, as Priestess I declare that we must follow the temple's holy rule. Untie their arms. What is sacred cannot be bound. *O Artemis, holy one,*' she declaimed, '*if what these men bring affords you joy, then take their sacrifice*' — however much we detest this disgusting ritual, she added to herself. 'Go into the sanctuary, you guardians. Prepare what we need according to the law.'

They all went into the temple, and some of the women went off into the sanctuary. The prisoners were set free. The guards stood around — but not too close; they had a healthy suspicion of goddesses and priestesses. 'What far home have you come from, strangers?' she asked. 'Who were your parents?' Pylades did the talking. Despite her earlier determination, tears ran down her face at the sound of his voice speaking in her own language. 'And your sister, if you have a sister? Oh you do, do you? Both of you gone away at once — so young and brave and you've left her brotherless at home? Let's hope she's safe, since troubles do strike — probably blind chance, but the ways of the gods are dark. Now you've landed up on this shore, you unhappy men, you'll have left your home for good.'

Orestes, rubbing his sore arms, spoke sharply. 'Whoever you are, why are you crying? You're making us feel worse, pitying us when you intend to take us in there and kill us. It's not kind to shed tears because *we* are so afflicted; in fact it doubles the trouble. We know and understand how this land worships its god, so stop weeping for us.'

The priestess, remembering her role, straightened her back. It would

71: Outside the Temple

be the worse for them all if King Thoas questioned her authority in the temple. 'First, which of you is called Pylades?'

'It's *his* name,' said Orestes.

'You also have a name: what is it?'

Orestes parried this. 'Take my body, if you will, but not my name.'

Relentlessly she questioned on: their town, their parents, their status. Were they brothers? 'In love we are sworn brothers; not otherwise,' returned Orestes. 'That's enough. Why all this, when we're about to die? Yes, of course we're from Greece; you can tell from our voices. Mycenae in Argos. But why all this questioning? Just get on with it, Lady.'

'From Argos ... ' Something was stirring in her memory. She murmured half aloud, 'Oh, how good to see you here ... '

'Enjoy it, then. I'm not enjoying it much,' said Orestes.

She ignored him. 'Then what about — Troy — yes, a war? Have they been defeated yet? What happened?' Names of people, places, were stirring in her mind. She spoke with rising excitement. 'After all, you're going to die soon. Stay and talk to me.' They hadn't much choice. 'It's coming back to me; someone called Helen. Where is she? I'm angry with her. I suppose she's back home by now, in Sparta? Safe with her husband, Menelaus, isn't it? And tell me about the army,' she went on. 'That seer, that Oracle, Calchas, wasn't it, a fake wizard? What of him? He's dead? Oh that's good news, praise the gods! And Achilles? Dead too — oh.'

'Whoever are you, asking all these knowledgeable questions about Greece?' Pylades was puzzled.

'Well, I'm Greek. Or was. I couldn't remember; but now, it's odd, it's coming back. Tell me about that poor war-lord, what was his name? Atreus' son: such trouble ... '

'I don't know him,' said Orestes sharply. 'Stop, that's enough questioning.' But she persisted. 'Well, he's dead,' conceded Orestes. 'And he's wrecked someone else's life as well ... ' He broke off. 'Why should *you* be so miserable about him? Was he linked with you in some way? Anyway, his own wife foully stabbed him and he died.'

This was a body-blow. But why should it be? Reeling, the priestess pulled herself together. 'Just one more word. Is she still alive, that wretched wife?'

'No. Her own son, her first-born, killed her to avenge his father. And Apollo, who ordered him to do it, has now sent him here, which hasn't helped him much.' That's it, thought Orestes; now I've told her everything.

But she missed the implication. 'Oh terrible! He was brave to do such a thing, but it was a false duty. Who's left now of that family of Atreus?'

'Well, there's Electra. She lives unmarried and alone. No more sisters. Except that girl they slaughtered long ago. There's no word of her. Just that she died there in Aulis.'

'Poor child. Wasn't it her father who lied to her and killed her?' The priestess had no idea how she knew this. 'And what happened to the dead king's son, the one you say slew his mother? Is he still living in Argos?'

'He lives all over the place, ill and bent and unhappy.'

The priestess turned away, her heart racing; she was beginning to remember. 'He lives! Goodbye to my dream last night,' she whispered. 'So you too were a lie.'

Orestes overheard. 'Know this, lady. The gods themselves aren't wise; they're nothing more than dreams on wings, streams of turmoil, exactly like men. Don't, like a fool, get blinded by them, nor by any priest. Go straight to whatever death you will die.'

Larysa, who had been utterly astonished by this conversation, broke the silence. 'But we are slaves here too. No one takes any notice of us.

72: The Prisoners by the Temple

We also have families we love. No one tells *us* whether they're still alive or not.'

'Wait, Larysa. Listen, you strangers,' said the priestess, 'I've had a thought. It might be useful if we could agree on it. I should be able to save one of you. Pylades — I've got your name right, haven't I? — would you go alone and take a message to Greece from me? I must have had friends there. I've forgotten. I can neither write nor read, being a woman, and only now, today, am I beginning to remember. But I have a scroll written for me here by one of the King's prisoners of war.

'This man knew it wasn't *me* who was craving for blood. I didn't want to kill these victims; it was the Goddess Artemis who wanted death for them. He knew my story, though I had no memory of it. He wrote down what happened to me many years ago, and I asked him to add my own prayer for help to any friend. He made me learn it by heart before sealing it up and giving it to me. But since that day no Greek has ever come whose life I could save by sending him home to Argos with it.

She turned eagerly. 'I don't believe you hate me, Pylades. You know Mycenae in Argos. You'll know the names that are beginning to fill my heart again. Help me. Be saved yourself. It would be your task to take the completed scroll … '

'But how can I?' said Pylades. 'I too am sentenced and under this altar's spell.'

'I can manage the King,' she said.

'It's a horrible job you have, priestess,' Orestes commented. 'It can't bless you much, a young woman taking a sword and stabbing men to death.'

'Well, what else dare I do? I have to obey the law. But I don't do the actual killing; there are men here in the vaults who do that. I just perform the ritual, touch your hair and sign your forehead with the water. Your grave will be a great gulf in the rock and holy fire.'

Orestes turned away. 'Oh, oh … how I wish it were my sister's hand that would close my eyes.'

'Alas, your unhappy sister lives under distant skies and all your prayers are useless,' said the priestess briskly. 'Yet you're from Argos. I will give you every possible care. I won't fail you. I'll make sure you're buried in rich clothing. I'll pour libations of oil to cool you and honey to die with you.'

She turned to Pylades. 'Oh, please don't hate me for what I'm condemned to do to him. For you, I'll go and find the scroll. I've hidden it in the shrine of the goddess; her Image looks after it for me there. Please wait while I fetch it.' Again, they had little choice. The guards closed in a little, glowering at the prisoners. 'Watch them, but leave them free.' She was thinking past all hope: perhaps my words will sail to Argos — yes, Argos — into the hands of people I love. Will someone not rejoice to know that here, on the edge of the world, I am alive after all and crying out for them.

She went back into the temple and Larysa took over with the prisoners. 'I ardently pity your tears, young man,' she said to Orestes. 'They'll splash holy water on you, deadly as drops of blood. I have to say farewell; and so do all of us Greek maidens.'

'For the record, I'm not crying,' said Orestes. 'But you're right, I don't want to die.'

'As for you, Pylades, for you we're happy. You'll reach your home again, sailing away from this place of slaughter.'

But Pylades had been having second thoughts. 'No, no, no,' he said. 'I've changed my mind. Not while the friend I love must die. No! That would be a miserable thing to do.'

'I don't know which of you to grieve for most,' said Larysa. 'Who suffers more, the one killed or the one bereaved?'

Orestes wasn't listening. He whispered to his friend. 'By heaven, Pylades, are you thinking what I'm thinking?'

'I don't know. What *are* you thinking, friend?'

'Who can this priestess be? Her questioning is so Greek. All that about Troy being overthrown, and how the leaders came back, and the wizardry of Calchas, and Achilles' fame. And she spoke with pity about poor unlucky Agamemnon, and about his queen and his children. This strange woman must be from Argos. What's got into her otherwise, with her scrolls and her questionings and her shaky memory, as though her own heart were beating with the joy or woe of Greece?'

'You've said it first. I'd say the same,' said Pylades. 'Though I suppose anyone living near a seaport would have heard of the fall of the great kings at Troy. But never mind that. I'm thinking of other things.'

'What other things? Go on.'

'I couldn't live for shame if you were dead. I sailed with you and I'll die with you. I'd be a coward, creeping about in Argos; or, come to that, out in the wind on the Phocian hills. And most people — for most are quite nasty — would whisper how I'd left my friend to die and made my way home. They'd say I watched the decline of your great House, plotted your death, married your sister and climbed on to your throne. I dread that. I loathe it. No. There's only one way: my last breath goes with yours. Let your grave in a fiery gulf be mine also. I love you, and I'm terrified of people's contempt.'

'Don't think such things,' cried Orestes, but *sotto voce.* 'I can just about bear my own burden. Your dying too would double it. Anyway,

73: Orestes and Pylades

all that scorn that scares you so would land far worse on my own head if I brought about your death. And after you've done so much for me. I don't really mind dying,' he went on. 'But you, you enjoy life, your house lies at peace with the gods — Strophius will come round, you'll see — while mine is all evil fate. And when you're safe, with my sister Electra for your wife as we agreed, your name and mine will live in your sons. That means Agamemnon's line too won't be cursed for ever, or its story blurred.'

He's got a point, thought Pylades. If I were in his shoes, I'd feel the same.

'Go back, my friend. Rule your land; let your soul live.' Orestes seized his hand. 'And when you come to Argos where the horsemen ride, greet Laodameia for me — and Theodore. Make sure my mare Zephyra is in a good pasture. Put up a gravestone for me. Electra will go and weep there and cut off a tress or two. Tell her how I ended here, prisoner of a king, killed by a young Greek woman in the sanctuary of the Goddess, purified in my own blood …

'It's goodbye, Pylades. I have no friend like you for truth and love. As a boy you played with me, took me hunting on the Phocian hills. My doom has fallen on you more than on anyone. Farewell. As for Apollo, that lord of lies, he's driven me far from Greece. No one here will notice how his prophecy turns out. I trusted his word, I gave him my heart, I slew my mother at his call. And now he throws me out to die.'

'You shall have your tomb,' said Pylades. 'I will marry your sister and guard her for ever. I am much stricken. I loved you living and shall love you yet more dead. But, though you stand on the brink, Apollo hasn't yet destroyed you. Think, how often the darkest hour breaks into the brightest dawn.'

'Enough. No god or man can help me now,' said Orestes. 'The priestess is coming back.' And as he spoke, she returned from the sanctuary.

'Now you go in, my attendants,' she ordered. 'Get everything ready by the altar stone for those who do the deed. Wait for me there.' Obediently Larysa and the women left. The guards drew back, shrinking a little from this priestess. 'You, Pylades,' she went on, 'here's the scroll. But one more thing. At this moment, when you're in fear of death, you're making vows; but when you're unafraid and safe you may forget them all. You'll carry my scroll all right, but I fear once you're free you'll forget all about me and what I have charged you to do. So swear an oath that you will carry this scroll to Argos, to the friend I name.'

'Well, you should swear in return, then,' said Orestes. 'Promise to send him away from Tauris safe and free from harm. Don't let the armies here catch him.'

'I promise. How else could he do what I ask? Don't worry about the king; I can bend Thoas to my will. I shall set your friend safely upon his ship. Now, Pylades, promise: "I will bear this scroll to your friend." Pylades obeyed, calling upon Zeus, Lord of Heaven. 'And I swear in turn I will save you beyond the end of this kingdom, as Artemis of Greece is my witness.'

'But supposing I'm shipwrecked?' he said, remembering the Clashing Rocks. 'If ship and scroll and everything are lost and just my life is saved, don't let this oath be held as something I left undone, to curse me.'

'Tell you what, then: you must learn the words by heart. I know them and I'll say them aloud to you now, so you can repeat them to the person I'm looking for. Then, if the scroll is lost in some rough sea, save yourself and my words will be saved with you.'

Pylades agreed that this was fair. 'How should the words go, then?' And with her coaching, he learnt the whole thing off by heart.

"Artemis saved my soul, I've no idea how, and gave a fawn to the altar instead of me. My father, not seeing this, killed the deer, believing that his sword was striking me. But Artemis had carried me far away and left me in this land of Tauris. Fetch me home to Argos, Brother, before I die; back from the Friendless People and the altar stone of Artemis, whose bloody rites I have to perform. Otherwise, one forsaken in grief shall, like shame, haunt you."

'And what is the name of the person I'm to find in Argos?'

'You must finish by saying this: *"To Orestes, Agamemnon's son, she that was slain in Aulis, dead to Greece yet still living, Iphigeneia sends peace."*

'Iphigeneia!' gasped Orestes. 'It can't be. Where is she? Back from the dead?'

'I am she.'

Dumbfounded he clutched his head. 'Where am I, Pylades? What do I say?'

Pylades whispered back, 'It's all right, Orestes.' She overheard him and agreed he had the name right.

'Well, Lady, it's an easy charge you lay on my soul,' Pylades told her 'You'll be glad yourself. I won't wait.' Portentously he went on, '*Right now I am fulfilling the service that I swore. Here you are, Orestes. Take the scroll. I am the messenger of — your sister.*'

A PAUSE: *There have been several coincidences in this story, and several delayed recognition scenes. As you will long have guessed, dear Reader, the captain's tale which had so infuriated Clytaemnestra in Aulis, of how the gods had substituted a deer for the princess, was the truth. Do you consider such phenomena to be from the gods, whatever you perceive them to be? Or are they mere chance? Or something else? Have you experienced such fateful events in your own life? How far are they linked with intuition? And how do you feel about them?*

* * * * *

CHAPTER 29

ANOTHER PLOT

'My sister! Never mind the message. How on earth … Iphigeneia? Surely you died in Aulis? Oh, may I hug you?' He moved towards her, while she stood speechless and Larysa jumped in to protest; to touch the priestess' robe would defile the goddess. Orestes took no notice. 'My beloved sister, my dead father's child, Agamemnon's daughter. Don't be afraid of me. Beyond all dreams, it's me. I'm your brother.'

'You? No, you're joking. My brother's in Mycenae, in Argos. I thought he was dead.'

'No he's not,' said Orestes. 'You have no brother *there.* I'm Orestes, Clytaemnestra's child. Agamemnon was your father and mine.'

Iphigeneia demanded proof. 'Ask me something about home, then. Tell me some story only Orestes could know.'

'All right,' said Orestes. 'I was sent away from home when I was four or five, but I remember how Laodameia would tell us about Tantalus, and about Atreus and Thyestes and their huge quarrels. Electra used to talk about you, her big sister gone away. How you'd weave stories on your loom. One had a huge sun in the sky'

'Yes, I remember that one, even the thread I used. Oh, that does touch me.'

'I heard how they brought back your hair as your dying gift and gave it to Mother to put on your memorial … Mother had given you holy water from home to take to Aulis.'

' … not so good a day when I drank that water,' interposed Iphigeneia. Her memory was recovering rapidly.

'I heard the robe I had in Phocis, covered in wild animals, was woven by you, my sister. Laodameia wrapped me up in it for the journey when I was small. Also, I saw something for myself as a little boy: our ancestor Pelops' ancient lance was hidden in your bedroom.'

That clinched it. Iphigeneia fell into his arms. 'Oh, you *are* my beloved brother. Here at last! You are long-lost Orestes.'

'And you. After such a nightmare you're back from the dead. Though we're still under a cloud.'

'Can this be that baby I knew? I remember — yes, I *remember* picking him up, light as a bird? Oh marvellous, though I fear it's just a dream. So what do we do now? If only we could stay like this for ever. Oh I bless you, Argos. He's alive, grown up, my own brother.'

'Yes, we are brother and sister,' said Orestes. 'But we're still going to need a lot of luck.'

'I certainly felt most *un*lucky when my father Agamemnon held his sword at my bare throat. I'm remembering what happened. He was miserable. This was no love-song from Achilles. Instead, my father's arms drew me to psalms and the sound of weeping; then finally to cold sleep and forgetting. Since then I have had no father,' said Iphigeneia.

'Oh, you unhappy one!' Orestes shuddered. 'Appalling, to think our father did such a horrible deed. And you yourself were going to spill your brother's blood today.'

'Yet more appalling. Oh Gods what a cruel deed I would have done,' cried Iphigeneia. 'How terrible! You've come all this way and I've nearly killed you. How have I put up with this dreadful role? And things are coming right by so frail a chance. What happens next? How can I help you sail away home to Argos from your certain death on this friendless shore? I've been so quick to kill. But how to save you? On your ship? Or by land? If you hurry off alone through the desolate countryside you'll be killed by unknown tribes. Surely the sea would be best — but there are the Clashing Rocks. O God, it's too far. What can bring us peace after our long suffering?'

'There's no time to talk now, Orestes.' Pylades spoke urgently. 'We must get free. The gods will only help us if we help ourselves.'

'One more thing,' cut in Iphigeneia. 'How is Electra? You and she are all I have to love.'

'She's happy. She's to be a wife,' said Orestes with a brief grin. 'This man here is to marry her. He's the son of King Strophius of Phocis and more than a relative. He's my true and only friend, he's my saviour.'

'And Mother! However did you dare?'

'I had to avenge our father. But don't let's think about that now.'

'You say she *killed* him? What on earth for?'

'Forget her. It's no tale for you.' Hurriedly Orestes explained how he had been driven by Clytaemnestra's Furies, outlawed by the Greek population for matricide, tried and pronounced innocent in Athens.

'Pallas Athene cast her own vote. She set me free from the noose at last. But not all the Furies accepted her offer of a temple. Some refused and hounded me back to Delphi, where I called on Apollo, "Lord, here I will die unless you save me as you have betrayed me."

'And he sent me here. "Go and seek the Taurian temple of Artemis, seize the carved Image that fell from heaven there and establish it on Greek soil. Only then will you be free," he said.'

Hearing this, Iphigeneia seemed to shrink. Was she not the guardian of that very Image for a dangerous king?

74: King Thoas of Tauris

'My dear, dear sister loved and lost, I think that Image is here in this temple. Could you help us? If I get hold of it I'll be sane again. And I'll bring you home to Argos in our ship. Without that statue from heaven, I'll never be free. And that'll be the end of the House of Atreus.'

I nearly killed him myself, thought Iphigeneia. Such horror! For years she had yearned for her forgotten family in Greece. Now, she wanted just what he wanted: peace for him and for her home. She also wanted to stop hating those who had abandoned her at Aulis. Steal the Image and there was Artemis to consider, never mind King Thoas who was bound to see the statue's empty pedestal and would immediately kill her and all of them.

'If only the Image and I could come to Greece together,' she mused aloud. 'No, too difficult. It's best I stay behind — which would be the end of me, but you'd walk free in Argos and by my own hand I'd have saved you. After all, you're worth more than me, a mere woman.'

'First my mother, now you?' burst out Orestes, feeling much as Pylades had done earlier. 'No! This hand has blood enough on it already. Whether we live or die, I'm with you. Either I take you to Greece and home, gods willing, or else I die here at your side. Artemis can't be angry, since it's her own brother Apollo who's commanded me to purloin her Image? Oh, he knew that we two would meet here. He's in charge, he won't fail us. We shall see Argos again, you and I.'

'Well, how to steal the Image for you, yet not die myself? I haven't much hope, though heaven knows I have the will.'

'We could kill your savage King Thoas,' suggested Pylades.

'I couldn't do that; not even if it saved our lives. He sheltered me when I was a stranger. But thanks for thinking of it. And no, you couldn't hide in the temple till dark and then escape. It wouldn't work. There are sacred watchers about who'd definitely see you.'

'What on earth do we do?'

'I see one dim chance,' said Iphigeneia slowly. 'I can say you're Greek and you murdered your mother, so we can't offend the goddess by sacrificing you to her as you are. You'll need cleansing in the sea. They're all terrified of sin and being contaminated. I'll say Pylades is equally guilty. And I'll make out you touched the Image and defiled her, so she too must be purified.'

'We could do the cleansing on the beach where the ship's moored,' said Orestes. 'But who will actually steal the statue?'

'I'm the only one allowed to touch it. As for the King, it's hopeless to try to hide things from him. I'll face him, make him give in to me.'

'Well, fifty oarsmen are waiting on the sea,' said Orestes. 'But will these friends of yours keep the secret? Can you persuade them? If so, heaven knows, it may all turn out for the best.'

Iphigeneia turned to the women. 'Comrades, this is my brother. I misunderstood my dream. Help me; keep the secret of our flight hidden. We're going either to our deaths — or to Greece? If it works, I swear to help all of you get home as well. Larysa, dear friend, if you turn away, I and my brother are lost.'

'Go and be happy, beloved mistress,' said Larysa. 'I swear we won't tell anyone, nor let anyone guess your secret. But Thoas is coming here soon to find out about the sacrifice.'

The friends were sent into the sanctuary to await Orestes' death with the arrival of the King; while at the shrine Iphigeneia prayed to the Image they were planning to steal. '*O Artemis, come away from this friendless shore, these cruel skies. Come home with us. What are you doing here, great Goddess, when over the sea a clean and joyous land waits for you, calls for you?*'

Orestes, awaiting his killers, heard heavenly music from the temple: Larysa was leading the chorus of women in a hymn. '*O for a kind Greek market-place again for you, Artemis.*' He could just make out the words. '*O for you the little hill above the sea, the olive-tree grey-leaved and glimmering.*'

Now surely that was his sister's own voice taking up the song? '*O by the island where you were born, Artemis, island where the swan sings, remember what happened to me, your priestess, Agamemnon's daughter, when there should have been a marriage and a child leaving her mother's side, her hair full of stars, dancing in rare garments, bright veils tossing in the evening light. O youth and the days that were!*'

He heard Iphigeneia's voice rising in sorrow as she sang: '*And towers were crashing and tears were blinding and angry men carrying me out to an unknown sea. They sold me for money and brought me, terrified, to this dark land to slave for you, O Huntress Artemis. But now a ship is ready to row you home to the seas of Greece, land of spring. Apollo sings joyously to his lyre as he guides you to Athens. O be with the ship and her fifty oarsmen; let the great sail swell before her as she reaches for the farther shore, great Artemis.*'

A PAUSE: *The protagonists' ideas come together in another plot. They pray this time not for vengeance and death but for home and freedom for themselves and their friends. The plan is there but its execution is still ahead of them, with all its dangers. Iphigeneia and her enslaved friends have all experienced tremendous homesickness. Have you any remedy for such a state? If you were estranged from home, what would it be like to return there now? What for you is home?*

CHAPTER 30

RELEASE INTO FREEDOM

Their song was interrupted by the sound of marching feet and into the temple strode King Thoas with a bunch of soldiers. 'Where is the Greek priestess, the warden of this sacred door? Has she dealt with those two strangers? I hope they're properly incinerated by now?'

At once Larysa came forward. 'Here she is herself, O King, coming to tell you about it.' And, right on cue, Iphigeneia made her entrance from the inner sanctum, carrying the Image of Artemis high above her head.

'What are you doing, girl?' cried the King. 'You mustn't shift the Holy One from her eternal base. You can't bring her out into the main temple in your own arms.'

'Go back, my lord,' commanded Iphigeneia. 'Do not come one step nearer. Don't say anything, don't do anything.'

'How dare you greet me like this? Has some rule been broken?' demanded Thoas.

'O King, the prey you caught was unclean,' declared Iphigeneia. 'When those two men were brought in, the Image juddered itself right off its pedestal. It wasn't an earthquake: the eyes blinked! Just for a second. I saw them. It's because those two men are very, very guilty and unclean. Not only did they badly hurt some of your herdsmen down on the shore; it was what they'd done back at home.' Iphigeneia moved nearer to Thoas and lowered her voice. 'These two men have killed their mother,' she told him.

'Good God!' gasped Thoas. 'And they're Greeks?'

'Well, they've both been hunted out of Greece. So you see I must take the Image into the sun, since the fire of heaven can lift all curses. I questioned them,' ('you and your subtle Greek arts,' murmured the King, admiringly) 'and they brought a wonderful message which moved my heart. They told me that I have a brother, Orestes, living there peacefully. Apparently my father is also living and thriving in Argos.'

'Yet even so you, a Greek, put the goddess first, and her laws.' Thoas was impressed.

'Well, I hate all Greeks — with reason, since they sold me as a slave, as you know. So now we must obey the Taurean Laws of the Goddess. First, I must shrive the men with something that will cleanse them of this dreadful sin. Salt seawater's best for that. It washes all the world's ills away,' she said. 'It'll need to be a secret place because I must do a hidden rite too. The Image herself needs purging; the stain of that matricide must be cleansed from her, or I certainly wouldn't have dared to move her. She requires it of me.'

The King, lost in awe, gave his consent. 'Your godliness and forethought are truly worthy. No wonder everyone holds you in such high esteem.'

'Well, I need you to bind both the strangers very securely. "Put not your faith in any Greek,"' she quoted. But Thoas was already calling for thongs and fetters and dark hoods and arranging for spearmen to accompany the priestess. 'And send a herald to command a curfew, my Lord, so that no one catches the contagion from this sin. They mustn't even *look* out.' How well this young woman cares for our land, thought the king as he obeyed.

75: Admired by King Thoas

'I'm doing this for one I am bound to love,' Iphigeneia told him. Thoas simpered slightly. 'Meanwhile, only you yourself, my lord, can purge this sanctuary with fire. You must wait here in the temple; and you must wear a blindfold as they pass, in case the evil of their crime enters you through your eyes. It'll take time; if I seem to be rather long away, don't get impatient. *And may the Goddess grant that this cleansing end as I desire,*' cried Iphigeneia. And the King agreed to everything, willingly joining her prayer as he bound his eyes.

The door opened and Orestes and Pylades, dressed in temple garments for the ritual, were led from the outer sanctuary. Attendants had young lambs whose slaughter would, as Iphigeneia explained, 'shrive the blood of sin. And,' she went on, 'here are the sacred flame of Artemis, and the secret power-items for cleansing the strangers.' She picked up the Image again and raised her voice.

'You people who live near these sacred gates, turn away; for something unclean will pass here,' she declaimed. 'Leave this road. Any man who hopes to marry, any woman who expects to have a child, run away with fear and awe. Run swiftly, otherwise, you may be defiled by what is passing. *Artemis, my wise mistress, hear my prayer.*'

King Thoas stood obediently by, pulling the veil more securely over his face, and the solemn procession passed out of the temple: first Iphigeneia with the Image; then the guards, also in veils; then Orestes and Pylades, tightly bound, hooded and clutched by veiled soldiers. With the rest of the men bringing up the rear, they moved off towards the sea. Larysa and the women locked the doors behind them and inside the temple they sang a long prayer to Artemis. Thoas listened, enchanted. Time passed.

* * * * *

At last a crashing and a thumping came on the doors. 'Hey, you watchers of the temple, guards of the altar. King Thoas, are you there? Unlock these doors. Call the King! We're looking for the King.'

'What's happened?' called Larysa from inside.

'The strangers! They've disappeared and gone. We've been tricked. It's some dark plot. That priestess, the Greek woman, has run away out of the country on a Greek ship. And they've taken the heaven-sent Image of Artemis with them.'

'I don't believe you,' declared Larysa through the keyhole. 'Your story's rubbish. Hurry up and find the King; he's only just left here. Follow him towards the town and you'll soon catch him up.'

'You're lying! You women in there, there's treason on your tongues. I don't doubt you're all in the plot yourselves. He's in there with you.'

'You're crazy,' cried Larysa. 'Why should those men mean anything to us? Find the King. Go to the palace — go!'

But the messenger, spying a huge knocker on the temple door, shouted, 'I will not stir till I've seen for myself whether Thoas is in there or not. Unlock the gates, you there inside. Tell him we've got a message for him.' He thundered at the portal till at last the great door opened and the King himself emerged from the temple.

'Who's that making such an uproar outside these sacred gates? How dare you men batter the door in this shameful way? Your noise has broken the ancient peace of the altar.'

'Ye gods,' cried the messenger. 'That woman! She swore to us you'd gone, told us to stop searching. And all the while you … '

Larysa, listening, murmured to the women, 'Oh no! O woe, Iphigeneia, should you fall into the hands of these men again, you'll see your brother killed and die yourself. I'm going to do something. You two, come with me.' And before the others could object, or any man spot her, Larysa had ducked behind her fellows and the three had slipped away.

'What was she after, that priestess?' thundered the King. 'What did she hope for, by such a trick?'

'My King,' said the messenger, 'I told you, the virgin priestess who looked after our shrine has run off with the sacred Image of Artemis — she and those two Greek men. All that about cleansing was a lie.'

'She's run off? What on earth's induced her to do that?' cried Thoas.

'She hoped to save him, her brother Orestes.'

'Orestes! What? Not Agamemnon's son?'

'Yes. That was Orestes, the promised offering to Artemis. You must trap them, my Lord, before they get away. Here's what happened,' he went on. 'The priestess told us to drop our end of their chains and wait. She picked them up and led the men out of sight to do some rigmarole for Artemis. We felt bad but we'd no choice. They walked off. Time went by. We could hear her wailing her weird incantations and droning as if she was struggling to do the cleansing. And we sat a long time waiting, till we began to dread that the prisoners might have slipped their chain, struck her down and made a dash for it. We were right above where their ship was secretly moored. But we were still too scared of seeing things we shouldn't. At last, we said, "Enough. Forbidden or not, let's see what's going on."

'So we did. There was the Greek ship, oars raised like wings on the sea, fifty men seated all ready to row. And by the shore, no chains on their hands, our two strangers, climbing into a small boat and the priestess wading out to join them. 'We rushed forward to seize the boat, grab the woman and drag her back to the shore, while two of us tried to get the men. Neither we nor they had weapons, but those two pushed us back into the water, raining blows on our heads. We retreated, damaged, to the beach and scrambled up a rocky bank. On top we found good stones and stood and pelted them, until the ship's archers sent a rain of arrows from the poop. That drove us back.

'Just then a big wave swept the boat towards the shore. Orestes jumped out, grabbed the young woman, slung her over his shoulder, put her in the boat and jumped in after her. Next, they were out to the ship, grabbing the ladder at the side. And there's our young priestess from Argos standing among the benches of the oarsmen. And the other Greek man too, clutching the carving from heaven, the Image of Artemis, God's high daughter.

'Someone on board yelled, "*For Greece, O oarsmen of the stormy shores, friendless beyond the blue Clashing Rocks. Lift the anchor, pull hard, for the prize is won.*" A glad roar echoed down the breeze, fifty oars dug in and away she flew. The harbour was calm enough, but in the open sea the weather caught her and there was a huge swell. A sudden squall right in her teeth gybed her, bellying the sail towards the stern, driving her back to us.'

And there among the oarsmen the priestess stood and prayed to the goddess. *O Artemis, save your chosen maid, bring me from this dark land to Greece. Forgive my theft for I seek to bring you home. And let these brave men live. You, Artemis, you love your brother Apollo; I also love my brother Orestes.*

'The sailors were pulling even more strongly,' went on the messenger, 'but in vain. They were being driven back, nearer and nearer to the rocks. Some of us rushed hot-foot here to town to look for you, my Prince, and tell you what's happening. Come with us now, Lord, bring grappling hooks and brass manacles and the strongest chains. Poseidon's winning and the wind and sea. Nothing can save this Orestes. We'll get him. The priestess, too. She's betrayed her goddess, whatever her cause.'

The messenger had delivered his message. 'Come on,' cried the King. 'To the harbour. Get your horses everyone and we'll catch the blasphemers. Take the boats. We'll pincer them between sea and shore. Chuck them down the cliffs or put up stakes for them; let the birds finish them off. And you can grab anything from the ship.'

He swung round on the women. 'You knew about all this. You'll pay. Each one of you shall know what treason feels like. Enough, no hanging about. Get on with it.' And he hurried off, more citizens shouting and running before and behind him.

But they stopped. For there in front of them, high on a rock at the roadside, arms out like wings, stood a figure in a great white robe, a sword brandished in her left hand. Light streamed from her eyes enough to blind them. Two more white-robed figures were blocking the way, thundering on huge drums.

'Where are you off to now, King Thoas, so hot after your prey?' The figure on the rock was speaking and fear was spreading among the men. 'It is I, Athene, who bids you stop. Calm yourself down, call off this flood of angry men. It is Apollo himself who has led Orestes here — yes, he is Orestes — telling him to escape from people who hate him. It is Apollo who has told him to bring his sister, alive and well, to Greece, carrying the holy Image which fell from heaven. He told him to bring that Image to dwell in Athens, in my own land. Only when Artemis of Tauris returns to Greece will Orestes' troubles end and only then will all be well for you here, O King. You may not kill Orestes somewhere between the cliffs and the rocky sea. Poseidon, for love of me, Pallas Athene, has made the huge waves gentle and let the oarsmen rest.'

King Thoas, in awe, fell upon his knees before the goddess, his men following suit.

'And you, Orestes, O far off one,' declaimed the goddess, 'go your way. Take the Image home from Tauris, and your sister too and your friend. When you come to my lovely city of Athens, you'll find a small and sacred cove, half hidden on the edges of Greece. Build a temple there upon a rock and set your Taurian Image in it, so that the world may know your tale of that Image. Throughout the whole of time, hymns will be sung in Greece to Artemis of Tauris. People will long perform rites for her there.

76: Poseidon at the Clashing Rocks

'Driven from Greece with a plague of Furies chasing you like blood-hounds, this is your story too, Orestes,' she went on. 'In Athens I saved you when the votes lay equal. From now on, when people bring their quarrels to court and the votes between life and death are cast equally, my law shall hold. That is, that clemency conquers, kindness leading to mercy. Farewell. Take your sister home from this shore in peace.

'And you, Iphigeneia. You shall keep the key of Artemis in Greece. You shall live and die by her temple there on the rock, and that's where you will be buried, with many gifts.

'Now, O you exiled women of Greece, true of heart and ever faithful, all of you shall soon accompany them in their ship, in peace, each to your own home. Take note, King: this is the will of Athene.'

At last the King spoke. 'Most high Athene, I bow my head to God's spoken word. Orestes will sail away with my Image of Artemis. But I bear no anger towards him, or his sister either. There is no honour in a battle fought against the gods; they are the stronger. Let those two go off to your land and plant my Image there. I wish them well. And you bond-women, too, I gladly free you. Return to Greece and to happiness. My galleys will stow their oars and we shall not try to burn your ship. This I will do, Goddess, at your command.'

'All is well then, O King,' said Athene. 'Fate takes as much notice of the high gods as it does of you mortals. *Winds of the north,*' she cried, '*that laugh as they blow, carry Agamemnon's son safely to Athens. I myself am with you, guiding home the hallowed Image of my sister Artemis over the long leagues.*'

And saying this, the goddess floated away with the two drummers in white.

'Go in bliss, Iphigeneia,' went up the cry from the soldiers. 'And your brother too. The Goddess Athene is shielding you. You'll get home safe and sound.' And they sang, '*O great one, Pallas Athene, we shall do your bidding. We have the joy and wonder of a word beyond our dream ... beyond our dream.*'

A PAUSE: *Iphigeneia shows no fear of Thoas, though he could kill her and her brother at any moment. Through courage and the confidence of love, she rises to the challenge, uses her skill to entice and deceive the king, and so brings about their escape. Again, what of personal integrity versus public necessity? How hard would it be to break one set of rules to bring about a higher outcome?*

* * * * *

And so Orestes escaped from Tauris with the women, his friend and his sister. As the poet told us, *his many-oared barque carried her safely home to Greece over the sundering waves.* They came back through the Clashing Rocks to Brauron on the coast to the east of Athens. When Iphigeneia had safely deposited the Image there, they all travelled to Delphi to give thanks to the gods. Electra was waiting for them at the shrine; Pylades greeted his bride and the two sisters met again. Home at last to Mycenae, where Orestes was welcomed by Laodameia and Theodore and his beloved horse Zephyra.

Iphigeneia with Larysa's help founded a temple to Artemis at Brauron and spent her life there in contented seclusion. Old Tyndareus died and Menelaus became bachelor King of Sparta, as Theodore had enjoined. Pylades married Electra and took her to Phocis, where Strophius forgave his son and blessed them both.

Thus through wisdom and justice the family curse was lifted from the House of Atreus and new life sprang from them all. Orestes, King of Argos, brought his bride Hermione home to the palace in Mycenae. I like to think they kept a dower house for Helen. Orestes and his Queen founded a new dynasty in Argos, blessed by the gods and, I trust, full of happiness.

* * * * *

77: The Mythic Tarot © Tricia Newell

POSTSCRIPT

The buck had stopped with Orestes. That was the end of his appalling double bind: damned if you do, damned if you don't. By challenging the gods, and also by embracing his fate, he had brought about the end of the curse on the House of Atreus. Yes, he had killed his mother, believing he was obeying higher powers. But when his conscience brought the Furies down upon him he'd cried out to Apollo, 'Over to you! I've done enough. I need help.' And he had been heard. The gods had sent Athene.

At Orestes' trial the god defeated the goddess. The masculine principle was re-established over the feminine principle; Agamemnon won out over Clytaemnestra, Orestes over the Furies. Once again, rationality trumped feeling. Was this a movement forward or back? For also, as a result of this same court of Athene, jury trial replaced revenge, banishment superseded stoning and the word came to outrank the sword. Thus there were two contradictory movements of the culture in this one story: because the Furies failed them, the status quo was entrenched for women; but there was a great leap forward for justice.

Together with justice are wisdom and mercy. *Give me wisdom that sitteth by thy throne, and reject me not from among thy children* (Wisdom of Solomon 9: 2), as the Apocrypha enjoined about three hundred years later. And in the light of wisdom, the curse of retribution began to fall away, first in Athens then in the wider culture. Vengeance gave place to justice. It was written later: 'Vengeance is *mine*,' saith the Lord. 'I will repay' (see Romans 12: 19), as if to say, *you* needn't bother any more. The opponent was no longer to be slaughtered as an enemy but treated with respect. Jury trial was set up and henceforth any casting vote was to be given in clemency (if not yet in mercy) to the defendant.

In our story, several people were willing to lay down their lives for their friends. However, over four hundred years later Christ went further still: love your *enemies*. The younger, capricious Greek gods, as well as the jealous, vengeful Old Testament God — all were outshone by that approaching vision, *God is love*. The tale of Orestes marks a tremendous step of the culture from harsh barbarity towards the God of Love.

* * * * *

ACKNOWLEDGEMENTS

My deep gratitude goes to Frances Aitken; you have gone way beyond the call of duty in going through every word with your practical friendship, help and wisdom. Gratitude too to Ian Thorp for being endlessly encouraging about Orestes and for publishing it. My thanks to my brother Adrian Marshall for your constant support and help. To Pamela Allsop, Monica Anthony, Les Ashton, Julie Brookes, Caroline Clarke, Petra Galligan and Navraj Matharu, my warmest thanks; I have hugely appreciated your staunch friendship and help. Thank you also to Robert Patterson for your steadfast backing in the project.

I am immensely glad to have had the chance to meet (just a little) the work of the great playwrights Euripides, Aeschylus and Sophocles. In immersing myself in eight of their plays, all around the same story, I found myself loving them all and wishing that people like me might become better acquainted with their ancient and tremendous tale-telling. The translators are splendid, and Robert Graves' books helped considerably; but the plays told their own story.

Many years ago, thanks to my Transpersonal inspirers Ian Gordon-Brown and Barbara Somers, I came upon the story of Orestes in *The Mythic Tarot*, by Juliet Sharman-Burke and Liz Greene. My thanks to them. I was touched by the tale they chose to illustrate the suit of Swords. Tricia Newell had done the illustrations, and they have stayed with me ever since — the lonely, sensitive boy with the weight of the family landing four-square on his shoulders, the double bind into which he was thrown, his hounding through the wilderness, and the eventual redemption that came about because he called upon the gods. I give warm thanks to Tricia Newell for letting me show those pictures here.

Hazel Marshall,
Rock Bank, Leicestershire,
April 2024

CREDITS

My thanks to the artist Tricia Newell for permission to reproduce her pictures from the Mythic Tarot.

BIBLIOGRAPHY

THE PLAYS:
Aeschylus (525-456 BCE.) *The Oresteia:*
Agamemnon, The Libation Bearers, The Eumenides.
Tr. Robert Fagles 1966, Penguin, London 1979.

Euripides (c. 480-407/6 BCE.) *Iphigenia at Aulis* c. 408-406, tr. Don
Taylor 1990, in *Euripides: The War Plays*, Methuen Drama 1990.
(Note: Don Taylor directed *Iphigenia at Aulis* for BBC TV in
summer 1990, with Roy Marsden as Agamemnon, Fiona Shaw as
Clytaemnestra, and Imogen Boorman as Iphigeneia; see
illustrations 14 and 17.)
Euripides *Orestes*, 408 BCE. In *Orestes and other plays*,
tr. Philip Vellacott, Penguin Classics 1972.
Euripides *Electra* c. 413-410, in *Euripides: Electra and other Plays*
tr. John Davie, Penguin Books 1998.
Euripides, *The Iphigenia in Tauris of Euripides* 414-412 BCE,
tr. Gilbert Murray, Aeterna Publishing 2010.

Homer (c. 1200-800 BCE.) *The Iliad,* tr, E.V. Rieu 1950,
Penguin, London 1961.
Homer, *The Odyssey*, tr, E.V. Rieu 1946, Penguin, London 1976.

Sophocles (c. 497/6-406/5 BCE), *Elektra* c. 420-414 BCE,
tr. Robert Bagg 2011, Harper Collins, Charlestown, MA., USA.

THE STORIES:
Robert Graves 1955. *The Greek Myths*, Vols. I & II, Penguin,
London 1957.
Charles Kingsley (b. 1819, d. 1875), *The Heroes*, Everyman's Library,
Dent 1910, London.
Juliet Sharman-Burke & Liz Greene 1986, *The Mythic Tarot.*
Illustrated by Tricia Newell 1986, Century Hutchinson, London.

ILLUSTRATIONS